Dee shrugged. "In my brief spell on Earth I have observed that there are many who proclaimed themselves messiahs. A few have followers, but nothing more than that. If Fawg is determined to convert believer and heathen alike, he will have his work cut out for him."

Dyckon held up the phial. "But none of them possess this."

Again Dee shrugged. "It could be dismissed as nothing more than a conjurer's trick. For every believer on Earth, there are a dozen disbelievers and doubters."

"The humani can worship what they will," the Roc snapped. "I do not care if they appoint Fawg set-ut as ruler of their planet." He held up the phial again. "This is a virus. Once it is released on Earth, it will propagate with terrifying speed among people who know nothing of it and are wholly unprepared for what it can do. Think of it, Doctor, think of the consequences. Think of the madness, of the mindlessness that will surely follow in its wake." He held up the phial again. "This tiny phial will destroy the world. And I can do nothing about it. But you can. You must stop Fawg set-ut before he destroys your planet, Doctor Dee. Bring him back here."

OUTRAGEOUS FORTUNE

THE MERCHANT PRINCE

Volume II

Armin Shimerman
with Chelsea Quinn Yarbro

POCKET BOOKS

New York   London   Toronto   Sydney   Singapore

This book is a work of fiction. Names, characters, places and incidents are products of the authors' imagination or are used fictitiously. Any resemblance to actual events or locales or persons living or dead is entirely coincidental.

An Original Publication of Pocket Books

POCKET BOOKS, a division of Simon & Schuster, Inc. 1230 Avenue of the Americas, New York, NY 10020

ISBN: 0-671-03593-2

First Pocket Books printing October 2002

10 9 8 7 6 5 4 3 2 1

POCKET and colophon are registered trademarks of Simon & Schuster, Inc.

For information regarding special discounts for bulk purchases, please contact Simon & Schuster Special Sales at 1-800-456-6798 or business@simonandschuster.com

Front cover illustration by Jerry Vanderstelt

Printed in the U.S.A.

This tale of John Dee wouldn't be possible without the input and blessings of Michael Scott and Bill Fawcett. *I* wouldn't be possible without the love and partnership of Kitty Swink.

OUTRAGEOUS FORTUNE

PROLOGUE

NOW HERE'S THE RUB.

I was born in the Year of Our Lord 1527, and it is now, as these people measure time, 2100—though, in truth, they have changed and altered the calendar to suit themselves so that even I am not entirely sure of the exact date. The positions of the stars, however, suggest that it is perhaps a decade or two later, which makes much mockery of their year-end Bacchanalian celebrations. The position of the stars also tells me that this is a precarious time, with malefics in stronger positions than benefics.

Riddle me this: If I am 573 years old, more or less—and looking remarkable well on it, too, I may say—why then do the history books insist that I died in the Year of Our Lord 1608? And how is it that I, who was a searcher after Truth and an explorer of mysteries, should now be a merchant prince in the eyes of many? I have no goods to sell, no merchandise, and I was not born to the purple, not even on the wrong side of the blanket, and so have no title to claim beyond astrologer and scholar. Yet so much is new to me in this time and place that I suppose it is fitting that I reinvent myself in accord with the times. It is a strange society that has shaped itself in this time, and I am in the position of seeking to find how to go on *here, in accord with the strictures of the age. Thus I am a merchant prince, raised by my knowledge to high position and wealth such as no one of my time could reckon. I deal in secrets, as I have always done, and I have become the master of the riches in my mind.*

There is one other question that rankles: I have always prided myself on having a logical mind and the logic runs thus: If the history books have me dying in my beloved Mortlake in 1608, and they are not mistaken in their recordings, that implies that I managed to return from this accursed place and time to mine own genteel and civilized world. Just the contemplation of my death being in the past fills me with such disquiet that I do not permit myself to contemplate it, for fear that specific knowledge of what no man may know will serve to fix me in this place, or bring about such an enormity that all the laws of Nature will stand affronted.

Yet I am dedicated to learning, to knowledge, to discovering the great arcana of Nature, and through these devices, I seek to make my way back to the place I belong without wreaking any havoc on this time greater than has been done already.

I wonder how I shall.

Extract from the Day Booke of John Dee, Doctor,
Dated this day, 25th January in the Year of Our Lord 2100

CHAPTER

1

AT FIRST IT HAD been nothing but a whisper, more vapoury lies on the Omninet: The legendary Royal Newton had been overthrown, defeated by a mysterious stranger who had assumed his role.

The rumours percolated onto the news groups and trickled onto the back pages of the tabloids as gossip column fodder before duly shifting onto the front pages and becoming news. By then, of course, the story had fractured into a dozen versions, all of them "exclusive" and from "sources close to the Newton family."

Royal Newton, the richest man in the world, was dead; no, he was in a mental hospital; no, he was living in penury in the devastated remains of Paris or New Rome or London; no, he had been incarcerated in one of the satellite prison cubes that occasionally fell out of their orbits; no, he had killed himself; he had been overthrown in a palace coup; he had given away his fortune and become a monk; he had changed sex and become a nun; he had joined a troupe of neo-hippies and was living in Alaska, tending the caribou; he had been seen at the helm of an outward-bound colony ship . . . the variations became more exorbitant and fabulous with every passing hour.

And none of the stories, no matter how outrageous, came remotely close to the truth.

Royal Newton had been overthrown and ruined by Doctor John Dee, a five-hundred-year-old mathematician, rogue, and astrologer from the court of Queen Elizabeth I. Dee, who had seen how such things were done, had modeled himself on the merchant princes of his day and achieved what no one else had been able to.

Lee Vantis, however, was one of the handful of people in the world who knew that Royal Newton had not been killed and was still alive—after a fashion. The electrician had been on call the day Newton had taken his heart attack, his plastic and metal artificial heart actually exploding within his chest. Paradoxically, even though Newton's artificial lungs had been shredded by the shards of chrome and Teflon, the heart's backup power cell had kept his blood circulating long enough for the doctors to hook him up to an artificial lung. The intricate Union demarcation rules on the Moonbase had dictated that an electrician had to handle the heart, and Vantis had been called in to remove the sparking and crackling artificial heart unit from Newton's chest. The myriad monitors and tubes draped from the man's body were proof enough that the richest man in the world was still alive.

Vantis had seen Newton twice in the weeks since the accident. Once when he had been back to the emergency ward to repair a faulty bed which insisted on folding itself shut at twelve noon every day—whether it was occupied or not—and on another occasion to reduce the pressure on the sliding doors which either closed with agonising slowness or snapped shut like the jaws of some rabid animal. On both occasions Vantis had been unable to find anything wrong with either piece of equipment and was beginning to suspect that the new religious movement which preached that God was in the machines might have something going for them.

However, on each occasion he had seen the small, dark man at Newton's bed. Vantis's attention had been drawn to the man because he seemed to be deep in conversation with the unconscious Newton. The small man paced alongside the bed, arms flailing wildly, fingers darting, dark eyes wild and bright.

Vantis asked around and eventually the rumours began to trickle back. Nothing remained truly secret on the claustrophobic confines of the Moonbase for long. The stranger was someone called Dee, rumored to be English, and he was the man responsible for Newton's heart attack—though no one was quite sure how. This Dee was certainly wealthy and obviously quite high up in Newton's organisation, Minuteman Holdings, because he had moved into Newton's apartment and installed new equipment in the communications room as well as new security codes and parameters.

And Lee Vantis couldn't help but wonder how much this information would be worth on the open market. Or, better idea still, how much Dee would pay to keep his name off the Omninet and out of the newsgroups.

Doctor John Dee read through the email twice, an overlong beautifully manicured fingernail following the words on the screen, lips moving in synch with the letters. If he lived to be a hundred, he would never come to terms with these too-regular letters shaped and placed behind glass. He grinned suddenly; actually he supposed he had lived to be a hundred—in fact, more than five hundred years. Well, no matter how old he was, in his opinion, a missive should be on vellum or, at the very least, on paper, and in a legible, nicely rounded hand. He always maintained that it was possible to tell much of the character of a person from how they shaped and wrought their letters. But this—this printing told nothing of the person's character, his state of mind, or the purpose; though, in truth, he acknowledged, this was one of those occasions when he didn't need to know more than the facts on the screen. Blackmail was blackmail, no matter how it was written or phrased.

"Doctor Dee, it is most urgent that we meet to discuss your relationship vis-à-vis Royal Newton."

Dee reached forward and touched the screen, and the email whispered out of the printer set into the desk. Settling deep into the antique high-backed leather chair, the small man steepled his fingers before his face, pressing the tips to his thin lips, and considered the wafer-thin sheet of transparent paper. How much did the person know? And how much did he want?

He looked at the header on the email—Lee Vantis. Real or assumed? Dee knew how difficult it was to acquire a false name in this time and place, but he was also aware that his assistant, Kelly Edwards, had prepared four different emails, names, and nationalities for himself for when he wished to send discrete messages.

Dee's fingers moved across the console, accessing the Moonbase records, and moments later Vantis's description and biography appeared. So the man existed, with an address in a four-by-four cubicle in the workers' quarters. Dee looked at the mail again; the headers certainly seemed to confirm that it had come from this Vantis person. Dee wondered if he would be so stupid as to make a threat and use his real address. Stupid or arrogant? Men could be dreadful fools through vanity as well as ignorance, he reminded himself.

On a whim he reached over and manually dialled Vantis's cubicle number. All the equipment in the room was voice- and presence-activated. Dee had discovered a brilliant septuagenarian to reprogram the communication equipment; she had not managed to completely remove Royal Newton's voice from the programs—with the result that some of the commands executed erratically or disastrously, and Doctor Dee was actually too short to activate some of the motion detectors which were set to Newton's height.

The call was answered on the second ring, the square panel rippling with liquid colour before showing Vantis's slightly distorted head and the hint of a filthy, chaotic cube behind him. Dee knew that Vantis would not be able to see him in the screen; only the golden Minuteman Holdings symbol was revealed, revolving sedately on a field of blue velvet. "Did you just send me a message, Mr. Vantis?" Dee said without preamble, the machine taking his flat, clipped accent and turning it into something female and liquid.

"Is that you, Doctor Dee?" Vantis spoke with the nasal twang of those who had spent too long in the recycled air of Moonbase.

"I speak for Doctor Dee," Dee said absently, one eye on the screen, while simultaneously watching another monitor which had begun to scroll Vantis's movements over the past months, his expenditures, and current financial status. "What do you want?"

"If that is you, Doctor Dee"—Vantis leaned close to the

tiny monitor in his cubicle as if he could peer into it to see the speaker beyond—"then I have a proposal for you."

"And what is that?"

Vantis grinned, showing perfect plastic teeth. "I'll not discuss it on an open channel. This is for a face-to-face meeting."

Dee tapped the second monitor with the back of his hand. There! Vantis has been in the infirmary on two separate occasions, one of them apparently in connection with a brawl—not a reassuring sign, but indicative of the man, Dee supposed. There was always a possibility that he had seen Dee and Newton. The man had meager savings, no prospects, and had been disciplined on two recent occasions for arriving at work obviously under the influence of pure oxygen.

"It seems I must place myself at your disposal, Mr. Vantis. Where would you care to meet?"

"Do you know the Unnamed Bar in the Sub-Levels?" He sounded furtive, but with a veneer of bravado to cover it.

"I do not. But I will find it."

"In an hour, then," Vantis said eagerly. "And come alone. If I see you come in with that black bodyguard of yours, then I'm gone and your story is splashed all over the Omninet."

"I'll be there," Dee said softly, his manner anything but threatening. "And I will come alone." He thumbed off the screen and sat back into the chair, an expression of absolute distaste on his narrow face. Blackmail was such an interesting sport—when played properly. In his time he had blackmailed and been blackmailed in turn, and really, the rules were very simple. To be blackmailed, one had to allow oneself to be blackmailed.

And he was not willing to acquiesce.

CHAPTER

2

"SHALL I TELL YOU what I have discovered about our employer?" Kelly Edwards struggled with enflamed, bandaged hands to move the headset microphone away from her mouth. She swivelled in the chair to look at Morgan d'Winter.

"Absolutely nothing?" d'Winter guessed, white teeth flashing in his ebony face.

"Absolutely nothing," Kelly agreed, standing and stretching, pressing her mittened hands into the small of her back and working stiff shoulder muscles. "The man simply does not exist." She stepped away from the huge computer console. "I've spent the best part of a week digging through every avenue and byway of the Omninet looking for some reference to him. I've even gone so far as to access birth records for people approximating his age; I've done hunts on people of his height and eye colour; I've voice-matched his vocal patterns and attempted to match them to a particular local. But even his accent doesn't exist. There is nothing. The man simply does not exist. And has never existed."

"Why do you want to know?" d'Winter asked, standing before the food dispenser and staring blankly at the menu. "This stuff is expensive, though some of this is *real* fruit!"

"When you're employed by one of the richest men in the world, you can afford the very best," Kelly said, joining d'Winter at the dispenser. The red-haired woman barely came to the bodyguard's shoulder.

"And yet our own Doctor has very simple tastes," d'Winter remarked.

"Did your own research reveal anything?" Kelly asked casually as she leaned forward to order up some orange juice.

D'Winter grinned. "I should have guessed you'd find out that I, too, am looking into the enigma of the good doctor."

"You left some fingerprints on the Omninet." Kelly grinned back, looking up into d'Winter's broad face. The fish-hook earring in his left ear took the light and sparkled menacingly. She tentatively opened the moon station dumb waiter and retrieved the orange juice. He took it carefully from her tender burned hands. "Thanks for this."

D'Winter moved away, the glass almost lost in his huge hands. He stood before the window and stared out at the desolate moonscape. He knew that what he was seeing was an image taken from some camera on the moon's surface and relayed deep into the heart of the moon, where it was projected onto this screen to give the impression of a window. "I went looking for our employer in places you wouldn't even know existed," he said, glancing over his shoulder. "Men like Dee are not that common. They may change their names, their faces, their skin colour, but certain things remain. An assassin may always work with a particular calibre of gun or type of explosive; a torturer may favour a particular method. There is a superstition to it, as if the weapon or method immunizes the doer from the deed."

Kelly shuddered. "Is that what you think Dee is: an assassin or torturer?"

D'Winter shook his head. "I don't know. We do know that when both you and I were incapacitated, he carried the fight right into the heart of his enemies' camp. We know he was captured and beaten. We know that when he managed to escape, instead of running, he turned right around and slaughtered half a dozen guards to get back into Newton's chamber. Doctor John Dee is not your average man."

"I've accessed every military and service listing I can find. I've tracked down Spooks and Silents, I've gone after wet-work artists and covert specialists. I've even looked up the records of those who are either dead or MIA, or so legendary as to be impossible to identify specifically. No one even vaguely approximating the Doctor has turned up."

Kelly nodded. "It is as if he simply stepped out of midair two years ago."

"A man like Dee," d'Winter mused, "cunning, ruthless, lethal—"

"And charming," Edwards added, "don't forget charming."

"And charming," d'Winter agreed. "Someone like Dee simply does not appear out of nowhere. There are bound to be records somewhere."

"Remember he has no biochip. Which means he has never been chipped or he managed to have it removed."

Kelly exhaled audibly. "Having it removed is difficult enough, but having it done covertly—"

"I checked with the doctors who perform that sort of surgery," d'Winter said. "There is one particular specialist in Kowloon, an artist of sorts, whom people with money use. The work is incredibly illegal and dangerous. If the chip explodes, it will kill everyone in a three-metre radius. But neither he nor his associates ever worked on a man of Dee's shape or appearance. There are approximately fifty people in the known world who are without biochips. I can account for forty-eight of them."

"And the other two?" Kelly asked eagerly. "Perhaps one of them—?"

"The other two are women."

"So?" Kelly demanded. "A sex change is a one-day operation."

"They were tall women." D'Winter was enjoying himself.

"Height reduction is also available."

"And black." He gave a vulpine grin.

"Okay, that's a little trickier. But not wholly impossible."

"Turning a thirty-something six-foot black woman into a five-foot white man is, I believe, beyond the capabilities of most surgeons. And there would be scars and surgical pins. Dee's scars aren't surgical."

"Which brings us back to the original question," Kelly said. "Who is Doctor John Dee?"

"And where is he?" d'Winter asked, glancing at his watch. "I thought we were heading back to Earth sometime today."

CHAPTER

3

WHEREVER MANKIND CLUSTERED, there would always be places like this. Doctor John Dee pushed through the heavy leather curtain and stepped into the cloying heat of the Unnamed Bar and then stopped, absorbing the atmosphere, allowing his eyes to adjust to the perpetual gloom. The bar was in the deepest part of the Sub-Levels, nearly two miles below the bitter surface of the moon. This close to the heating reactors, the temperature was unpleasantly warm and fetid with a multitude of odours that the Recyclers would never cleanse. It reminded him of the stews and brothels of Southwark in his own time, of London during a visitation of the Plague. They, too, had smelt like this; but then, he supposed that misery and despair carried its own horrible aroma.

The bar was crammed to capacity, men and women of all ages and races, most of them wearing coveralls that indicated their rank and profession. A profusion of orange coveralls crowding the horseshoe-shaped bar suggested that a Dockers shift had just changed, while the shabby white of the maintenance crews mingled with the distinctive white-collared coveralls of the administrative corps. Dotted through the crowd, the grey and black or olive green of off-duty police and military officers sat generally alone or in small groups, the chairs angled to turn their tables into barricades against the other patrons. Wandering through the crowd, men and women in garments designed to show pallid flesh moved with trays of oily-looking drinks.

Dee grinned suddenly and took a deep breath. The scene was so familiar it was almost making him nostalgic. The costumes may have changed, and perhaps there were more dark-skinned folk here than there would have been in his own time, and there should be a roaring fire against one wall, some class of meat turning on a spit. There should be sawdust or rushes on the floors, dogs growling under the tables, but he had stood in places like this in practically every city in Europe; and he doubted if he could recall a single time he had done so out of pleasure. It had always been business; perhaps he was doomed to forever wander the stews of the world, conducting some nefarious business—it was a fate he didn't view with dissatisfaction.

A space at the bar opened up, and he slipped in alongside a hugely obese man wearing the yellow and black of the recycling staff. Dee's sensitive nostrils flared; he caught the distinct odour of faeces and urine from the man's clothing. At least he hoped it was from the clothing, and that the man was not so far gone in strong drink that he was unable to control his body. This was a most unpleasant place, Dee thought, and decided that made it appropriate for the work he had to do. It was also condign that this place should be where the Recyclers met, for who better to deal with such offal as Vantis than these workers? The paradox of the Recyclers was that they held one of the lowliest, least popular jobs on Moonbase, and were also the highest paid. They controlled the air, water, and sewage maintenance, and Dee guessed that the man beside him was in the sewage department. Just as well, Dee thought. He would have work for him shortly.

The bartender, a small man, missing the lobe of his left ear, caught Dee's eye, and the doctor pointed to the drink on the bar beside him and raised a single finger. The bartender nodded and turned away. It was a trick the doctor had used time and again. It never mattered what the drink was—he had no intention of drinking it anyway, and when he walked away from the bar, the person he was sitting beside would inevitably pick up the drink, assuming it was theirs.

Dee turned slowly, taking in the room, eyes hidden beneath a long-billed cap. Most of the attention in the room was now centered on a low stage upon which a young woman was performing a fire-eating act, drinking peculiar-coloured liquids, and squirting multicoloured flames over the head of the audience. It was only when he looked again that he realised that not all the flames were coming from her mouth. Dee forced himself to look away. Not everyone was concentrating on the stage. The small group huddled in the corner were obviously plotting some sort of scheme, possibly criminal, sketching it out on the back of a scrap of paper; alongside them in the next booth, a woman who was an extraordinary example of the surgeon's art—d'Winter had told him about such things, and it had taken quite a stretch of the imagination to believe it—was negotiating with a one-eyed rogue. And if the man wasn't careful he was going to lose the other eye as well. Farther along, three professional trollops, obviously foot-sore and off-duty, drank in silence and waved away potential customers. And—there! Finally!

Lee Vantis sat in a booth close to the door, an untouched drink on the table before him. Now that he had placed him, Dee allowed his gaze to move on, looking now for people watching Vantis. It would be out of character if the man had arrived alone. There were two others, easy enough to spot, wearing the off-white coveralls of the maintenance crew, with lightening flashes over the breast indicating that they, too, belonged to the electricians guild. The fact that none of them had reacted to his appearance confirmed his suspicions that they did not know what he looked like, though he had taken the precaution to disguise himself in the drab nondescript uniform of a petty clerk.

As he moved into the seat, Vantis looked up and raised a hand. "This seat is taken, pal," he said menacingly.

"I know," Dee said smoothly, "by me. You were keeping it for me, Mr. Vantis, were you not?"

Vantis blinked, eyes automatically darting over Dee's shoulders to where his companions waited. Even if Dee had not been aware of the others, Vantis's movement would have given it away. The doctor was almost disappointed. There would be no sport to be had here today.

"You're Dee."

"Little escapes you, Mr. Vantis," Dee said softly, his sarcasm lost on Vantis; he maneuvered himself into the corner of the booth, where he could both watch Vantis and see one of the men guarding the door. The other was almost directly behind him, but there was little he could do about that. "What do you want?"

"I know all about you, Mr. Dee," Vantis said quickly, in a lowered voice that was intended to be threatening.

"I doubt that."

"I know you had something to do with Newton's heart attack." Vantis ended the statement with a faintly upward inflection.

Dee stared at the man, saying nothing.

"I've seen you at Newton's bed."

"Listen to yourself," Dee said abruptly, "listen to what you're saying. You know I had something to do with Newton's heart attack and you've seen me at his bedside. Just what exactly are you accusing me of? Of visiting the sick? Visiting the sick is a Corporal Act of Mercy: Is it a crime now to be a Good Samaritan?"

Vantis frowned, apparently not entirely sure what a Samaritan was. "I know you caused the heart attack. I had to be called in to pull the burst heart out of his chest. And I've been asking around about you, Mr. Dee. And guess what—no one knows about you. I reckon that if no one knows about you, it's because you want no one to know about you. It's not happenstance. Maybe it's because you're a really private person, or maybe it's because you're shy, or maybe it's because someone is looking for you. But either way, you do not want your name out there in the public domain. And you know the press are already sniffing around Newton's disappearance; they will pay handsomely for any new information. And I reckon they would pay handsomely for your name." Vantis took a deep breath. "And I reckon you would pay even more handsomely for me not to tell them."

"What is to stop you giving the press my name after I have paid you?" He considered Vantis archly. "You could collect twice then. I don't imagine you'd turn away from such an opportunity."

Vantis's eyes flared as he considered the new idea. He hadn't thought of that. "Well, of course, I wouldn't do that; I'm a man of my word, Doctor Dee."

"I'm sure you are, when it suits you." Dee sighed. "But it seems to me, Mr. Vantis, that you have very little to sell."

"But I have—I have." Vantis's voice went up a notch in alarm. "And once I give the press your name, you know they will dig and dig. God alone knows what they will find. And what they don't find, they may invent."

"True," Dee admitted. "Very true. Tell me," he said suddenly, "how much do your two friends know?"

Vantis eyes once again moved beyond Dee. This time he caught the movement himself and smiled sheepishly. "Nothing. I told them I was collecting a debt, and I was afraid you might get a little rough."

"Do I look the sort to get rough?" Dee asked innocently.

Lee Vantis looked down at the small man and grinned. "Not at all. I could take care of you myself."

"Not the first time I've heard that." Dee smiled. "Tell me," he asked, "how much do you want?" He moved in his chair, shifting position, and slipped his hand into his jacket. "I presume you want only hard currency."

"Absolutely. No credit transfers. Too easy to trace, and too easy to stop." Vantis's plastic teeth were yellow in the gloom. "I was thinking perhaps ten thousand. It seems a reasonable sum. Particularly if it buys you a lifetime of peace."

"Very reasonable," Dee agreed. He slid out of his seat and moved in alongside Vantis. He lowered his voice, drawing Vantis closer to him. "However, I was thinking of a slightly higher price."

"You were? How much?"

"This much," Dee said, and slid the Italian stiletto between Vantis's ribs, forcing the razor-sharp blade up and into his heart. Putting his hand over Vantis's mouth to stop the death rattle, he watched the man's eyes widen in that last eternal look of shocked surprise, and then his throat worked and a tendril of dark blood appeared behind Dee's fingers. Dee twisted the knife, ruining the heart, waiting for it to stop so that there would be no surge of blood, and then, in one deft movement, pulled the knife out and plugged the wound with the man's coverall.

CHAPTER

4

IN HIS LONG AND often adventurous life, Doctor John
Dee admitted to several remarkably stupid mistakes. The
incident with Mary, Queen of Scots, that almost cost him
his head; he should have known better than to undertake
such a venture under the baleful influence of Saturn. And
there was the occasion when he had insulted Sir Walter
Raleigh in court, that incredibly stupid mistake with
Princess Elizabeth before she had risen to the throne and,
of course, the foolishness with the de' Medici woman
which had, in its own peculiar way, been the catalyst for
everything that followed and which had been responsible for his encounter with the Daemon Roc, who had
transported him five hundred years into the future. However, even he, who was loathe to recognize his own shortcomings, had to admit that he had now committed a
remarkably stupid error, more impulsive and ill-judged
than any he had made before—possibly a fatal one.

If he had been more careful, and not quite so arrogant, he would have realised that Lee Vantis had brought
more than two companions.

Slaying the man had been a mercy killing; the fact that Vantis had survived for so long in the world was a mystery. From the moment he had slid the knife between the blackmailer's ribs, twisted it to ensure that he was in fact dead, to walking out the door had taken perhaps ten heartbeats. Dee had been through the leather curtain before the two guards had realised that anything was wrong. All they had seen was Dee moving in to sit beside Vantis, a brief conversation, perhaps money changing hands under the table, and then Dee casually and calmly walking away. The doctor had almost reached the end of the corridor before both men had appeared, their shouts echoing off the metal walls. Glancing over his shoulder, Dee had grinned and rounded the corner. And ran straight into the two huge men in the white coveralls of the maintenance department. One had been lounging against the wall, a broad-headed wrench tapping idly against his leg. Dee caromed off the man and sat down hard on the metal floor. While he had been struggling to his feet, Vantis's two companions appeared, shouting and pointing at Dee. The man with the wrench lifted the heavy tool as Dee rolled forward. His guttural shout turned high and feminine as the smaller man drove the point of his stiletto into the man's groin. The maintenance man collapsed, legs tangling around Dee, and then the second man was on top of him, swinging out with a short length of pipe. Dee stabbed with the blade, wishing now he had something with an edge to it. He felt the blade strike home twice, but not to any useful depth, and then the pipe struck him an agonising blow on the shoulder, numbing his arm; he felt no pain as the next blow cracked his elbow, the sound loud and popping in the echoing confines of the corridor. The Doctor managed to drive the dagger into the fleshy thigh of his assailant and twist it savagely before the other two men were on top of him. He saw, in vivid, frozen detail, the pattern on the sole of the boot that rendered him unconscious.

The pain brought him awake, a hideous clarion that could not be denied. Pain was like a flower, he had once written, a delicate ephemeral bloom, something to be welcomed, examined, enjoyed, and then put away. That was before he had experienced true agony that set talons deep in his flesh and plucked at his very vitals. He realised now how ludicrous those words had been. This was not the pain of a hangover, of raw grapes and bitter mash, the pain of a stomachache, of sour wine and unripened cheese. This was not the pain of riding, when every muscle ached and burned with exertion, and the spine felt hammered. Nor was this the pain of lovemaking, when his muscles were deliciously aching, when his knees and elbows were burned and scraped raw. No, this was pain, proper raw suffering. If Dee survived this encounter, and he was beginning to think that he might not, he would pen a proper treatise on pain, and acknowledge it as the single greatest emotion.

His arm was broken; he could actually feel the bones grate together, sending shards of hurt up his shoulder and into his jaw; from the tightness in his chest, he imagined that at least three of his ribs were similarly damaged, for breathing was an exercise in anguish. All the fingers on his left hand were immovable, swollen, and discolored, and he guessed that they had been stamped upon. There was the tart copper taste of blood in his mouth. He examined his teeth with his swollen tongue, but at least they all seemed to be intact, though his upper left canine was loose.

Lying absolutely still, he made himself aware of his surroundings. He was supine on metal so cold that it actually burned his skin, and from the ambient nature of the stillness that surrounded him, he guessed that he was in some metal chamber of sorts; probably a cell. Which could mean that he was under arrest for the murder of Vantis, if he was fortunate: He was a wealthy man, and wealth could buy many things in his own time, even freedom. And he guessed that this time was little different. But if he was in a cell, then why had he not been attended to by physicians?

When Doctor John Dee opened his eyes, he realised that he was in no holding cell. He had seen these chambers throughout Moonbase in the last few weeks; he recognised the circular logo on the door.

As he struggled into a sitting position, he saw Vantis's two companions staring at him through thick porthole glass. And then the air began to hiss and vent, and Dee supposed that he was in a decompression chamber—one that lead out onto the airless surface of the moon.

"So now it ends," he said, oddly satisfied to die on the moon.

CHAPTER

5

"THEY THREW HIM OUT of an airlock." James Zhu passed the single-page report to Morgan d'Winter and stood back. The two men turned to look at the disheveled and bloody group of Maintenance workers who stood and crouched against the wall of the holding cell.

None of the terrified electricians would meet their gaze; d'Winter tall, black, and menacing, silk-soft leather jerkin and trousers whispering menacingly as he moved; Zhu equally tall, but broader, immaculately dressed, his flat Asian features impassive. Zhu they knew by reputation—he had been Newton's Head of Security, a Mongol who claimed direct descent from Genghis Khan—and a man who could kill with a single touch. But the fact that Zhu deferred to the black man with the shaven head frightened them even more.

"I'm looking for an explanation," d'Winter said slowly, surprised by the depth of emotion he felt at the death of the doctor. He stared at one man, forcing him to look up. "What happened to Doctor Dee?"

"He killed one of our people." The electrician, his

white coverall splashed with the dried blood of his wounded companion, braved d'Winter's icy rage. Looking from him to Zhu, he continued hurriedly, "There was a struggle; he pulled a knife. Bob's here got cut bad. . . ." His voice trailed away. Then, taking a deep breath, he pressed on, "It was self-defense. And you have no right to hold us here against our will." He looked about, as if seeking help.

Zhu moved forward, soft-soled shoes making no sound on the metallic floor of the holding cell. "I want you to have no doubts as to the seriousness of your situation," he said calmly, his cultured British accent lending his words a deeper menace.

"I want my lawyer," the speaker said abruptly.

"Of course you do." Zhu touched the man on the side of his face, the movement blindingly swift, the touch gentle, almost caressing. "But I am afraid that you are not going to get him." The man's jaw cracked and dislocated with a dull popping sound. "I am the law on this moon. I will ask you questions and you will answer them. You will answer truthfully and completely. This is simply nonnegotiable," Zhu said reasonably. "And please believe me when I say that whatever I can do to you is as nothing to what my dark friend here wants to do with you."

"Five of you against one small man," d'Winter sneered. "What were you afraid of, that you took so many? Yet one of your number is dead, another lies gravely wounded, and a third needs major reconstructive surgery, so five may have been prudent."

"He started it," one of the electricians whispered.

"Who did?" d'Winter demanded.

"The small man. He—"

"You mean you don't even know his name?" d'Winter asked incredulously.

"We were never told. Just got a description. It was Vantis's deal all along. He said he was going to collect on a debt, and he asked us to come along in case things got rough. The small man killed Vantis. I saw him do it. Just slipped a dagger into him, cool as you please. We chased him, there was a struggle. He still had a knife—I think it was the same knife he used to kill Vantis. And then things, well, things got out of hand."

"So you threw him out of an airlock!"

Zhu touched d'Winter's arm, and the two men stepped back. "That's how disputes are solved in the lower sections. You know it as well as I do. It's difficult to hide a body down there; the recycling isn't so good. So they push them out an airlock. Get rid of 'em. The equivalent of pirates making their victims walk the plank, or soldiers fragging unpopular officers." He glanced at the electricians, his look chilling them, even though they could not hear his words. "What do you want to do with these."

"Push them out of the same airlock!" d'Winter said without hesitation.

"That is, of course, an option. Though it achieves nothing," Zhu added. "A good lawyer, if they could afford one, might make a case for self-defense. It seems clear that the Doctor stabbed this man Vantis first."

"But what was Dee doing meeting with Vantis in the first place?"

"With both Vantis and the doctor gone now, I presume we will never know." Zhu's lips moved away from his teeth in what passed for a smile. "I presume from the little I've discovered about you and the woman Edwards in the past few weeks that Dee is as much a mystery to you as he was to Newton and myself."

D'Winter nodded. "A truly remarkable man," the bodyguard agreed. "We know nothing about his life."

"And even less about his death," Zhu said, dipping his head and covering his mouth with his hand—an old habit to prevent a lip-reader from recreating his words off the scanners and monitors that covered practically every inch of the moonbase. "I've examined the airlock where these men claim they flushed Dee. And the scanners do indeed show them pushing him into Airlock 22, and no record of him coming out. So I have to assume he went out onto the surface. People do different things when they hear the first hiss of air beginning to seep out of an airlock. Sometimes they run out onto the Moon's surface when the doors open. Afterwards you will find that the dust outside the airlock is churned up, or there will be scraps of cloth and bone, perhaps strips of dried flesh, even a desiccated corpse close by. Though I do know of an escaped prisoner who managed to run five metres before he finally succumbed. God knows where he was headed," he added. "However, if they huddle inside the airlock, then you'll find that the interior is gory with the bits and pieces."

"I've a feeling I'm not going to like what you're about to tell me."

"As I've said, I've checked the records. I've got tape from the moment Dee entered the bar, to the second they put him, unconscious, into the airlock. I've got the record of the airlock cycling to a full flush and vent—that means it was fully opened, all breathable air gone." Zhu paused for a sigh.

"And there was no sign of Dee," d'Winter guessed.

"None," Zhu said, pinching the bridge of his nose to ease a sudden sinus headache. "Either he wasn't in the airlock—in spite of all the evidence that suggests that he was—or he was in the airlock and managed to somehow survive. And that is patently impossible."

D'Winter turned away from the huddled electricians and strode down the corridor, a broad grin on his face. "Why should that surprise you? Dee's very existence is patently impossible!"

CHAPTER

6

"GOOD DOCTOR DEE, this is becoming a habit." The voice echoed as if it came from a long distance.

He had been dreaming. Of England. A green and pleasant land. Of perfumed breezes and gentle rains. And then he had been drowning, or something worse. Standing in the middle of the maze at his beloved Mortlake, arms wide, head thrown back, desperately trying to suck in God's own breath. But there was none to be had. There was no air. And, as he looked around him, the maze was withering, the leaves crisping, curling, grass yellowing, dying, the world turning white and sere, the soft earth melting, reforming, turning hard and white, cold beneath his touch. Blue skies and white clouds were burnt away as the sky itself turned metallic. . . .

"Doctor—"

He was not in Mortlake, not in England. He was far, far from home—and dying. Dying in a time and place beyond his wildest imagination, a mass of battered flesh and broken bones, more carrion than—

"Doctor Dee, can you hear me?"

And why could this voice not let him die in peace! What now tormented him in his hour of extremity? Doctor John Dee opened his eyes, squinting against the harsh white lights, and looked into the face of a nightmare. A long, narrow, and leathery reptilian head was inches from his, slit-pupiled eyes staring unblinking at him, a thin tendril of spittle drooling from between scores of razor-sharp teeth. The mouth worked and Dee heard words, though they did not synchronize with the movements of the mouth. "Ah, Doctor Dee, you are back with us." A razor-taloned claw offered a metal cup brimming with viscous green liquid. "Drink this. You need to replenish some vital electrolytes and rehydrate."

Dee accepted the cup and swallowed the liquid in one quick gulp. It tasted as foul as it looked. "Dyckon," he whispered, astonished at how weak his voice sounded, "though you be one of the ugliest creatures ever to grace God's earth, I'll allow that I am mightily glad to see you."

"Beauty, as they say on your planet, is in the eye of the beholder." Dyckon grinned alarmingly. "On my planet there are some who consider me handsome. It is all a matter of perception."

Dee reached up and gripped the alien's leathery skin. "At this moment, my friend, I think you are beautiful."

And then the face of the creature dissolved into a thousand tiny shattered fragments, and the blackness closed in again.

When he awoke, he felt marginally better. He sat up slowly, aching muscles protesting, but without the sickening sharpness of broken bones, the deep, abiding torture of shattered organs. He traced the lines of his ribs with his fingers, and, although the flesh was tender, the ghost of a bruise, green-yellow and faded on his pallid flesh, the bones were whole. He worked his arm experimentally. It was stiff, but, like his ribs, was whole again.

Dee swung his legs out of the bunk, remembering the last time he had lain in this cot. Then his state of mind had been one of absolute terror; he had been convinced that he had died and gone to Heaven. And when he met Dyckon ab-ack na Khar, of the Roc, he had been convinced that he had gone to Hell.

Two years ago, as he measured time—and five hundred years as the rest of the world counted it—Dee had been sentenced to die by the de' Medici. Walled into a tower, he had been slowly starving to death when Dyckon had rescued him. Now—and he grinned widely at the irony and symmetry of the circumstances—the Roc had done it again. Dee's grin faded. This save had been much too close. He was obviously losing his touch. In his youth he would never have ended up in such terrible circumstances.

He dressed slowly in a loose-fitting shift and then came unsteadily to his feet, swaying slightly on the chill metal floor. The door facing him irised open, and Dyckon stepped through, talons clicking on the metal floor, long serpentine tail hissing behind him.

"You are awake."

Dee touched his throat and found he was wearing the thin metal collar which enabled him to communicate with the Roc. "I am, thanks to you. I am obliged to you." He bowed, in the formal courtesy of the court of the first Elizabeth of England. "You are indeed my Guardian Angel."

"I understand the concept," Dyckon said. "In fact, I have reason to believe that one of my own ancestors introduced it to your world some many thousands of years ago. The legends of your peoples speak of the Shining Ones and Angels; I am sure they are referring to my people."

"My friend," Dee said kindly, "I believe you will find that we called your race Demons."

"Indeed?"

"Indeed!" Dee's certainty was convincing to Dyckon.

"Well, if that is so, it will warrant research. There might be an analytical presentation in it." Dyckon turned away and Dee followed him. "A good presentation will bring honour to me and my family."

"And how goes your attempts at advancement?" Dee has spent some time instructing Dyckon in the fine art of lying—a talent unknown on the creature's homeworld.

"I have been marked for advancement, and there is talk in the Collegium that I have been recommended for a Chair of the Collegiate. If it comes to pass, then I will be the first ever Roc to hold such an exalted position and the first of my clan ever to achieve any Notability."

"And this is important to you?"

"Notability is always important."

"Anonominity is much more so. The anonymous, the unknown, the discrete, the hidden, can achieve so much more than those in power and high office."

"It is an interesting concept, and I will consider it accordingly."

"Do so."

They came out into the large central chamber of Dyckon's craft, and the Roc folded himself into a tall, narrow, angular chair, his tail curling around the tall central post, locking him into position. From experience Dee knew that he would not be able to sit in the facing chair, and he took up a position against a wall covered with what he had once taken to be windows, but which he now knew to be screens.

Dyckon opened his mouth, but before he could speak, Dee said, "Tell me, what are you doing back in this part of the galaxy? From what you told me, I would have imagined that you would be back on your homeworld, striving for political preferment, attempting to bring honour to your family."

Dyckon's narrow head dipped in a bow of the first degree. "Your tutelage has served me well. I have done more and advanced further than any of my race. The whole concept of 'lying' is fascinating. I have found that people will believe the most outrageous untruths, provided that the words are delivered with sincerity and eye contact."

Dee smiled. "It was ever thus. There is nothing easier to get away with than the big lie. But never forget the cardinal rule of lying—the cardinal rule of all politics."

"Memory is everything and leave no witnesses," said Dyckon.

Dee nodded. "Exactly. Liars need a good memory. Once you have been caught in a lie, the whole house of cards begins to tumble. Thence it is but a short step to ruin. But if you are caught, then stop at nothing to remove the witnesses."

"It is a brutal way," Dyckon acknowledged, "and yet effective."

"The old ways are the best," Dee agreed. "But you have not answered my question. What are you doing back here?—aside from rescuing me, of course, for which I will be forever in your debt," he added hastily.

Tiny spots of purple appeared on the Roc's bald skull, and the sacs beneath his red eyes darkened and filled with liquid. "I have a problem that needs to be sorted."

"I'll wager it is a serious problem if it has shipped you back to this world."

"Serious enough. You should know, Doctor, that I am not the first Roc to study your people, nor was I alone in my studies. During my tenure watching over your planet, I was accompanied by a young student, Fawg set-ut. Like me he was ambitious but, whereas I was prepared to watch and interact only with you, I discovered that Fawg set-ut was more proactive in his experiments. He would travel to Earth and walk amongst the people, conducting experiments upon them, eliciting responses to his appearance, cataloguing how the human body would react to excessive heat or cold, hunger, thirst, and fright."

"Charming fellow," Dee remarked.

"When I began to move in political circles, I took your advice to heart," Dyckon continued, "I sought out those who could prove detrimental to my career and either removed them from office or rendered them ineffective." The Roc watched Dee's razor-thin eyebrows rise slightly and shook his head, a humani habit he had picked up from too many years observing the mammals. "No, I did not kill them. Allow me to explain: I had announced— lied if you will—that I had never failed a presentation, so I had to send the lecturer who once failed me to one of the outer planets to head up a new library. The last four librarians all perished in mysterious circumstances. I have no doubt that he will, too." The Roc showed razor teeth. "Furthermore, I had cultivated the air of a Roc successful with females, ensuring—as you suggested—that I should only be seen in the company of the most beautiful and powerful women of my clan. So it was necessary to send any female of my clan who might, shall we say, call my reproductive prowess into question, to one of the Rimworlds. I created a research project specifically tailored to one particular female whose revelations might prove embarrassing. The research project is completely fascinating, but made all the more difficult because communication with the Collegium is rendered practically impossible because of the denseness of the suns and the solar radiation in that part of the galaxy."

Dee pushed away from the wall. "It is my experience that those who preface bad news with minor items of success have very bad news to impart. It is usually an effort to sweeten a very bitter cup, and to keep the bearer of such tidings from parting company with his head or his freedom. Which brings us, I think, back to this Fawg set-ut?"

The Roc hissed, forked tongue flickering on the air, and Dee was once again reminded of the classic description of a Daemon from the holy books of the Bible and the hell-fire descriptions of the saints. "He knows about you," Dyckon said simply.

"Ah," said Dee.

"And he bears me some enmity."

"Ah."

"And he has disappeared."

"Oh dear." Dee looked about in dismay. "Do you know anything more?"

"I believe he has gone to Earth."

Dee's thin lips curled at the unintentional pun. "There are few places that someone like him could hide. Your appearance is, if you will pardon my mentioning it, remarkable."

"Ah, but he has this." The Roc's claw opened. A narrow oblong glass phial embossed with what Dee recognized as an Aegyptian glyph nestled in the creature's leathery palm. A clear jellylike substance rolled slowly into the phial.

"I have the distinct impression that I am not going to like what you are about to tell me," Dee said, watching Dyckon remove the stopper from the phial. The clear gel immediately curled out of the phial and wrapped itself around the Roc's hand, coating it with a clear, slightly rainbow-hued sheen. Twisting sinuously, the liquid coiled up his arm, and within moments the large Roc was covered in the shining gel.

"Now let us say," Dyckon said slowly, voice sounding muffled and distant, "that I wished to appear as one of you humani. That I wished to appear as male, tall, and blond, about thirty—"

As he was speaking the gel coating his skin began to twist and coil, ripples of colour sliding across it.

"—with a long flowing beard—"

Beneath the gel Dyckon's appearance was changing, altering, hard reptilian skin giving way to soft white flesh, razor-tipped claws folding away, drawing back to tapering fingers with flat square-tipped fingernails. A mouthful of razor teeth pulled back into a strong square jaw, a long straight nose appeared between two slit-pupiled eyes. The beard was like swan's down and the same colour.

"—and with white wings, for example—"

Wings sprouted from Dyckon's back, like the wings of a dove, huge and luminescent, each feather precise and distinct.

"Or perhaps you would prefer this image?" Dyckon said, a forked tongue flickering in the perfect human mouth. His image changed again, altering fluidly, his great height shrinking, skin darkening and weathering, hair greying and curling—Doctor John Dee found himself looking at his own perfect image.

"Remarkable," Dee said, shaken. He took a deep breath and steadied himself. "The illusion is not without flaws," he said, looking at the image of his own naked body. "There are no nipples, no navel, no genitalia, and the skin is too smooth; there should be blemishes. I have my share of scars."

As he was speaking, clothing formed on the body, a simple white shift, which subtly altered and changed into a simple black suit, then into the more ornate clothing of Dee's Elizabethan age.

"Remarkable," Dee said again. "But the eyes?" he wondered aloud.

"Yes," Dyckon said, his rasping voice sounding incongruous coming from Dee's own mouth, and as the Doctor watched, he could see the forked tongue flickering behind the thin human lips. "The liquid tissues of the eyes and the material of the tongue and mouth will not change. So no matter what form I assume, my eyes and tongue and the inside of my mouth will remain unchanged."

"Perhaps you would care to change into something else?" Dee suggested. "It is too curious a sensation to look at myself. I had barely grown used to the brightly lit and too-clear mirrors of this new age, and now to be looking at mine own image—but with the addition of a serpent's tongue and lizard's eyes—is too disturbing. No offence meant to you," he added hastily.

"None taken."

The surface of Dyckon's skin ran with liquid silver as he held out his right hand with the small phial. The viscous gel ran into the bottle, revealing Dyckon's Roc form beneath.

"What is it?" Dee asked, his scientific curiosity aroused.

"A virus. A disease, if you will, culled from one of the Ancient Homeworlds. It feeds off the electrical impulses generated by thought. Wearing this gel, one can assume any image one wishes for a brief period of time. For those unschooled in its properties, it can bring about spontaneous and uncontrolled changes of body, often abrupt and disorienting. Prolonged exposure to the virus is dangerous, for it disrupts identity, and, for most experiencing its effects for any period of time, there is a sapping of character and a breakdown of what you regard as personality. "

"And you say Fawg set-ut is on Earth with some of this liquid."

"Just so."

"I do not see the problem. He may slip unnoticed among the people of the world and not cause panic. Where's the harm in that?"

"Fawg always maintained that the Roc were superior to the humani. He subscribed to the theory that we were the original gods that the humani worshiped. I believe he has gone to establish himself as a god amongst the people of Earth. He had made a study of humani religions and has decided he is among the heros described, that he must assume the role of that hero in order to bring this virus to humani, so that they will become his true followers and servants. He believes he is destined to do this."

Dee shrugged. "In my brief spell on Earth I have observed that there are many who proclaimed themselves messiahs. A few have followers but nothing more than that. If Fawg is determined to convert believer and heathen alike, he will have his work cut out for him."

Dyckon held up the phial. "But none of them possess this."

Again Dee shrugged. "It could be dismissed as nothing more than a conjurer's trick. For every believer on Earth, there are a dozen disbelievers and doubters."

"The humani can worship what they will," the Roc snapped. "I do not care if they appoint Fawg set-ut as ruler of their planet." He held up the phial again. "This is a virus. Once it is released on Earth, it will propagate with terrifying speed, among people who know nothing of it and are wholly unprepared for what it can do. Think of it, Doctor, think of the consequences. Think of the madness, of the mindlessness that will surely follow in its wake." He held up the phial again. "This tiny phial will destroy the world. And I can do nothing about it. But you can. You must stop Fawg set-ut before he destroys your planet, Doctor Dee. Bring him back here."

"How dangerous is this virus material right now? In this room? To me?" Dee asked.

"I don't know," the Roc confessed. "I notice that you do not seem to have the same limitations and debilities of many of your fellow creatures."

"Um," Dee grunted. "Pray tell, is that why you've selected me for this thankless task?"

"In part, yes, and in part because I have asked you to, and you have an obligation to me," Dyckon said mildly, "and because I believe Fawg set-ut has cracked the code on a Ancient's timeslip device."

Dee shook his head. "I do not comprehend the words."

"In simple terms, Doctor, I believe Fawg set-ut has the means to send you back to your own time."

"Thank God fasting," said Dee devoutly.

"Truly, one does increase faith through adversity," said Dyckon, evading Dee's steady gaze. "And there is one more thing."

Dee sat very still. "All right. What is it?"

Dyckon turned to Dee, his face a mask of gargoyle chagrin. "Fawg may have an accomplice."

CHAPTER

7

STRATEGY BROOKS SAW THE bullets hit. Two shots spaced within half an inch of one another, dead centre in the chest. Her shooting instructor would have been so proud.

It might have been the light, the blinding flare of the shots in the gloom, but the woman had the distinct impression that when the bullets struck, the seated man's form rippled in slow viscous circles. His form distorted, and for an instant, an eye blink, there was something else, something dark and wet revealed. Then it was gone.

The intruder who called himself Yeshua Ben David reached up and touched his chest, then held out his stone-white hand to Strategy. Nestling in the palm of his hand were the two .255 bullets. The woman noted absently that the bullets were perfect, not deformed as if they had struck a bulletproof vest of impervium.

"Once," the man said, "I would have allowed such things to harm me. But I do believe I was taking the flesh-made-man concept a little too far." He smiled again, without opening his mouth.

Strategy thumbed back the hammer and brought the

red dot up to rest on the intruder's forehead. "Who are you?" she asked shakily.

"I am who I say I am. I am the Messiah." He spoke as if accompanied by a fanfare of heavenly trumpets.

"And I am Joan of Arc!" Strategy snapped. "Do you know how many nuts approach the station on a daily basis claiming to be the returned Christ, to have been kidnapped by aliens, or to have just seen Elvis? And sometimes a combination of all three: Elvis was an alien; he was the Messiah, but he was kidnaped by aliens. You're the third messiah this week."

The man's elegant fingers moved, holding up the two bullets. As Strategy watched, the lead flowed and melted, to be replaced by two perfectly faceted, glittering diamonds. He tossed the two diamonds to the woman, who snapped them out of the air with her left hand. They clicked together in her palm.

"Once it was water into wine. And I can do that, too," he added, "but in this material age, I do believe the traditional rewards of gold and jewels will be more attention-getting. Wouldn't you agree?"

Strategy ignored the question, moving the pistol in her right hand, shining the laser light into the diamonds. Shards of crimson crystalline light scattered around the room. "They look real," she said dubiously.

"Believe me, they are," Yeshua Ben David said. "I do not deal in lies. That's the other fellow's territory."

Strategy pocketed the diamonds and brought the gun back to bear on the man. "A trick, a magician's trick," she announced. Maybe this was a trick by a rival newshow, set up to embarrass her. Was she being filmed even now? Was her rival, Gloria Gonzaga, going to pop out of a door or poke her head in and say, in that smug tone of hers,

"Strategy Brooks, Newswoman Extraordinaire, you're caught." Then she would point to some innocuous object in the room and grin. "Say hi to the watchers all over the world."

Yeshua suddenly stood up. He was surprisingly tall, she noted. "This is not a trick, not a joke. This is the truth, Strategy. I have come again, and, whereas once I had Peter to build my Church, now I have you. The new gospels will not be on parchment skins, it will be written on the airways and spread through the Omninet. You will be the author of my new gospel, Strategy Brooks. You have the ear of the whole world. Will you do this for me?"

The woman started to shake her head.

"Like Thomas, who once doubted me, eh? What will convince you? Do you want minor magics, or miracles?" He touched the table, and, from his finger, a sheen of solid gold spread out, swallowing even the bottle and glass, turning them to hard orange gold. "It is an interesting trick," Yeshua remarked, as if talking to an inquisitive child. "Midas could do it, but he could not control it." He reached down and touched the chair; the leather flowed to a green greasy-looking stone, which Strategy recognized as jade. "Always a favourite in the East. They say it contains the soul of the wearer." Yeshua stretched out his hand and touched the gun in the woman's hand. "Watch."

She did as he ordered, in a mixture of fascination and horror, as it turned orange and translucent. Yeshua smiled again. "Do you want insects in your amber?" he asked. Tiny spots appeared in the gun-shaped blob of amber: an ant, a perfect wasp. "I can do this all night," he said quietly. "Do you want me to show you more?"

The woman took a deep breath. "No, let's quit now—

while I have some of my apartment left intact." She tossed the gun onto a couch and nodded towards the gold wine bottle. "Do you think you could turn that back into something drinkable?"

"I can do better than that," Yeshua said. "It wasn't drinkable in the first place." He sat back into the jade chair, and it immediately turned soft and liquid, the hard green stone appearing to flow back into him. For a single instant he was outlined in green, as if his skin had turned to stone. Resting his hand on the table, he tapped the surface gently; the gold flowed away from the table, turning his right hand into a shining glove. She watched the glowing gold flow up his arm; it vanished before it reached his elbow. Reaching for the bottle, he poured a glass of clear honey-coloured liquid into the glass.

"What happened to my wine?" she asked numbly.

"I think you will find this more interesting," he said, passing the glass over.

"What is it?" she asked, bringing the glass to her nose and breathing deeply. She smelled honey and cloves, exotic spices, and other, less identifiable odors, complex as good wine and more intriguing.

"This is the nectar of the gods. It has not been drunk on this Earth for lo these many, many years. Taste of it, Strategy Brooks, and know what men have sought for ages."

The newswoman thought of herself as a risktaker, but she'd be damned it she'd just up and swallow something offered her by this nutcase. "If you don't mind, I'll have some later." She smiled her best polite smile and set the drink on the floor.

He shrugged the matter away with the aplomb of a practiced maître d'. "Not at all—perhaps once you learn to trust me." His expression was utterly benign as he adjusted his sunglasses.

"All right." "So you're God?" she said, then giggled with the absurdity of the question.

"Not God, with a capital G, but rather god, with a small g, I am," Yeshua said reasonably, continuing with an innocent eagerness that disarmed her. "Now, tell me, Strategy, how are we going to bring this message to the world?" He waved his hands around the room, and immediately a small rainbow arced across the ceiling. "What do I have to do to convince a disbelieving and cynical populous? I can't spend all my time making gold and precious stones—no one will listen to me if I do; that's what people will want from me—riches and tricks."

Strategy crossed her long legs. She was on surer ground now. If there was one thing she could organize, it was a publicity campaign. "First, and most important," she said evenly, "what's in it for me?"

Yeshua sat back into the chair, the dull light in the room running like oil off his antique RayBans, "You remind me of someone—long ago—who once asked me the same question. She, too, was used to selling her services. I will give you the same answer I gave her: You can have anything your heart desires."

"And what did this woman want?"

Yeshua gestured vaguely. "Mary wanted money, jewels, fine clothes, a little power, youth, the usual."

"Always acceptable," Strategy remarked. "Speaking of power, a show of my own would be nice."

"But after a while she realised that what she really wanted was me." This statement was so candid that it didn't strike Strategy as outrageous at first.

Strategy's grin was pure ice. "Let's get this straight from

the start: I've never allowed my personal feelings to inter-
fere with my work. I will be paid."

"That's what she said." He smiled at her, no trace of
guile in his eyes.

"And don't flatter yourself; you're not my type."

"That's what she said, too."

"What happened to this Mary?" Strategy was becoming uncomfortable, her emotions squirming just below
the surface, which troubled her.

"You're not a believer then?" Yeshua asked, and answered before she could summon up a response. "No,
no, of course not. Very wise, too. Put not your trust in
gods, for their jokes are cruel and their ways are incomprehensible." He moved restlessly, then turned toward
Strategy. "What happened to Mary? Well, she eventually
decided that she was indeed my type. You will, too," he
added confidently.

"I only believe in what I can see and smell and
touch." Strategy was feeling a bit queasy from the lunacy of the situation and thought about having some of
the wine instead. But she hadn't made up her mind
about this Yeshua yet. Even though he couldn't possibly
be for real, her instincts told her there was a great story
here.

Yeshua moved his hands again, and the rainbow reap-
peared across the room. It abruptly hardened, then shattered into tiny bursts of light. The lights died to countless
crumpled white dots which slowly seesawed to the
ground. A dozen fell on the seat beside Strategy. She
reached over and touched them, half-expecting to touch
nothing more than air, and discovering that it was a ball
of tightly rolled paper. Unfolding the paper, she discovered it was a new hundred-dollar bill. The next ball she

opened was also a hundred, and the next was a new five-hundred-dollar note.

"I think you will find there are a million new dollars scattered around the room," Yeshua said. He stood up smoothly. "I'll leave you to tidy up."

"Where are you going?" Strategy said, panicked now that she was going to lose the man who had apparently casually dropped a goodly sum of money in her lap for no reason. This was well beyond caprice. She scrambled to her feet, hearing new dollar bills crackle beneath her. She nearly tipped over the wine as she reached down to retrieve it.

"Why, to rest of course," Yeshua said reasonably, nodding towards the bedroom. "Even gods have to rest. Oh," he added, "and we do not like to be disturbed." He walked past the woman, trailing a vaguely musky odor, sweet-sour, slightly reminiscent of herpetology tanks, neither pleasant nor unpleasant, but a reminder of his presence. When he stepped into the bedroom, she distinctly heard the double lock engage, and then the mag-locs snapped shut, sealing the room.

Standing in the middle of the room, Strategy Brooks looked around at the countless crumpled balls of money. "A million bucks!" she whispered, and drank the warm wine in a rush. The drink tasted sickly sweet and cloying. She could actually feel it moving down her throat, setting her insides afire. Then she wondered where the maid kept the sweeping brush.

In the darkened bedroom Yeshua stripped back the covers to give the impression that the bed had been slept in, then he lay facedown on the floor and sighed deeply. His figure flowed and shimmered. Silver-white globules formed on the surface of his skin and dripped away, puddling on the floor, before moving together where they joined in a slowly pulsating puddle.

Fawg set-ut of the Roc sighed again, a slowly rasping hiss, and the incongruous-looking RayBans slipped off his reptilian face. Holding the human form for the female had taken an extraordinary effort of will and had exhausted him. Resting his head on his crossed claws in the Sleeping Posture, he noticed that a tiny portion of his iridescent scales looked white and decidedly fleshlike. He blinked, slit pupil widening to focus, but when he looked again, the impression had passed. He would rest now, and on the morrow he would play god again. He thought he might like to raise someone from the dead, call him forth from the tomb, so that the restoration could not be attributed to medical skill. That should convince even the most hardened sceptic. Within a matter of days he—and his disciple, who, even now, was going about the task Fawg had given him—would have this planet eating out of his hands.

CHAPTER

8

KELLY EDWARDS WAS DREAMING of blood and fire and pain. So much pain. Pain so intense that it became an environment in itself. Sometimes she was the one in pain, and the blood was hers, thick and red against pallid flesh, and then the dream would twist and warp, and she was standing outside an airlock tube, looking in, and the walls were coated in gore, and the burst shape of what had once been a man was familiar. So terribly familiar. The ache of loss was so much more horrible than the lacerating sense of fire and pain. She gasped for air. The sudden reminder of her scalded deformity burned her more.

She was surprised by her vanity in the midst of such horror. But it was a part of what made her human. Even in the midst of her dream, the depths of her feelings surprised her. After all, John Dee meant little to her. He was a stranger—truly a stranger, for she had never met anyone who combined his peculiar mixture of genius and naïveté, of learning and impulsivity, with his extraordinary mix of genteel manners and coarseness. He could be aloof, friendless, and distant, a stranger in a strange land, forbidding and capricious. And, she reminded herself firmly, he was her employer. Nothing more. And still she dreamed of the small dark man, now gone, grotesquely eviscerated on the moon. The moon seemed to her to be as distant to her as any faraway sun in an outlander galaxy. She sensed herself now standing just outside the air chamber and Dee was *inside*, staring *out*. He continued to stare as his body like a inflated balloon just released flung itself about the evacuated escape hatch. His hooded eyes, dark and mysterious, watching her clinically, almost coldly, as she listened to the ominous hiss as the air was sucked from the chamber. Though blown about the airless room, Dee's questioning eyes never wavered, hanging in the air like mesmerizing bubbles. What did he want? How did he want her to *help*? How was she supposed to do that? It was too late to do anything, if there were anything she could do. Her lungs spasmed, her throat constricted as she fought for breath. But there was no breath. No air. Nothing but the austere sterility of the moon.

Only Dee, his disembodied eyes *watching* her, asking her for *what*? As she struggled to breathe, desperate to pull air into her straining lungs, there was only Dee . . .

. . . watching her. Dee.

Kelly Edwards snapped awake, head twisting, automatically biting at the gloved hand pressed over her mouth, bright green eyes wide with terror. She strained in the dark to see her attacker. There was a figure bending over her, a hand pressing lightly over her mouth. As she started to scream, the hand firmly muffled the sound but allowed her breath. In the diffused light from the screen to the side of her bed, a face rose over hers, it looked like—Good Lord! Dee.

So she was still dreaming. This dream was better than the last. He seemed more real. The figure raised a black-gloved finger to his lips and smiled, and the eyes were bright and grey, twinkling in the reflected light of the screen. His eyes, reassuringly back in his face, were still questioning. "M'Lady," he whispered, his accent and tone archaic, quaint, and completely, unmistakably Dee, "I fear I have startled you, and for that I apologize. That was not my intention, but I could not permit you to scream."

"Dee!" Kelly Edwards whispered, now sure that reality was more inexplicable than any dream, "But you're—"

"Dead? Not yet. Be of calm and quiet mind," he reassured her. The Doctor removed his glove and with his free hand tentatively smoothed Kelly's wrinkled brow. "Rumours of my death, like mountain echoes, are not to be trusted, M'Lady, particularly on so untrustworthy a body as the moon, which is known to be a source of deception. Oh, not that there wasn't cause for concern. I agree that I have been sorely tested. I think my soul a rich thing and, being of an overly miserly nature, was loathe to part with it so easily. Death is an overrated commodity. Though it is true that I should be dead—dead these many years, and yet ,by God's grace, or His whimsy, I am not. So here I stand, hale and reasonably hearty, albeit in need of a bath."

With that, he spread his arms wide and stepped back from the bed and theatrically pronounced, "My life's a miracle—that's certain. What the meaning of it may be I cannot say." He playfully posed for her in the half light, his palms raised high, his one leg semi-bent in front of the other, his head uplifted, his eyes twinkling towards heaven, allowing the woman to have a good, long look at him. He played the fool for her. His elan cheered her heart, and she began to relax. She took stock of him, giving herself the chance to see him clearly: He was one of the smallest men she had ever seen—at five-foot-two inches, she was taller by at least four inches, and yet he exuded a presence that lent him stature, in both senses of the word. He had always affected a slightly antiquated style of clothing, but now he was dressed in a simple black one-piece, vaguely military style ensemble, replete with a long tunic with countless pockets. The black boots on his feet were small enough for a child; the one black glove that covered his hand shimmered with a vaguely iridescent glow. His demeanor and his outfit were completely at odds. But there was no question that he was charming, and his charm excused all his faults. She smiled in spite of herself.

Suddenly conscious that she was lying naked in her bed, she pushed herself up on the pillows, awkwardly bunching the blankets up around her chin with her bagged and burnt hands. They stung with the contact. The sudden reminder her employer was seeing her scalded injuries burned her more than the fire in the tender new flesh. She was surprised by her vanity, which she thought she could not have. She lashed out. "How can I trust you? You're like mercury. You're unpredictable, arrogant. I suppose it would be foolish to ask how you got in here in the first place," she demanded, and then added, "and what you were doing with your hand over my mouth. I thought I was drowning."

"To answer by the book, in the order asked," Dee said as he moved to sit on her bed. "One"—raising a thumb—"have I no right to be here? I think I do—is this

not my fortress? Two"—showing her his index finger—
"have I not all the access codes including those to the
chamber below, the priest's hole, that leads to my study?
Is there some reason I should not use them? No?
Three"—holding up his middle finger—"consider my
position: Was it not wiser to wake you without rousing
our large black friend?" Dee smiled, showing his small
teeth. "For how could I know that I might wake you
without your coming back from the realm of Morpheus
ready to shoot; Fourth"—he smiled, indicating his
fourth finger—"I am in no hurry to have my presence
announced, no matter how flattering your opinion of
me may be. However, Fifth"—he presented her with his
now fully extended hand and gently laid it on her
mouth—"must I not thus put my hand on you to prevent you from shouting your head off, lest you rouse our
friend in the next room?" Kelly tried to interrupt, but
Dee's hand prevented her. It lingered there still smelling
of the glove's leather. "With d'Winter, I could not take
such a chance as I have done with you. He'd more than
likely to shoot me first."

Kelly Edwards felt the heightened sensitivity of her
lips and took a deep, uneven, shuddering breath. Dee released her uplifted chin and lips. His hand caressingly
moved higher and brushed strands of damp red hair off
her forehead. Although it had been completely burnt off
in the attack some months previously, it was growing
back, and now she kept it buzzed short, except for a single curling tail that hung down the back of her neck. She
let him minister to her for a moment, unsure of how she
felt about his touch and the sudden sensitivity of her lips.
And very concerned about what he thought of her hair.
Then she reached in under her pillow and pulled out a

small silver fletchette pistol. "And what was to stop *me* from shooting you?"

With a theatrical feint of fright, Dee smiled sadly, nodded at Kelly's still healing hands. "I knew I would have a little more time with you than I'd have with d'Winter." He cocked his head at her and teased, "With hands like that, is it possible for you to pull the trigger?" He looked at her poor swathed hands and made a face. "I think not." At that moment he wished he had not laughed at her. But he had.

The woman dropped the gun on the bed and struggled to tug the blanket around herself, though not before Dee got a glimpse of the stretched, bright-red patches of healing skin that mottled her pale flesh, then slipped out of the bed. In the final days of his campaign against Royal Newton, the industrialist had brought the battle to Dee, and both Kelly Edwards and Morgan d'Winter had very nearly perished. Only the most advanced, expensive medical care had replaced Edwards's burnt flesh, and d'Winter's broken left leg and right arm had been set and his burns treated. D'Winter, who may have been many things in his lifetime, usually a bodyguard, sometimes private hired muscle, other times military mercenary, but never, at least not so far, an assassin, affected the depilatory habits of professional fighters, so had had no hair on his head to burn off, though the fishhook he wore in his left earlobe had melted into his skin, leaving an unholy mass of scarred tissue as a reminder of that close call.

Moving noiselessly, Dee followed Edwards as she moved, naked, a blanket clutched to her bosom, down the corridor. She was already calling out Morgan d'Winter's name as she approached his room. High on the walls, gun cameras tracked her movements, programmed to a combination of her DNA and retinal pattern, pheromone scent and body pattern, to recognize her as a friend. Anything else moving down the corridor was going to be cut to pieces. Dee shutter-stepped around her trailing blanket, careful not to step on it. A bad angel prompted him to take advantage of the idea. Her body was well-formed and pink, an excellently trim, fine-made woman. If he were bold enough, what a glimpse of Heaven might be his reward. He deliberately turned his thoughts away from such speculation; there were more pressing matters to tend to.

Morgan d'Winter appeared suddenly, an indistinct shape in the gloom. A silhouette in the doorway. Even in the gloom, the black .60-calibre Wolverine Magnum was enormous. "What is it?"

The woman flashed a quick smile. "We've got a visitor," she said, and stepped to one side. Morgan d'Winter saw a shape moving in the gloom behind the woman, black on black—a fleeting smudge in the night—and the enormous pistol coughed like a wounded lion. The finger-length piece of ceramic bullet took Dee in the centre of the chest, punching him the entire length of the hallway.

CHAPTER

9

"KNOW YOU," Doctor John Dee said, still painfully alive, every breath laboured, "in my time, I was considered Fortune's favorite. I was born under most astonishing stars—no one had ever seen the like." He clucked, and coughed at the agony it gave him. He couldn't help but be amused by the irony of the situation. "This assumption was held far and wide, and familiarity made it known as truth. In that error I became a touchstone of sorts, a paragon. Should a wager be laid, the wagerers would come out and rub my head; brides on their way to the altar would beg a kiss; mothers would proffer up their babes-in-arms so that I might touch them, in the hopes that my charmed existence might pass to them. There were also those who looked upon me with fear, and would not meet my gaze for fear of a basilisk-stare." Dee took several shallow breaths. He lifted his head, his body still splayed out on the floor. The shock of the assault was clearing from his mind. His hands and arms braced to lift his upper torso. "But since coming to this cursed situation, this calamitous, lie-spawning, foul, dung-hilled, infected epoch . . ." His friends watched the color return to his face, and the Doctor begin to wind himself up like a spring. Words tumbled out barely ahead of his shortness of breath. "I have been harassed and harried, shot at and beaten by mine enemies, chased by brigands, delivered unto the void—and now, to crown the lot, a pox on it, shot by mine own people. Nothing in the Heavens accounts for it, but that we were on the moon and did partake of her lunacy." Dee paused for a moment to catch what air he could, and then his eye fixed on his distressed bodyguard. "Thou sodden-witted, arse-bussing . . . you nearly made worm's meat of me!" he roared.

"I said I was sorry," Morgan d'Winter apologized as he slipped his arms under the panting Doctor Dee. He braced his legs, straightened his back, and, with a grunt, hoisted the little man and carried him into the next room, privately reassured that it was a room that Dee would approve of—his library.

"Sorry? Sorry! 'Forget, forgive, conclude, and be damned!' " said Dee, cradled like a colicky baby in Morgan's arms. "You shoot me with something that looks like it should be mounted on the side of one of Raleigh's ships, and you fob me off with you're sorry. God's teeth, man, you bollixed up all!"

The big man lowered him gently into a leather chair. The air sighed out of the cushion under Dee's weight. "You're still alive, aren't you?"

"Aye, so it seems," Dee said cynically. "No thanks to you."

D'Winter shook his head, wanting to relieve some of his shock; he could not blame his employer's crankiness. He walked to the liquor cabinet, saying under his breath,

"Hell, I was just doing my job. I shot at an uninvited intruder."

"Does this exonerate you?" Dee asked edgily.

This was more than d'Winter was willing to accept. "Well then, you should not have come creeping in here in the middle of the night. And you're lucky you didn't come creeping into my room first. I'd have probably shot you in the doorway—and more than likely tried for a headshot. So your fancy suit wouldn't have been able to stop that."

"Is that what saved him?" Kelly Edwards asked loudly, forcing both men to turn to her. Now that they were settled in Dee's ornate, book-lined study and library, the room a combination of styles and periods, crammed with the scientific instruments of another age sitting alongside the latest high-tech equipment. Walls of books and maps—real books, printed on genuine paper, and folded paper maps were bundled together with flat-screen readers and cheap disposable book-e-s and read-e-s.

She was sitting in a deep leather chair, wrapped in a thick blanket, before a simulated fireplace, which radiated heat while projecting the holographic image of a burning log. He had originally objected to this seeming illusion, demanding the real thing, but Kelly had countered explaining about county housing restrictions outlawing smoke and fumes and open fires. Dee had acquiesced, reluctantly.

The color was beginning to seep back into her face; the hand holding the shot of brandy had stopped shaking. She stared at the holographic fire and replayed the scene. When she had stepped aside so that d'Winter could see Dee, she had been momentarily confused by a deep bark, although why she didn't recognize the sound, she still couldn't think—until she realised that d'Winter had shot Dee and that the small man was flying down the corridor on his back. The memory made her shudder, and she used both hands to hang on to the glass. She forced the recollection out of her thoughts, shifting her focus back to the present. She'd seen too much death recently. She didn't want to see any more.

D'Winter shrugged, then walked back to Dee, bringing the Doctor a glass of his favorite tipple—iced milk. John Dee gave him a withering look. It was a silent, blaring accusation. "Hey, no matter what you think, it was the right thing to do, shooting. That's what you pay me for."

"Shooting at *me* is not part of your job," Dee told him sharply.

"But—" d'Winter began guiltily, "when I saw Kelly in the corridor, with the shape behind her, I thought it was some sort of trick. I thought someone had a gun to her back and was coercing her. When you stepped aside, I saw the opening and took it." He shrugged again. "That's how I've stayed alive these many years."

"And how many innocent men have you left for dead in your wake?" Dee snapped, rubbing the heel of his hand against his sore chest.

"Enough," d'Winter said flatly, "though I doubt that most of them were innocent—merely stupid," he added. He hesitantly offered the drink to the Doctor.

"And your suit," Kelly Edwards asked abruptly, as she saw the doctor open his mouth to respond, "that protected you? How is that possible?"

"Yes . . . yes, so it appears," Dee said, taking the milk with one hand and rubbing his hand down the silklike material with the other. He had come to crave milk, although in his own age it was the tipple of infants and used more for cream and cheese than providing something to drink, for milk soured quickly and became unwholesome. The suit regained his attention. In certain light, the countless tiny overlapping scales, like the skin of a serpent, were clearly visible. "It turned the shell." He, too, wondered how the suit had saved him.

"More than turned it," d'Winter said, opening his palm. Nestling in the deeply lined skin was a piece of what looked like melted glass. Reaching into his pocket, d'Winter produced a .60-calibre ceramic bullet and placed it alongside the melted blob. "This is what it should look like."

Dee, his scientific curiosity aroused, touched both bullets with his tiny, long-nailed, elegant fingers. "I do not entirely understand the properties of this suit," he admitted, "though it *seems* that this bullet has been melted by some intense heat."

"Doctor," d'Winter said quietly, "this is a ceramic bullet, traveling at subsonic speed. It can punch through half a metre of solid prestressed concrete without shattering until it hits something soft. It can even get through impervium. It should have gone right through that fancy suit of yours, smacked into your sternum, where it would have shattered into hundreds of tiny pieces of pottery, and shredded your insides. I could hit you almost anywhere with this, and you would be dead before you hit the floor."

"What a . . . vivid picture you draw. If that be so, it follows, then, that this pretty piece of snakeskin somehow purloined the energy generated by this same shell and transferred it back into the shell itself. If it had done nothing more than stop it by simple strength, then the shell should have shattered and left me a bloody corpse."

D'Winter nodded. "Even double X impervium will not stop this little baby."

Dee was not entirely sure what double X impervium was, but he was not prepared to betray his ignorance. "Witchcraft, eh? Or alchemy."

"Doctor," Kelly Edwards said solemnly, "I think it is time for some answers."

Dee turned to the woman, a vague, irrational snap of anger in his eyes. How dare she demand—and then he realised that this was not his own age, his own era, where women—certain women—were little more than chattel. Where women's prerogatives were defined exclusively by the men who housed and defended them, except, of course, for the Queen's Grace. Here, in these modern times, all women had the rights of his queen, and the law gave them protection undreamt of in his own age.

"Kelly is right," Morgan said, moving around to lean against the fireplace, resting a bandaged arm against the mantelpiece. "I think we both knew, from the very beginning, that you were no ordinary man. Not simply because you were displaced in time, a living anachronism—that took months to digest. For a while I thought you were some criminal—Tong-Mafia, New Yakuza—on the run from your employers. Then I thought you might be government—maybe from the rumoured Free-Illuminati who are gearing up to take over this world, but in the end I realised that you were none of these. You were—are!— unique, Doctor Dee. You're an impossibility. You and your gadgets contradict everything science and my mind tells me makes sense."

"Then haply your science is wrong," said Dee.

"It must be." In a tone of complete mystification , the very practical d'Winter admitted," Kelly and I have no idea what makes you tick. And now the time has come to tell us."

Dee neither moved nor spoke. His face did not betray the flurry of racing thoughts that filled his mind. His awareness of how hard it had been to breathe all but disappeared. "I think you owe us that," Kelly said softly. "Our association with you has cost us dearly. I lost my brother, and both Morgan and I were very nearly killed. And you, good Doctor Dee, you," she said, again shaking the recent scenario from her head, "should be dead."

Dee sank back into the deep leather chair, allowing its wings to shadow his face, and brought the glass of milk up to his lips. The white was startling and incongruous against his black suit, a gift from Dyckon

Kelly and Morgan watched him, saying nothing then they saw that the material of the black suit was changing, altering slightly—what had once been solid black had now altered subtly to match the deep wine-colour of the leather chair, while Dee's black boots, which did not quite touch the floor, had taken on the vague outline of the Oriental rug beneath it. Within a dozen heartbeats Dee had become practically invisible against the chair. Dee, unaware of the change taking place and mistaking his watchers' rapt attention for concentration on what he was about to say, took a deep breath, then let it out again.

Amazed by the changing garment, neither Edwards nor d'Winter said anything. They watched transfixed. They had asked this chimera for his innermost secret and was he now revealing himself? They had long since learned that he was capable of the unimaginable. Would not all be revealed?

"I don't know where to begin," Dee admitted, wanting

to tell them the truth and not certain how do it. All his life he had lied and never thought about it. There were lies and there were lies. Life for him had always been a lie. He had lied to survive, at court, on his missions, at home. He had lied to protect himself, to protect others. He had sold his soul to protect his country and his Queen from their detractors and their enemies. He prayed Heaven would understand. He intended only the most admirable results from his deceptions. Admittedly, there was no Tudor England to protect now. Then he had lied to betray his foes, and sometimes his friends. He had lied to serve the Queen's gracious realm. He had lied to keep himself from prison. Did not falsehood, falsehood cure? Lying was as innate in him as the instinct to stay alive. And now he was faced with a dilemma: Which version of the truth, or which lie, would he tell? These two would scarcely believe his present-day Truth. It would seem to them like nothing but an unimaginable conceit, the assumptions of a man from another time who was, by their lights, woefully uneducated. Therefore, the Truth, as he understood it, was out of the question. What was needed was the virtuous lie. Kelly and Morgan were all he had. He could not bear to lose them. But which lie could he afford to tell? And was there a fixed line twixt truth and lie, for there were even occasions when he himself could not tell the difference. "Tell me, my friends," he asked softly, "do you trust me?"

"We have trusted you with our lives," d'Winter answered for both of them. "What more do you want?"

"Now, that is something to consider," Dee allowed.

"And now we're looking for a reason to trust you further; we can't go along on the expectation that everything will be all right because you say it will," Kelly bravely added. Her sense of reality challenged by what she saw in front of her. "Because if you expect us to stay with you and survive, we need to know what you are and what we are up against." She punctuated her last word with a swallow of brandy.

"There is a truth in that," Dee agreed.

"You've been lucky so far, way more lucky than you have any right to be, but you can't tell me it'll last forever, no matter what you say your stars promise," d'Winter pointed out. "You can't rely on that kind of luck forever, especially if we don't know what we're dealing with—if we knew more, I wouldn't have taken a shot at you."

Dee nodded. "Your argument has merit."

"We can't afford another mistake like that," said d'Winter. "Suit or no suit, you're taking too many chances. I don't want to kill you unless I mean to do it."

"Certainly," Dee said, chuckling. "All right. All right."

And so he told them the truth. All of it.

CHAPTER

10

EXTRACT FROM THE Day Booke of John Dee, Doctor, in the year of Our Lord 2100:

Whoever is born possessed of a sound mind is naturally formed by the Heavens for some honourable work and way of life, or so the Church of England teaches. That is believed to be certain. Those of us who study the stars have a different view. Therefore, despite Divine Intervention and to the extent that you can, whoever desires to live in the way shown in the Heavens, let him undertake above all else the way of life that he was born for; let him pursue his bent zealously, for the Heavens favor this Natural directive. That activity which from tender years you choose, speak, playact, dream, imitate; that activity which you try more frequently, which you perform more easily, which you enjoy above all other, which you leave off unwillingly, that which is written for you in the stars; that assuredly is the reason why the Heavens and the ruler of your Horoscope gave it to you from birth. Within this frame-

work, you will promote your life and your chances for Heaven by being diligent to the road that you were born to travel.

I was born to lie. With that God-given propensity come the graces of double-dealing, promise-breaking, gaming, counterfeiting, and intelligencing. I have prospered in all these seeming vices for the betterment of others. I twist the truth to find the Truth, but that is what Mercury destined for me from the hour of my birth—Mercury moving retrograde, in trine with Mars. What else could I do that would not deny my destiny? So I have never been troubled by the concept of falsehood.

Truth is as we perceive it, and the perspective of the viewer colours Truth's interpretation. When my Protestant England stood firm in Church controversy against the Irish and Spanish Catholics, we believed, in our heart of hearts, that our Way was True and Holy, and they, the Papists, were spiritually deceived. And if any doubted this, they did so at great peril, and paid for their temerity dearly. But verily, if I may use so honest a word for this work by a double-dealer such as I—for I had leisure to parlay with the O'Neill when he was hard by Windsor Castle—that he and his fellows believed with equal rigor that their Roman Vatican was in the right. Consider also Galileo and Bruno who were once judged godless for their beliefs, although now they are hailed as prophets and visionaries: No one would have dared to endorse their opinions when they first gave voice to them. Truth, not unlike Proteus, changes its shape as every man and every age tangles with it.

I feasted with vipers in the Royal court of our Virgin Queen (what be that title, but a National counterfeit? I can say this now, but then, my head would have been forfeit had I so much as whispered so traitorous a thought) by giving the lie, about myself and others. It was a necessary feint, for I desired to survive, yea, prosper in that inimical snakepit. It was given out that in my studies as a mathematician, I dabbled as a magician, and could decipher the secrets of the stars. Therefore, I was called sorcerer and a magus, but I was neither, wanting, as I did, the initiation that such practitioners must pass through. Yet, I allowed my countrymen, and by extension all of Europe, to perceive me as such. Verily, in my studies, I was naught but a diligent scholar and Elizabeth's own poor astrologer; my other studies I stumbled upon by happy accident. Now that I am in this place where the religion of empiricism prevails, my work is accepted as the purview of science, but to my mind it is still the clandestine and black learnings frowned upon by the Church that I first undertook when other men, less favored than I, went to the stake or the dungeons for their curiosity.

No amount of pulpit pounding could ever dissuade me from my belief that by breathing my innermost thoughts to others, I exposed myself, betrayed my weaknesses. The blabbing of simple truth is naught but simplicity. Maintaining a virtuous veracity in that tempestuous court, was tantamount to penning my own death warrant. My ambition was made of sterner stuff. In the accomplishing of my career, there was no more charity in me, than there is milk in the Tyger. In the shadow of the English court, I learned the value of the planted rumour, the secret whisper, the allusion to a competitor's indiscretion, the uncloaking of another's unacceptable desires, or the delineation of an upstart's over-

weening pride. Well-placed suggestions I scattered like seeds. Some there were that would find fertile ground, grow, and take on a life of their own, and in doing so become accepted fact. Opinion has ever made the listener a fool. It cozens the unwary into scanning the outward habit for the inward man. I became a master craftsman of that stately craft. At second glance, mayhap, there was Truth in my being called Sorcerer. For most assuredly the power to alter appearances was mine.

All I learned, I learned from mine governor, my lord, Her Majesty's own Secretary of State, Sir Francis Walsingham, Spymaster par excellance. I also had a nodding acquaintance with Kit Marlowe, and all his little schemes; clever as he was, he was no match for Walsingham, who could damn a man with faint praise, indeed. He was my Chiron. But here's the rub: Doubtless he never studied the value of truth or rather the value of truth-speaking. Nor was he tutored in the loving clasp of fellowship.

I had friends at court, though there perhaps the word was used even more loosely than it is bandied about now; I had allegiances and alliances at court. After all, friendship oft has no more substance than an airy word; either of which is naught but nothingness. In those days I gave myself the lie that I had friends aplenty. Rather I had those who would hail-fellow me one day and stab me in the back the next, I allowed as friends, as did many another. Marlow at Mistress Bull's in Deptford fell victim to the same dangerous illusion and so died, stabbed through the eye—an apt death for a flawed and foolish vision of the world.

There were women, too, who would call me friend

*and some would call me lover, and I paid for their
mouthings with favours and sometimes with coin. But
had I friends? Friends I would trust with my life? The
question continues to haunt me.*

*Mayhap, insofar as true friends are rare, I was pos-
sessed of only one; that Irish whoreson rogue, Edward
Kelly, whom I dearly loved. But even to him, who partook with me in diverse schemes and visions, who
abided in my bosom more than any other, I never
utterly unmasked myself. For I was ever wary that he
was, by Nature, and by his stars, a thief, an oppor-
tunist, and a mercenary, selling his skills and his information to the highest bidder and so far did I trust him.
I am not so blind but I do see in him the very book
where my sins are writ. But in defence of my soul's sal-
vation, I did all for country and Queen. Edward was
not so scrupulous. His stomach and his purse were ever
his inspirations. But leave him be, he has been dead too
long for me to give him bad report.*

*And these other two? Are they in truth Friends?
Friends I would trust with my life? This night, they
chided me for withholding the secret of my true identity. They made demands of me of my secret life, as if
they had some sovereign right to my Truth. By being
secretive, they said I was unjustly false to them who
had more than proven true to me. Make no mistake, I
had paid them well in coin for service and owed them
no other recompense. Nature and custom prompted me
to lie and dissemble, for I had no doubt that I could
spin a fiction that would have soon satisfied them. But
the lie went stillborn. Some nagging scruple, born of
this last year, forbade me. Their devotion went far
beyond the pittance I paid. They had given their blood*

for me and, in the woman's case, the life of her brother. These are sacrifices that weight heavy on me. Those days when we fought together were dangerous, and their Loyalty never wavered. She was my counselor; he was my cudgel. They comforted me in the darkest of times. Their love was ever manifest. Yet Sir Francis was wont to remind me that times of adversity oft may hoop together the dog and the cat. And manifest Love may be feigned Policy. Yet, when the hunt for Newton was over, they ministered to my fledgling organization even when I had vanished from their sight. They dutifully expended their wherewithal in desperate search for me. Here was no self-interest to be gained. Here was no feigned playacting to curry favor. Sith, for all they knew, I might well have perished. Therefore it seems that in these two, Love and Loyalty are truly demonstrated. And what is friendship but Love and Loyalty. I could not but reason that both had oft been tested and always proved to be aurum ultima, rare metal indeed.

I was forced to ask the question: What bitter scene should stage itself out if and when my friends were to learn the truth? Sure, I would lose them both, lose their trust and their love. Such a loss, I realized, should undo me and leave me a drowned man, bereft of air and life. This is a play not to my liking. I have discovered (a discovery that gives a man like me more than pause to here acknowledge) that these two are as important to my ease as rest and nourishment. For I am lonely in spirit. Lonely as those last days in Venice, walled in with my world only peopled by wretched bleak thoughts. Lonely these four hundred years. Lonely for my former life that has vanished as surely as a dream, for a London that can be found no more, for the slyness and *rapacity of the court, for the churchyard nights. No, I write too quickly. Wanting of true companionship, in mine own time, I ached with loneliness. Now, miraculously, twenty score years in the future, I have found two boon companions whom in the way of friendship I love and cannot believe but that they love me. My soul rejoices in the discovery.*

And, reasoning thus, though perhaps not so rationally as this age would dictate: that as they had demonstrated their friendship and love to me, then surely, if I had any humanity left in me, I must do something in return for them. I must needs tell them the truth. The whole truth. Without bark or polish on it.

Yet, old ways run deep in me.

It took perhaps four hours, from start to finish, from the de' Medici castle to the gargoyle's rescue of me in the airlock on the airless moon and my return to Earth. I recounted my first mission, and I spoke of my second mission, which now had a two-fold reason to it, to bar the spread of the virus and to make good if Fawg is indeed in possession of a time-journeying device.

I had expected questions. To my great surprise there were none. Nor were there any loud expostulations denying my Truth. Nor was there a wringing of hands of the coming Apocalypse. Nor were there any doubts in me expressed.

When I was finished, exhausted with the telling, they both stood confusedly to take their leave of me. They, with few words between them and some nodding of their heads, said merely, "Good night."

D'Winter squeezed my shoulder gently, and Kelly's lips brushed my cheek, and both said that they were

*weary and would see me in the morning. Then they
retired.*

*How am I to interpret their reactions? Is there a
magic bonding in truth-telling? Or was the old repro-
bate, Walsingham, right in his universal distrust? Was
I wrong to abandon my true self?*

*In mine own time, if I had told such a tale, I would
have been burnt as a witch, or dismissed as mad. But
these are mad times, where even madness is deemed
sane. So, here I scribble, alone with my unhappy
affairs, awaiting the dawn and their reaction.
Certainly, as if a weight removed, I have a great relief
for having shared my story with them. In my heart, this
truth-sharing topples the last wall that stands between
us. Yet, it harrows me with fear that by blabbing what
should have remained hid, I have lost their precious
love that I have but late acquired. What will they think
of me? Have I doomed myself once again to a sterile
loneliness? I feel I am a prisoner in London's Tower,
awaiting the verdict from the Privy Council, either to
newfound joy or to the block and the axe.*

CHAPTER

11

THE WIDOW WAS DRESSED entirely, dramatically, and very fashionably in black. Perhaps the hat was a little too large, the half-veil a touch too much, the dark glasses too chic, and the skirt just a little too short, the high-heels a little too high. But, Leeta reasoned, this was her day, her day to take centre stage and, who knew, perhaps one of her late husband's producer friends would be in the audience—sorry, amongst the mourners—and would spot her obvious talents. At least a pair of those talents had been bought and paid for by her late husband, Romulas. Leeta O'Connor locked her slender legs together as the chauffeur opened the door. Silk slithered across butter-soft leather seats as she slid out and took Clive's leather-gloved hand and straightened, facing the enormous gothic gates of Forest Lawn Cemetery, Elysian Fields Development sitting high atop the Hollywood hills. A blast of copper- and sulphur-tasting heat from the naked afternoon sun washed over her. The city below and to her right was coated with a bilious yellow haze from the Pit. The raven-haired young Englishman kept his eyes firmly fixed on the top of the woman's hat, unwilling to meet her eyes, which he hoped would be sparkling with wicked humour and lust. There was everything to play for now, and all they had to do was to play it cool for the next couple of weeks—if he could only keep her from blowing it.

Mother Petronella O'Connor appeared in front of Leeta. Hatched-faced and grim, the old woman must have been at least one hundred and twenty, but five husbands—and five fortunes—and countless plastic surgeries had kept her looking not a day over eighty. Her priceless emerald necklace spread like a banner just above her reconstructed cleavage. Although she had lived in America all her life, she had deliberately cultivated an Irish brogue lifted from VTV shows and movies, that would have been unintelligible in what remained of the island of Ireland.

And because Mother O'Connor had married her way into successively *richer* relationships, she instinctively recognised Leeta and knew her for what she was. And there was no way this tart was getting hold of her Rommie's fortune. Smiling bitterly, the plump old woman latched a clawlike hand onto Leeta's arm and fell into step beside her. "Lend me your arm, can you? I'm a bit stiff today." The old lady's vise grip on the younger woman's arm just above the elbow made resistance futile. "You must be just devastated," she said in her mock-Irish accent.

"Completely," Leeta said, hoping the death-grip would end soon. She was sure she was getting a bruise. Judging the moment to be appropriate, the leggy honey-brunette extracted a tiny square of antique silk from her cleavage and patted it against her eyes. The tears came then, large and lustrous, like moonstones, brought on by the pepper-spray she had used on the handkerchief. "Rommie was everything to me."

Mother O'Connor nodded without a trace of sympathy. The friends and well-wishers that had gathered to pay their respects to Romulas O'Connor, entrepreneur and businessman who had made his fortune in the fish restaurant business—"If it ain't O'Connor's, it ain't fish"—would have seen nothing more than the pretty young trophy bride dutifully escorting her grieving mother-in-law up to the grave site. They nodded courteously to their well-wishers. If they had been very close, they might have seen that Mother O'Connor's grip on Leeta's arm was white-knuckled in its intensity. They might have been greatly surprised that Leeta's pain was more physical than emotional.

"I'll cut you a deal, girl," the old woman said, through smiling teeth. The word *girl*, distorted by the phony brogue, sounded more like "ger-rrel." The elongated diphthong set Leeta's teeth on edge.

"Deal?" Leeta sniveled. "I don't know what you mean." Her brown eyes widened appreciably in surprise. She had never been able to get along with Mother O'Conner, not since she landed in Angel City and had found Romulas O'Conner at one of his restaurants, just ripe for the plucking. Since that hour the two women had been locked in genteel, mortal combat.

"Oh, aye, you do. You know exactly what I mean." Mother O'Conner took her daughter-in-law's powdered chin in her hand and examined her face. "I was about your age when I married Morrie Senior, your Rommie's father. Well, I suppose the difference between you and me is that I was a wee bit more patient than you. Wasn't

I? I made sure he knocked me up before he had his heart attack, eh? I had custody, did I not, of his fortune and little Rommie's, too." The old lady released the widow's chin.

"Why, Mother—"

"Don't mother me, *girl*; I'm no more your mother than you are Saint Bridget," the old woman snapped, elongating the word a little longer than usual. Their discussion was interrupted by the swish of metal car doors opening. She then turned sadly to watch the hearse unload its coffin. The two women observed silence while the solid oak—real wood—casket with genuine imitation gold fittings was wheeled out onto the gurney. A wreath of flowers in the shape of an enormous fish—"From All the Staff at O'Connor's Fish Restaurants"—was placed on top. From the street level, the casket and all its trappings slowly made its way up the hill.

"Here's the deal, now. I'll cut you in for twenty-five percent of Romulas's fortune. You take it, you disappear: I want *never* to see you again. Go back to Texas, or fly to the moon, just leave L.A. Basin forever. If you don't, I'll fix it so you never get a dollar from the estate. Think about it. We needn't fight about this. Sure, you'll come out with about eight million before inheritance tax if you're willing to take my offer. But that's not bad for fifteen months on your back, eh? And you won't have to pay a lawyer a single dime." The couple had been married for fifteen months. There had been no sex before the marriage; Leeta had demanded that.

"Twenty-five percent?" Leeta asked icily, all pretense of grieving now gone. "And why should I settle for less than half when I can have it all?"

"I'll contest it is why," the old woman said firmly.

"Rom was a schmuck, he was, for not getting you to sign a prenuptial agreement. I warned him about you, but would he listen? He was fat and he was an idiot and he was always a sucker for big-haired brunettes with big brown eyes and a little-girl-lost attitude. And double-D gahzoolies to dangle in front of him." The old dowager blinked repeatedly in mock imitation of Leeta's style. "Easy t'is to legally claim he was not of sound mind when he changed his will to make you sole benefactor. bejesus, he was being treated for depression!"

"Only because you depressed him." The sweetness was gone from her smile now, leaving only a display of teeth not unlike a snarl. She had known women like this, back in Texas: Her Aunt Opal was just such a woman as Mother O'Conner, and Leeta had made a study of her from her youth. The only difference here was that Opal had been on her side, while Mother O'Conner was plainly her enemy.

"Aye, but its enough to throw a spanner in your works." She chuckled. "Don't think I won't do it. I can and I will. It'll go to the courts and stay there for years, that it will. I can wait. Can you? It'll cost you millions in lawyer fees."

Four of Romulas O'Connor's employees, who had taken part in a lottery at the restaurant to see who would get the privilege of carrying the coffin, walked past with the heavy box astride their straining shoulders. O'Conner had been as big as a whale. The faintest aroma of stale fish wafted after them.

The two women fell into step behind the coffin. Leeta returned the silk hankie and the pepper spray back to her eyes. Her eyes gleamed. "And while it is that we're waiting," Mother O'Connor continued, "I'll just continue my

investigations into just who Leeta Robertson is really."
She felt the involuntary twitch of muscle in the younger
woman's arm in a vain attempt to escape her clutch; she
pressed her advantage. "You see, I happen to know that
Leeta Robertson never existed; but I do know of a Rita
Lee Roberts, from Paris, Texas. Her mother a waitress in a
breakfast bar, and her father unknown. Four brothers,
three sisters; DNA testing confirms that all were sired by
different men. Looks like little Rita Lee took after her
mama, except she was a wee bit more clever than her
waitress-mother, and aimed higher than a diner owner.
There ain't much I haven't got on you, girl." As the diphthong in 'girl' was enunciated, Leeta saw all the perfectly
crowned teeth of her mother-in-law's mouth. Too bad,
she thought, that when you lose a spouse or divorce him,
you legally keep the in-laws. "I can paint you blacker
than black in any court, I can. But sure I don't want to do
that—not because I've got any feelings for Romulas, dear
girl—but because it would be bad PR for some of my
own business interests. Wouldn't it, now?" She patted
down her lipstick with the edge of her hankie. "So my advice to you, little girl, is to take your money and run."
She emphasized the thought with a sharp head turn towards the cemetery road. There something caught her
eye. "Sure, if you've got a brain in your head, and if you'll
take a bit of advice from someone a bit older and a lot
more experienced—you'll dump the feckin' Brit chauffeur first chance you get."

"I had intended to," Leeta said softly, wiping away her
tears. "He's amusing, but he's starting to cling."

"Good girl." Mother O'Connor smiled as she finally
released her daughter-in-law's arm. "I knew you were
sensible. Why else did you marry my son?"

"I didn't kill him," Leeta said suddenly, "I'm sure of it."

"Oh, are you, now?" The old woman was not going to allow the baggage to ease her conscience with any easy self-deception. "Well, bejesus, I think you did, girl," Mother O'Connor said evenly. "A pretty young fancy bit like you; my little idjit wouldn't have been able to keep his hands off you. And we both know that my Romulas needed to lose some weight and that he had high blood pressure." There was devilish delight in the old lady's eyes as she piled on the guilt. "You killed him, you did. Killed him as sure as you're standing here. I've seen the doctor's report and the autopsy. I know what he was doing the night he died. Heart attack was the official verdict. And it would probably stand up in court, but for Rita Lee. So make up your mind: Agree now, or lose everything. I'll do it, for the memory of my boy as well as his fortune, which you got most shamefully. But, *girl*, we both know he died happy," she said with a wry smile, and then added, "My second husband went the same way. Died with a smile on his face, he did. I guess it's a family curse."

Leeta O'Conner, unable now to harbor any illusion about what a schemer she was, reflected on what she had done; she had to admit the old woman had a point. A nearby relative would later report that she had heard the young widow plaintively say to herself, "Oh, Rom." And that a tear fell from her eye.

They climbed up the cemetery path to the graveside, past headstones that time and acid rain and radioactive wind had rendered illegible, past pointing angels and wreath-wrapped crosses that had wilted in the elements. Here and there in the cemetery, bright splashes of colour, artificial flowers under Plexiglas shields, told of other interments of Old Money. This Forest Lawn Development had been closed to new occupants for nearly fifty years now, and only family interments into established plots were permitted. A conservative estimate put the value of each plot at something approaching three-quarters of a million, making it a final gesture of conspicuous consumption. The mourners fell in behind the two women, men who would have been of an age with Romulas. They were accompanied either by wives as old as themselves or younger second or third trophy wives. Either way, many of the men looked worried and tired.

At the edges of the crowd were some of O'Connor's less respectable colleagues: a sullen group of bulky Russians, illegal traders in fish culled from the *Hot Waters*. This was the local name for the coastal offshore sea between L.A. and San Diego. The underlying seabed had been so polluted with factory debris and atomic waste that the surf above was slightly radioactive. The core meltdown at San Onofrio had made it worse. Monstrous fish, squid, and abalone had been pulled from *Hot Waters'* depths. But stripped of their hideous skins, the marine freaks had often been gobbled up in O'Connor's Fish Restaurants, usually as the "Catch of the Day." Beside the Russians, there was a larger group of Chinese from the New Territories, Aleuts from the Red Island Republic, and an international crew of boatmen who manned the distinctive O'Connor green, white, and gold fleet. Most of them knew that more than fish came ashore in the monofilament nets that they harvested from the Pacific. Moving through the crowd and part of it were the police photographers surreptitiously taking pictures. Everyone knew that Rommie wasn't as dumb as he looked and that there was no way he'd made a pot of money out of just selling fried fish. Therefore he had to be doing something a little illegal—and although they had been investigating him for more than ten years, they still hadn't managed to find out what he was into. The Narcs suspected drugs and the Feds were reasonably sure about illegals, but there was nothing that either agency could pin on him. Maybe, the cops thought, the funeral might attract some interesting new leads. Some were wondering if the young wife might now take the reins in the company. However, they all agreed that the real power lay with the terrifying mother. At the back of the group, nestled under a withered copse of trees, a GNN news van hummed .

CHAPTER

12

"FRIENDS, WE ARE GATHERED here today to pay our last respects to our brother, Romulas, though," Father Wallace, the stout, florid-faced priest, added with a condescending smile, "we all knew him as Rommie." Father Wallace had a high voice with a prominent lisp; his bulbous nose overwhelmed his face. The portly priest stood behind a portable transparent lectern, upon which he had placed his notes and his Bible. The Father wasn't very tall and his balding head could barely be seen above the podium. Directly in front of him, the heavy wooden coffin now sat on the hoist that would lower it into the freshly opened ground. An enormous mountain of flowers, real and artificial, lay to one side, ready to be piled on top of the heaped earth. Mother O'Connor and Leeta sat on folding chairs to the priest's right—and the priest was having a hard time keeping his eyes off the young widow. He'd heard the rumours about how old Rommie had met his end—and though he was a man of the cloth, and supposedly celibate—though who believed that anymore!—he decided that was how he wanted to go. Going out with a bang came to mind, and he immediately raised a white handkerchief to mop his brow as well as the top of his exposed head. He hid the knowing smile and licked his wet lips. Seated and standing beyond the widow and mother were collected the usual group of friends and colleagues; the women overdressed, the men sporting the obligatory black tie or armband. Some checked their sports watches; others chatted up deals with business associates. None of them seemed too happy to be there, and they were all conscious that in a couple of hours the Santa Ana Devil's Breath would swirl up a lethal cocktail of radioactive dirt and poisonous air around the Hollywood Hills. The late afternoon wind wouldn't kill you immediately, but it eventually took you down, turning your lungs into soup and your skin to boils.

"Romulas was a good man," Father Wallace continued. "A family man; he looked after his mother." The congregation turned to look at Mother O'Connor and, as one, decided that she didn't need looking after. "And of course the tragedy here is that Rommie leaves behind his bride of fifteen months." The assembly turned to look again, and most of the men decided that Leeta certainly needed looking after, and wondered if they should volunteer for that task. The women decided that they would rather look after her as she walked away.

"We know not the ways of the Lord. We know not why he has taken our brother from us at this time. But there will come a day when all will be revealed to us."

"And that day is upon us now." The voice was low, commanding, powerful, and it echoed flatly across the still cemetery. The assembly turned to look at the man who was moving, almost gliding, through the gravestones towards them. He was tall and handsome, some would say even beautiful, jet-black tightly curled black hair atop a high tanned forehead, eyes hidden behind dark reflective glasses, and dressed entirely in white, even down to his boots. Behind him followed a GNN news crew, with Strategy Brooks herself in the lead.

Father Wallace took a deep breath and tried to regain his composure. "Sir, this is a funeral service—"

"Not anymore." The voice stilled any further questions. All eyes were on the man now, the three GNN vids rolling silently, capturing a perfect three-dimensional image, while Strategy, who had prepared a script, remained silent.

"I have come again, my people, come again as I promised you, and this time I will not abandon you."

The man moved through the congregation until he was standing at the foot of the grave, his voice ringing out as he neared the coffin. "I asked myself what would utterly convince you that I had returned, for I am only too aware that there are many who use my identity in vain. Once, there was a man called Thomas who had to touch my wounds before he could accept the truth. I am here today to demonstrate proof to all the present-day Thomases—before they have a chance to doubt my second coming."

Crossing himself quickly, "This is blasphemy," the priest whispered.

The two Mrs. O'Conners scanned the crowd for the funeral director, affronted at the cemetery staff for allowing this publicity stunt. After all, they had plunked down a hundred thousand for the ceremony.

"The truth is never blasphemous," the man in white said. "I have chosen this poor sinner at random, and I have come here to show the world that my message is for rich and poor alike, that no one is exempt from my great love."

"Who is he?" Leeta whispered; she was now prepared for all manner of shenanigans from her mother-in-law, and supposed this must be part of her plan to keep Leeta from claiming the fortune she had earned.

"He's pretending to be Jesus Christ, he is," Mother snapped.

"Oh," Mrs. O'Conner, the younger, murmured. She'd been raised En-Pagan, but had stopped attending Sabbaths before she's turned three. She only vaguely knew the story of Jesus of Nazareth.

The stranger turned his proud head towards Mother. "Not pretending," he said, though there was no way he could have heard her whisper. "And this is for you, and the others like you" he added mysteriously. Crouching down, he caught the edge of the coffin lid and pulled. With a snap of splintering wood, the lid went sailing off across the graveyard, leaving the coffin gaping open, revealing the pasty corpse dressed in his best summer suit.

A shocked murmur went around the crowd. All eyes were now fixed on the man claiming to be Jesus Christ, and the police cameras had given up on their detective work and turned to record the bizarre events.

"Romulas" the stranger said, "Romulas, rise. It is not yet your time. Come back to us. Come back to your loved ones." The stranger stretched out his hand and touched the dead man's cheek.

Romulas opened his eyes and sat up in the coffin.

Leeta squealed and fainted into an unseemly heap at her mother-in-law's feet. All Romulas's mother could say was "Shi-i-ite!"

CHAPTER

13

DOCTOR JOHN DEE was still sitting in the same chair as dawn washed bitter acidic yellow over the blasted Angel City landscape. In the corner of the room an ornate Austrian pendulum clock circa 1730 struck six on the mantel. Each reverberating toll inspired Dee's preparedness to accept his fate. He had studied the stars and their meaning was clear to him. Six was the appointed hour for reconvening with his friends. He drew in a deep breath; he heard them coming. He sat a little straighter and smoothed his hair.

Kelly Edwards was the first to enter the chamber. She was dressed in simple green military fatigues made fashionable by a GNN newswoman, and her pallid flesh and shock of red hair were in stark contrast to the drab green and brown. She had changed her clothes, but it was obvious she had not slept the night. Morgan d'Winter strode into the room with his usual dogged resolve and moved to the chair he had vacated some hours previously. Neither of them looked directly at each other but kept their focus on the Doctor.

Kelly spoke first. "John, why don't we open the blinds? There's no light in here." She moved towards the window.

"No. Pray don't." Dee quickly raised his arm to wave her away from changing the mood. "I like the gloom. I've met all my moments of crisis in darkness. Truth is I've never gotten use to your time's overlit rooms. A taper to dispel the immediate blackness is all one really requires. Besides, the garish brightness hurts my eyes."

Kelly acceded to the Doctor's objections and took a seat on the nearby couch; d'Winter sank into his chair as if he intended to take root there. The three sat in uneasy silence, each wanting to break the tension, but not knowing where to start.

The Elizabethan favourite thought to himself, "Fortune, thou strumpet, turn your wheel if you must. But do it apace. I am racked with waiting." He coughed and spoke aloud: "Well, you have returned to me, and that, I hope, is a fortunate sign." Neither of his listeners seemed to have heard him. Neither made any response. "I would not have been surprised if, after hearing my fantastical tale, you had packed your bags and fled into the night," he said, this time a little louder.

"Believe me, I thought about it," d'Winter said sourly, his eyes riveted on the man sitting across from him. "I've worked for madmen before; I don't like it. They usually end up getting you killed just before they're taken down themselves."

"True enough, but sometimes they end up as kings," Dee benignly observed.

"There is that, yeah. There are those rare occasions," d'Winter agreed. "But even then, the King often conveniently forgets about his guys that put him in power."

"Granted, Mr. d'Winter. But let us not dwell on royal manoeuvres, rather ponder the questions before you. Are you with me or not? More to the point, do you believe me or not? Am I mad? Or does my story merely make me seem so? And what have you decided to do? I have watched the night turn to day in anticipation of your responses. The wait has not been an easy one."

Kelly readjusted herself on the couch and curled her long legs up under her. "We've spent the night on the Omninet libraries," she told him. "We've discovered that there was indeed an Elizabethan courtier called Doctor John Dee, born in 1527 in the reign of Henry VIII, six years before the birth of his daughter, who grew up to be Queen Elizabeth I of England." She consulted the flat crumpled paper-screen cupped in the palm of her hand. "Physically, you resemble the descriptions of the man. He was a mathematician, scholar, astrologer, trader, and spy for the Elizabethan court. Doctor Dee even advised the Queen on the most suitable day for her coronation. She held him in high regard, most of the time." She looked up quickly. "And he was also accompanied on his travels by an Irish mercenary named Edward Kelly."

The Doctor nodded. "Also a redhead."

Kelly Edwards continued, "Their capture by the de' Medicis is also recorded and dated as—"

"1575," Dee supplied.

"1575," Edwards agreed.

"I checked the celestial, church, and secular records for Venice for that same year. Curiously, it records the destruction of the de' Medici tower by a bolt of lightning and the disappearance of the England Thaumaturge, Johannes Dee. This same Doctor Dee is also credited with creating a language called Enochian because he believed he was in communication with Angels."

Dee shrugged delicately. "So I believed at the time. The Roc deceived me. "

"He died in—"

"Nay, no more!" Dee barked, raising both hands. "You damn me by exposing the date of my death. Thus far, I have been careful not to learn when 'tis that I die; do you not spoil it for me now. Nor man, nor any living creature, is privy to that appointed end. There's Divine kindness in that; for to know is to abide in a waiting Hell."

Kelly shook her head angrily. "More of your bullshit! This Dee died a long time ago, in the past," she exploded.

Her incredulity was visible to Dee; their sense of disbelief was palpable, and he could hardly blame them. He could see that she could not mask her disbelief. Gradually his self-assurance slipped away. Perhaps he had pulled the wool over their eyes—Kelly's and Morgan's.

Kelly's realisation that she might have been deceived by this old fool flamed her fury. She sprang up from the chair needing to get away from him.

Dee became more disheartened. What reasonable man—in this time that made so much of reason—could accept his story? His heart sank; he had lost them forever. How ironic, he thought, that as a spy he had never told a lie this bold, and had always been trusted. Now by telling this monstrous Truth, his friends were going to abandon him. "Perhaps that is only an antiquarian's assumption," he started, "a surmise based on a guess. Surely a mind of the Renaissance could not conceive of a man stolen from his time as anything other than tales about the Little Folk, who are known to be gone from your world. Yet, here I am. Does not my substance give the lie to your Omninet?"

"So how do you explain," d'Winter demanded, "that you died in the past and you're here? That's an impossibility, Doc. 'Sides, they got your grave, man. You've been buried deep for a long time. You didn't have DNA retrieval back then, so reconstructing you wouldn't be easy. Someone could have broken into your tomb and found some viable cells—"

"Indulge me," Dee said, suddenly very excited by this new revelation. "You are very sure that there is a grave site?"

"No question about that, man."

"I have thought about this for . . ." His hands gripped the arms of his chair. "Yea, many is the time when I have thought of naught else. But it would seem to me," he said distractedly, "if it is given out that I was uprooted in mine own time in the Year of Our Lord 1575 and planted here in 2099, and now I learn that I died and was interred in mine own time; therefore"—his voice almost exultant rising in hope—"is it impossible that I returned to that same time by some means and lived out the remaining span of my years? That my journey is an aberration that will one day be mended, and I will be gone back to my own century?"

"You're talking about time travel," d'Winter snorted "and no one has successfully perfected it. When the Australians ran that Aboriginal experiment a couple of years ago, two of the scientists came back dead and the third was a raving lunatic. And you're just as meshugga."

"And yet Dyckon tells me that the Old Ones had perfected time travel, and they have simply lost the secret." Dee steepled his fingers and regarded d'Winter over the tops of them.

"Dyckon? That's your dragon-gargoyle buddy? Right? Right," grunted the bodyguard.

Kelly was still angry but allowed him to work it through, persisted, "And if we are to believe that you are who you say you are, and *if* we believe the historians, we must assume that you returned to your own time to die there—and therefore"—she turned to Morgan—"time travel would have to exist."

"Yeah, that and the Easter Bunny," hooted the big man.

Kelly Edwards shook her head. "I feel as if my head is about to explode. I'm so mad at you I could spit." In despair, the former publicist felt completely confused. She wanted to believe in the man she had so trusted, but it was utterly unbelievable. She had sacrificed so much for this perplexing man who might conceivably be a lunatic. Self-flagellating guilt grew in her about what she done to herself and her poor brother.

"I am sorry, my dear, that my being here seems so unreasonable. It grieves me to have lost both your confidences. S'truth, I knew I gambled on the loss of your trust by telling you my tale," Dee said, "but I felt that it was time to be candid with you." He moved the diary that was sitting on his lap to a nearby table. "If naught else, at least, it will explain some of my diverse peculiarities," he added with a grin. "If, in your hearts, you cannot truly believe this portion of my tale, by all that is holy, you must credit the rest. For upon my life, I swear to you there is a deadly contagion, which you name a virus, abroad in your world, and I must get to it. I have seen the Plague, and I know what it can do. This pestilence exceeds anything I have encountered before—not any pox, not any depredation of war can deal the blows this so-called virus can. I must have you believe that much of me. The world's future depends on it. Moreover, if I am to do this, I must once again have your good help, for I cannot track down this mad Roc without you."

"But how can we believe you?" implored Kelley Edwards. "Why do we assume you mean this now when you've told us half-truths and who knows what else?"

"Aye, that is the question," he conceded. "But I believe I have the answer. In last night's investigations, did you not uncover the whereabouts of my bones, my last resting place?"

"Yes." She looked directly at him.

"And your time, does it not have the power of testing identity through the mechanism of the very building blocks of our body's cells? I have heard of various methods you can employ to that end."

"You mean DNA testing," Morgan D'Winter responded immediately, seeing where Dee was leading. "Assuming we can do it, you want it done?"

"Aye," acknowledged the Doctor. "Take what sample of me that you require and make comparison with my remains."

"But the research says you are buried—"

"Please." He spread out his palms toward them. "I don't want to—"

"No. I wasn't going to tell you where. Only that you are buried where no one is going to allow us to just dig you up." D'Winter shrugged. "They still frown on grave-robbing, you know."

"Is there any way to manage it?" Kelly asked, her resentment of Dee lessening.

D'Winter just grinned. "Honey, you just leave that assignment to me. I'll be in and out of there before anyone's the wiser." He stood. "I've got a DNA scanner in the back." Turning to Kelly, he cautioned, "We'll know for sure by this time tomorrow. I'll catch the next flight. Here's my Glock Viper. It's my spare. You use it if you have to." Kelley took the weapon in her hand but without much conviction. Now turning to Dee, d'Winter said, "Listen, Shakespeare, I sure hope to hell you are who you say you are. 'Cause if you ain't, you'll be in psych deck the moment I get back." With that he left the room.

Dee just stared at Kelley; she returned the little man's stare. She wanted to believe, but she didn't want to be made a fool of again. She made no attempt to keep him at gunpoint. She rested Morgan's gun on her thigh. "The very fact that I'm still here should suggest to you that I'll want to think about helping you," she said reasonably in what she thought was a little too lenient a concession.

"That charitable desire is all I hoped. *Si la fortuna me tormenta, la speranza me contenta.*"

"Is that Latin? What does it mean?"

For the first time in that already long day, her former employer laughed. He was regaining some of his habitual confidence, for he laughed with a heartiness that surprised her; she granted him a tiny smile in spite of herself. "No, my dear," he finally said, "it's Italian. Forgive me for laughing, its just so delightful to hear that I might even stand a chance of being in your good graces once again."

She smirked at his constant use of anachronisms. She reminded herself that she had gotten used to his language and his constant use of aphorisms. They had been cute. She shook her head at her own susceptibility to his charm even now, when there was so little in him to trust. She reprimanded herself but couldn't help liking him; he was a lovable little coot, nut or not. Wouldn't it be weird, she asked herself, if he really were who he said he was? A Renaissance astrologer sent by a gargoyle five hundred years into the future to prevent a worldwide epidemic? She shook her head at the sheer incomprehensibility of it; she uttered a small but audible chuckle.

He nearly cried. "The translation is 'If fortune torments me, hope contents me.' "

"Oh, I see."

"Kelley," he said; this utterly took her by surprise—he so rarely used her Christian name, "if you have any cause to distrust me or think me mad, I'll quit you and lock myself within my sleeping chamber till Morgan returns." He rose to leave.

"No," she said quickly, not sure she wasn't making a mistake, "I want to trust you." Not wanting to be deceived again, however, she added "At least, until we have proof otherwise."

Dee could not remember ever being happier. Slowly he sat again. "Thank you."

"You're welcome."

She sat with him for a moment, watching the sunlight brighten the room. Motes of dust danced in the golden air. She turned her head from side to side, giving her an excuse to look away from him. She concentrated on her upper back, right in the middle of her shoulders, where the dull ache of tension was stored. She hair fell in front of her face. She looked down at her feet, and saw they were firmly planted on the ground. She felt awkward in his company, like an adolescent. The floor below the windows gleamed honey-yellow, the light creeping toward where he sat. She could think of nothing to say. She was tired but no longer so completely lost. She finally looked up at him and saw at once that he was as relieved as she, and their long night of doubt was nearly at an end. He was facing the window, and, like the floor, it was awash in early morning light.

"Doctor, after all this time, what made you tell us who you are? Why now?" She leaned forward as if she half-expected him to whisper the answer.

Again he was surprised by her directness. "As I've said, I could not bear the guilt of playing false with friends. Friends of the heart. Oft have I lived a lie. But here with you was not the time nor place. This morning I have learnt a weighty Truth. I must tell you the baring of one's inner self with friends works two contrary effects: It enlarges joy and nips grief." The power of this realization sat with him, and he mentally reviewed a lifetime of secrecy. "That is the Why of it. The Now is the easier of the twain to answer. Presently I need your help and could not ask you to put yourselves in harm's way again without revealing what was your right to know. I inquired of myself if not now, then when?"

"John, if you are who you say you are, you are a miracle. I've said it before, and I'll tell you again. It will take me time to get used to that," she admitted, trying hard to make him see her point of view, though she doubted she had been able to. She pouted in indecision.

He leaned towards her, which only momentarily made her think of d'Winter's Glock Viper in her lap. She felt guilty and loosened her grip, carefully placing the Doctor's hand on the settee, obviously not wishing to overstep his bounds. "I quite understand," he reassured her and then added, "Time's glory is to smooth all and bring Truth to light."

"You have an aphorism for everything, don't you?"

"I had an excellent Latin teacher. Master Alistair. He beat into me the appreciation that Cicero and Quinapalus had conceits for all things. We learned to catalogue all the lessons taught by life through the writings of Roman rhetorticians."

"Did they have an answer for a universal virus?"

"No, unluckily, belike they did not. In my day such a thought would have been heretical at best. The Chinese spoke of the vermin of vermin, but it was the extent of the inquiry. All men knew that disease spread in an invisible, deadly cloud, like smoke." Dee saw a mixture of fear and uncertainty inhabit her eyes. He knew he had given her a fearful amount to digest. He leaned back in his chair. "As I am a Christian man, I am as truthful in this as I am in the story of my journey here. I have only now learned of this virus and what it can do."

She took this in and in fatigue rested her head on the plush arm of the couch. The coolness of the leather helped to calm her nagging thoughts. She stretched her neck back and studied the ceiling. "All we have to do now is to figure out how to discover the whereabouts of an alien who can change his shape at will."

"Oh, I think he will reveal himself to us," Dee said confidently. "He has to, for his plan to succeed."

Kelley glanced at him. "And this 'he' is a gargoyle with wings and a tail?" She laughed to herself. "This is going to take awhile."

"Aye, it is," said Dee, trying to be reassuring, and added, "but then, friends are the thieves of time. You must use the time to good effect."

CHAPTER

14

"AND THERE YOU HAVE it, ladies and gentlemen, the extraordinary vids from the Forest Lawn Cemetery earlier this morning."

Behind Strategy Brooks the image of Romulas O'Connor stepping out of his shattered coffin was frozen laser-sharp on the screen, although the image of the man calling himself Yeshua Ben David was slightly blurred, jagged pixilization fuzzing his image like a cheaply done special effect. Strategy folded her perfectly manicured hands and stared straight into camera. She had rewritten this piece a dozen times and had no need of the auto-prompt.

"What we who were blessed to be there saw this morning was miraculous. In this age of science, we were privileged to witness something outside its purview. There will, of course, be many who will question the events and suggest that some sort of trickery took place." Strategy's voice dropped, and she leaned forward slightly, and all across the globe, viewers, watching the perfect three-dimensional image of the woman's head and upper body, automatically leaned forward and stared into the woman's dark eyes, hanging on her every word. "But let me assure you, ladies and gentlemen, this was no trick. No illusion. This was a genuine Act of God, witnessed by a large gathering. This reporter was on hand to personally verify to you that like Lazarus, Mr O'Connor did, indeed, rise up from the dead. There is no doubt whatsoever that he was dead and no doubt that he is once again alive."

A sheaf of thin plastic sheets appeared in the woman's hand. "This is his death certificate, duly signed and authorised by two County registered doctors. Because Mr. O'Connor died in somewhat unusual circumstances at home, there was an autopsy. Here is the autopsy report, also duly signed and noted. Here is the insurance company's—Global-Mutual ('We're Assured You're Insured') Fawcett Insurances—own doctor's report." Here is the Metro Police report. The undertaker's report— and bill, the florist's report and bill, and the invoice for the coffin. A statement from Leeta O'Connor, Rommie O'Connor's erstwhile widow, who was with him when he died. Here is another testimony from Mr O'Connor's mother, who formally identified the body. An account from the chauffeur who comforted Mrs. O'Conner in the Bel Air household when the Metro police arrived." Strategy dealt out the reports of Romulus O'Connor's death like playing cards.

"Rommie O'Conner was without question dead. Dead and gone. Except now he's come back, summoned back from the dead by a man calling himself Yeshua Ben David. And for those of you who don't know, in his time Yeshua Ben David was better known as Jesus Christ. Yes, ladies and gentleman, this is the Second Coming. And you heard it first, right here on GNN. And now we'll catch you up on what went down in Sports today."

The screen behind her faded, and the next reporter began to give his account of a riot in Uruguay. Strategy gave it only a little attention, waiting for the reaction to her piece to begin. She hadn't long to wait; in the response box on her station screen, a message flashed:

"This is a trick, and you were taken in. Selma J., Spokane, Washington."

"Why aren't you staying with this wonderful man? Homer D., Wellington, New Zealand."

"Pretty pathetic, No name, Ottawa, Canada."

"This man could not be the Second Coming. Jacques Fate of Rouen is the Second Coming. Michelle la S., Calais, France"

Strategy toggled onto the graph, showing percentages of approval, disapproval, and other. She saw the disapproval was slightly ahead of the approval and nodded. She was sure of what she had seen, but she knew what tricks could be done with cameras and the manipulation of images. It would take time, but she wanted the story to build. She left her alcove of the studio and went across to the editor-in-chief's office, knocking once and entering without waiting for the summons.

"What's up?" Franco daRocelli said, eyeing Strategy suspiciously.

"I think we turned out better on this first go than we expected, and that's good." She folded her arms. "We were thinking we'd get a sixty-forty split and it's closer to fifty-fifty, with a tiny percentage for other."

"Trying to keep the story off the spike," said daRocelli.

"Well, wouldn't you, if you were in my shoes?" Strategy said with false sweetness.

"Okay, okay," daRocelli said, making a gesture of mock surrender. "You can have another two spots with it, and if the percentages improve, then we'll talk. In the meantime, you do your best to keep up with him, and see if he can do anything even more spectacular than raising a fish salesman from the dead." He laughed aloud, enjoying himself. "Not that it wasn't fun to watch. Where'd you have the effects done?"

"No effects," Strategy said firmly.

"Hey, you got the story in L.A. What else could it be?" He nodded to the door. "Well, if you've got the balls to file the story, I've got the balls to run it."

"Oh, you're so brave," Strategy cooed sarcastically.

"I am, aren't I?" daRocelli asked. "Out you go, Strategy. I got a meeting."

"That's 'I've,' " she said, and left triumphantly.

Before she could get away from deRocelli's office, his voice stopped her, spoiling her well-timed exit. "Strategy, you don't actually believe any of this, do you?"

"What do you think?" She didn't linger, hurrying on to her own office to begin work on the follow-up to her story. She resisted the urge to call Yeshua ben David to get his reaction to her piece, for she was fairly certain he would think she hadn't been strong enough in her account.

Half an hour later the first solid figures were in, and the positives were forty-four percent, the negatives at forty-nine percent, the remaining seven percent registering for other. The feedback remarks ranged from credulous to out-and-out offensive, just about what Strategy had expected. She sighed and stared blankly at the display of awards on the far wall, but nothing came to her.

"So tell me," she said to the air, "how am I going to improve on this? I can't tell Yeshua what to do, but I need something spectacular, better than the raising of the dead, to get the world's attention. And Franco's right—it can't be in L.A." There was no answer to her musing, and she was about to go get a cup of coffee when a strange stillness came over her, and she had a flash of understanding, a comprehension that was so encompassing it took her breath away. She beamed. Now she knew exactly what she had to do. She would begin with an interview with Leeta O'Connor—how did she feel about the return of her husband? How were things now that her husband was back? She could probably manage an innuendo or two about sex, which ought to boost their viewer reaction a couple of percentage points. That done, she'd get an interview with the virago of a mother, and then, if it was at all possible, with the raised man himself. No one had done that yet—he'd been whisked away in the limousine and taken to the hospital at once and had been holed up in his house ever since. Maybe she could even work out a meeting between Yeshua and O'Conner—the old thank-the-man-who-saved-your-life scenario. It was always popular. She pulled up her unlisted directory—she wasn't supposed to have one, of course, but a grateful engineer had given it to her, four months ago, and she supposed most of the codes were still valid.

The first number rang three times, and then a breathless voice answered. "Yes?"

"Mrs. O'Connor? Mrs. Leeta O'Connor?" Strategy made her tone as friendly as possible, but to no avail.

"Yes?" Leeta said dubiously, a guarded note in her voice.

Deciding to make the best of it, Strategy plowed

ahead. "This is Strategy Brooks, Mrs. O'Conner. I covered your husband's . . . resurrection. I was hoping you and I might have a talk about—"

"How did you get this number?" Leeta demanded.

"One of your staff gave it to me, at the cemetery. After you . . . um . . . left." It was becoming awkward.

"Whoever did that will lose his job," Leeta promised, and broke the connection.

She's toughening up, Strategy told herself, trying to be philosophical about her failure to make better use of this opportunity. She decided it might be more prudent to wait a while before calling Romulas O'Conner, fairly certain that Leeta would put him on guard against her. So she found the number for O'Conner's mother, reminding herself that the Widow O'Conner was a thick-skinned old bird and wouldn't pluck easily. While the rings were sounding, Strategy prepared her tactics for the conversation.

"Hello?" The old woman's voice was clear and definite—no fuzzy thinking here, no elderly need to please.

"Mrs. O'Conner, this is Strategy Brooks—"

"The newswoman. I remember you. I saw your report on my son." There was an underlying note of satisfaction that Strategy found a little off-putting.

"Yes. I hope you didn't find the coverage too distressing," said Strategy.

"Sensationalistic bullshit, if you ask me," she said, "but that's nothing new in your business, is it?"

"I wouldn't put it quite that way—" Strategy said defensively.

"Why should you? You're not on the receiving end."

Fully expecting to be cut off in the next second, Strategy made a last attempt. "I was wondering if you'd like to tell your side of the story. No strings, up to slander and libel, but otherwise, full reporting on the event. And what's happened since?" The last, hopeful note in her request was more tentative than she had intended.

There was a short hesitation, then Mrs. O'Conner said, "Well, girl, what kind of money are we talking about?"

CHAPTER

15

Extract from the Day Booke of John Dee, Doctor, in the year of Our Lord 2100:

> Our life's weave is of mingled yarn, good and ill
> together.
>
> Since arriving here, I have always held mine own
> good time to be that of an age of genteel refinement
> and moral civilization, and this godless Tomorrow,
> which is my current Present, no more than a barbaric
> pageant, filled with marvels to be sure, but wanting the
> divers delights and dignities that illuminated my age.
> The Quest for righteousness and honor in the emula-
> tion of Divine Grace that inspired all the best of my
> peers is dull now. In its stead stands an unmanly trick
> of sloughing off responsibility to God, one's fellow man,
> and one's immortal soul. We held honor more precious
> dear than Life.
>
> And yet, perhaps, now I am forced to some new reck-
> oning of my views. In my time, even if a Solomon had
> come to me with a tale as wild, as outrageous as my

current History, I would have deemed him mad or, worse, possessed of a demon and had him brought before the ecclesiastical courts, there to be made whole again. After I had recounted my strange adventures to my companions, they had, with little credence, listened. There was rage in their eyes and mutiny in their hearts. Morgan visited my bones where they were interred in England. Their long-dead DNA and my living being proved a match. When he made return, he was like a solemn Judge—so too was Kelly. It was plain that each for their own part had searched the credibility of my life's History, and had found me guilty of telling Truth. And then—and this is the mystery!—on the morrow, they accepted all the particulars of what I had imparted without so much as a quibble. Accepted the most moon-calfe allegations of alien beings, and world domination, and how very devils with the power to assume whatever form they choose, harbored a deadly contagion to loose upon the world.

"We will help you," Kelly Edwards had ventured. There was neither guile nor cunning in her voice.

"Why, would you?" I asked, for I was truly aston-ished by her charity.

"Because you are our friend," Morgan d'Winter had answered.

And that was the end of it. What qualms or doubts they had died. Their passive charity exhibited a noble spirit more in keeping with the Good Book than any cleric of old. In that moment, God's benefice enveloped me. I was as the seafarer who after a long journey espies safe harbor. They sat no more as Justices but as argonauts before an English Jason eager for honorable adventure, naught in their demeanor but resolution, comradeship, and trust. A man may have many things—houses, land, coin and jewels—but if he is without a friend, then he is possessed of nothing. And what a pair had I been blessed with.

And, so, we fell to planning, trying what actions might be done to flush this Roc and his malignant virus. We conversed for hours having divers disputes and petty reservations as we planned, but slowly from these thorns we plucked out a stratagem to bring down the foe and to ensure the success of our endeavor. I was convinced by the moderns that my inclination to hunt him as one would course a wild boar in France was not sufficient to the problem, for this Roc had the mischievous power to change his outwardness completely, and evade any pursuit dictated by appearance.

D'Winter it was who hit upon the exceedingly good notion of tracking him by DNA. This substance is still a most perplexing concept to me, but Kelly maintained that it is more reliable and more true than any other method of identification, and so I am of a mind to consider it as a ready means of locating this Roc, and, with him, the virus as well. If we but find this virus, its signature DNA, they say, will supply the means to defeat it. Theirs is a most fervently held belief: that DNA is the key to all life, rather like the materia prima, from whence all living things are begot. That which the alchemists of the East proclaimed is the most potent force on earth. Induction teaches us that from like instances, the mind draws good conclusions. Mayhap, this monstrous Roc who is splenitive and rash lies under the planet Pluto, a cold dark place, which I am told was but late discovered some eighty score year ago. That thesis may be sound, for this DNA is also but recently identified, and it may be that there is some kinship between the two. I will cast a chart or two and perceive if my thesis holds. Meantime, my friends will delve into their Science and their computers hoping to find some telltale clue to prime our attack. They are even at it now, while I am for bed. Some must watch, whiles others sleep. I will prepare in the morning. We must not venture all in one ship. Thus, in earnest, make we ready our pursuit of this Roc.

But, in all truth, I cannot choose but think on the Time device that our quarry possesses. My thoughts ever and anon harken back to Mortlake and my heartsick hope of returning.

CHAPTER

16

THEY WERE ON THEIR way to see a drug dealer.

"In my day," Doctor John Dee remarked quietly, fastidiously leaping over a noisome puddle of something that looked suspiciously like blood, "men took their solace and found their dreams in strong drink."

"Oh, yeah, we still do that," Morgan d'Winter grunted. "We've just jacked up the options. There's a hundred different ways to get high. Booze is only one of them." He was moving cautiously through a narrow stinking alleyway, a fat-bodied silenced pistol in his hand. He was dressed in full body armor from steel-capped boots to reenforced titanium helmet. Tiny sensors set into the helmet relayed a wealth of information to the single lens that hung, patchlike, over his left eye.

"Certes," Dee continued absently, nervously watching a rat the size of a small dog keeping pace with them, "other substances could quicken visions. I myself partook of a blend of mushrooms, laudanum, and a tincture of certain spices. And the Crusaders had brought back a rather pleasant paste from Arabia which had much the same properties. Mine own researches had indicated that diverse rotten fruit and breads had a very like giddying effect upon the theatre of the mind. Moreover, I was one of a faculty of scholars, Warner, Harriot, Marlowe, Chapman, and poor John Lambe, who had frequent and open discourse with the Wizard Earl, Northumberland, and Sir Walter Raleigh, and like men of honour and high repute. Their chief bent was for the study of science, mathematics, and philosophy, which the vulgar termed 'magick.' These principal personages of the Realm came to us as supplicants to be schooled in the metaphysical arts. But they in turn tutored us in the mysteries of tobacco and opium, which aided us in piercing the veil of Truth. The churchmen, had they any knowledge of our experimentations, would have been horrified, and the consequences could have been most unwelcome. Our secret gatherings we dubbed the School of the Night." He was glad now he had left his journal back at his Library, for the area through which they traveled was increasingly unwholesome.

"That's great, Doc, but can you keep it down?" Suddenly d'Winter held up a hand in warning. In the infrared display of his helmet, he could see bodies moving at the far end of the alleyway. Three glowing shapes, crimson and amber, shot through with yellow-white. Behind them a ill-defined orange carpetlike swath heaved on the ground. Morgan adjusted the spectrum, shifting from infrared into ultraviolet. The shapes turned blue-black and the carpet colours disappeared. Figures scrolled down the tiny screen over his eye, as Kelly Edwards, sitting twenty miles away and a mile underground, momentarily hijacked the nearest satellite—a GNN traffic bot—and grabbed an ultra-high rez image of the area. The traffic bots scanned traffic. They read the serial numbers embedded in the windshields of cars to solve traffic snarls. They transmitted driving instructions to drivers to optimize travel time; they identified the location of car-jackers ; and they controlled signal lights to redirect traffic patterns. It was rumoured they could read a lot more, too. Conspiracy theorists argued that the GNN traffic network was really up there to spy on human traffic, inasmuch as there was not enough vehicular traffic on the roads for them to monitor anymore. The lunatic fringe of the conspiracy theorists suggested that the bots were beaming down paranoia-inducing radiation, which wasn't entirely impossible, given the way in which riots occasionally erupted out of nothing. Kelly cycled the image through the filters and allowed the computers to do the weapons match.

"What's going on?" D'Winter whispered.

"We have three hostiles, armed to the teeth. All solid projectile weapons, all Egyptian manufacture, Sphinkz Mk 2s, and one Mk 3. The handguns are Texas Republican Equalizers. There are also assorted knives, nunchakus, batons, and I'm picking up one toxic reading on the chart. One of the hostiles has either an acid pistol or a toxic gun." There was concern and strain in Kelley's voice as she diagnosed the situation. The small palm-sized pistols squirting either a cocktail of acid or toxins were fearsome weapons. The effects on human flesh were not pretty. "But that's not the real problem."

Morgan d'Winter stopped. And Dee, still muttering to himself, nearly ran into him. "Okay. What is?"

"The real problem is behind the men. There are, according to this report, at least one hundred very large rats blocking the way. Please be careful, Morgan."

"No problem, Kel," d'Winter said. "We've found what we came for."

"You are pleased?" Dee whispered.

"Sure," said d'Winter, just loudly enough to be heard. "It means we've found who we're looking for."

"In my day," Dee remarked, "London's wharves teemed with legions of rats, and they were excessively large and fearsome monsters, but these . . ." Dee focused on a black rodent, more the size of a terrier than a rat, that stood on its wrinkled grey hind legs about three yards ahead, now blocking their way in the alley. "S'blood, but that's a filthy piece of work," he muttered, and then, in a louder voice, continued, "These are beyond belief, beyond reason, beyond beyond! These are behemoths, a pestilence in their own right, a blight upon the land." He was not slow to note another two dog-sized rodent creatures that had joined the rat that had been keeping pace with them. Getting away from the hoards of rats was part of the reason he chose to take up residence at Mortlake rather than risk living in overpopulated London. At Mortlake the rats were kept in check by cats and terriers, and confined themselves to the stable and the pantry.

"These aren't garden-variety rats, Doctor. Genetically modified," d'Winter said, then, realizing that Dee might not understand the term, added, "Artificially grown to this size, and then implanted with a tiny device in their skulls which allows them to be controlled. In some of the larger ones an eye is replaced with a miniature camera, allowing them to act as unnoticed spies. Some of them even have tiny speakers implanted in them, allowing for a two-way communication."

"More DNA, I suppose?" Dee stopped and turned to the look at the giant rats. "These beasts unnoticed!" he squawked. "That I cannot credit. One would have to be sand blind not to see this monster."

"You'd be surprised how easily they can crawl in and out of places without anyone the wiser." Dee's security chief chuckled. "They're great at getting visuals."

"Certes, someone might even now be viewing us through the mechanical eye of this rat?" Dee asked.

"Well . . ." d'Winter began, and then said simply, "Yes." It was easier than trying to explain.

"And might this rat actually have parley with us?"

"Someone could talk to us through the speaker implanted into the rat," d'Winter explained patiently.

"By all that's holy, a secret pestilent familiar indeed," Dee said, aghast.

One of the rats darted ahead of the others, and leapt up onto a pile of putrid packing cases, tiny claws clicking metallically onto the wood. From his perch, the brown giant snarled.

"And some," d'Winter added nervously, "have had their claws and teeth replaced with titanium, an enormously powerful metal. Rip you to shreds. You do not want it to bite you." d'Winter warily raised his pistol.

"Rats were ever enormously powerful assassins," the Doctor reciprocated. "During the pox years, they chewed thousands." Dee felt abruptly nauseated. He'd give anything right now for a pouch of ratbane to keep the monsters at bay.

"Hey, d'Winter, we've made some other changes, too." The new voice came from the rat. The words were tiny and metallic, vaguely squeaking. Dee was horrified by it. He was numb with uncomprehending wonder: A talking rat, the size of a possum, was too much for his Elizabethan mind to accept. He stood utterly transfixed, his eyes riveted on the rodent's black and pink eye. Its long wormlike tail twitched. It crouched on the top of the box and stared at them malevolently. The right pink eye contracted.

D'Winter stopped. The viewscreen over his left eye abruptly magnified the creature, and he could see that the left eye was in fact a small irising lens, and he could just about make out the tiny grill-like speaker in the long hair beneath the throat. Adjusting the viewscreen to x-ray allowed him to see that more than fifty percent of the rat's body was composed of metal and electronics.

The speaker crackled. "I've made some refinements to my pets."

D'Winter shuddered. "So I see."

"It's been a long time, Morgan. I heard that you bought the farm. Taken down with the Preacher."

"Well, I'm alive and just as pretty as ever, as you can see; but, you know, it was a close-call thing."

"Someone still taking potshots at you?" the tinny voice asked.

"Nobody with a current address," d'Winter said ominously.

"Ah, yes, the fearsome Morgan d'Winter reputation. Tell me, Morgan, what are you doing creeping down my alleyway, and who's the old runt with you?"

The sudden reference to himself made Dee suddenly readjust to the improbability of the situation. He struggled to regain his composure. Conversing with a brown rat did not seem unusual to his bodyguard. As he had many times in the past, Doctor John Dee told himself he must acclimate to the wonders of the Twenty-second Century.

"Back off, Ratman, I'm not creeping down your

alley—you and I both know that's not gonna happen. I'm here to do a little trade. Sell a little information. Keep in touch. And Dr. Dee here is my current employer. He pays me well. So don't embarrass me. "

The rat tilted his head to look into Dee's eyes. "Ah, would this be the Doctor Dee we've begun to hear about? The cipher Royal Newton was after?"

"News travels fast," Dee said, politely replying to the rat as if he were a functionary of Elizabeth's court.

"There's always a rat somewhere about," the voice said. "You can put the gun away, Morgan, and come on in. You're safe with me for now."

"Safe!" Dee whispered as the mercenary holstered his weapon. "Define for me once more this word *safe*."

The big rat turned and darted down the alley, metallic claws clicking on the slick stones. It stopped, turned his pointed head, and ordered, "Come on. Step on it. I haven't got all night."

"We're right behind you," answered the mercenary as he quickly moved after the twisting tail of his host.

"I'm following a talking rat. You can't tell me this isn't Black magic," Dee said uneasily, but nevertheless following the vermin. "Back home, they'd burn me for sure. Doubtless, I would deserve it."

CHAPTER

17

IF HE CHOSE TO turn a blind eye to the heaving mass of vermin that gathered in the darkened corners of the long vaulted room, the heavily armed guards with vaguely—and in some cases more than vaguely—ratlike features, the solid wall of tiny monitors, each one flashing a different scenario, some in garish colors, others in subdued monochrome, and the constant high-pitched chittering, a combination of human speech and rat squeaking, Dee decided that he could almost be comfortable in these surroundings. What was most disconcerting were the very audible snippets of different conversations he heard all at once being broadcast around him. None of them surprisingly having to do with either his or d'Winter's arrival.

Doctor John Dee was a creature of habit. In his own time, he had always risen in the dark an hour just before the dawn; he had always bathed, whether he needed to or not, and then broke his fast with the same simple breakfast of no more than four courses, suited to the manner of the present age more than his own. Although he possessed an extensive and costly wardrobe, much of it was in the same style—simple black and grey clothes trimmed with ermine or crow's feathers; his cloaks were lined in fox fur, and he owned six pairs of identical court shoes, and six pairs of identical boots. All of them equipped with built-up horseman's heels.

He eschewed surprise. When he traveled to London, he avoided the dimly lit narrow streets and the dangers they hid. He journeyed by way of the Thames, with the same ferryman, and with the same bodyguards who always looked up as they passed under bridges. The same servants had tended to his house in Mortlake for many, many years. His favorite pastimes were the study of mathematics and the casting of star charts, neither of which could be said to be surprising. When he went adventuring into Europe on behalf of Walshingham, the British bureaucrat in charge of spies, or on less covert official junkets for his own dear Queen, it was always in the company of Edward Kelly. He was truly glad of Kelly's company; the man, for all his faults, was a steadfast companion and willing to back Dee to the hilt. They traveled with the same baggage boxes each trip, and carried the same weapons. He always prepared his reports in the same way, using his neat, precise, and distinctive hand, the same tiny writing, the same unbreakable code of his own devising. Walsingham's secretary, Thomas Phelippes, had insisted that Dee use the more cryptic double-blind system being employed with great success against Mary, Queen of Scots. But Dee stuck to his own codes based on the mathematical studies of Abbot Johannes Trithemius great book, *Steganographia*. Dee, like most educated men of his age, preferred the simple ease of an ordered life in an unpredictable world, the calculated niceties built up after years of habit, the astrological pre-

ciseness of practiced observations. Nature's clockwork
majesty was grounded in basic fundamentals that held
true no matter what upheavals were visited upon the
world. Mankind's earthly duty was to probe those natural
principles and adopt them, thereby aligning themselves
with Divine Purpose. Doctor Dee also subscribed to the
theory—and was it Socrates who had first proposed it?—
that man could best cope with new, unfamiliar experiences by comparing them with existing familiar ones.
This was the core of Aristotelian logic.

And, truth to say, he had been in a disquieting situation like this before. Once, long ago, he had sought to set
up a ransom exchange with an unusually large Ethiopian
slaver who made his camp in the rank sewers of Rome.
The man had abducted one of the daughters of the newly
appointed Ottoman governor of Rhodes and was offering
her to the highest bidder. In truth, the girl was no prize,
cursed with an unfortunate set of features, and a match-
ing personality, but Walshingham felt that it would be to
England's good if the Queen were to be able to return the
potentate's daughter to him on his next visit to the
British court. Strategically, all of Europe marveled and
fretted at the rapidly expanding Ottomans in Asia Minor,
especially since Christendom had just lost Cyprus to
Islam in 1571, the slaughter at Famagusta horrifying all
who heard of it and providing a triumph for Selim the
Grim that boded ill for Europe. England's Secretary was
convinced a diplomatic coup of this sort would increase
commerce and friendship between the two island na-
tions and possibly lead to opening trade relations with
the Ottomans. Elizabeth had finally been won over to au-
thorize the expenditures.

Thus it was that Dee had ended up in a damp sewer,

surrounded by a motley crew of slavers, brigands, and mercenaries. With water dripping monotonously in the background, and large Roman rats scuttling in the gloom, Dee had first tried to effect a legitimate business transaction—English crowns for the princess. But the hulking African was intent on keeping both. The Doctor had instructed his man to initiate alternate plans, and after agreeing on their strategy, they separated. Kelly bribed the girl's keeper and the Irishman had cleverly managed her escape disguising her as a male prostitute and taking her out through the servants' entrance, along with half a dozen acrobats. Despite being alone with vermin crawling around his legs, Dee had held his composure and charmingly entertained his host and his entourage with ribald stories of Elizabeth's paramours, all the while giving the escapees the time they needed to make their getaway. At the last moment the escape had been discovered and Doctor Dee had barely made it out with his life by scattering English coin throughout the dank passageways. But, as it turned out, the entire affair had been for nought. Though he had rescued the girl, she did not want to be rescued; more important, her father had never wanted her rescued. He was more than happy to have one less ugly daughter to settle a dowry upon, and had no intention of taking her back. Walsingham had much to explain later on to the Queen for the needless expenditures

Then, as now, the leader sat in a high-backed wooden chair, with the light behind him, so that he was in shadow. Obviously, Dee thought, there must be a handbook somewhere for brigands who kept camps in sewers.

"You are smiling, Doctor Dee. Does something here amuse you?" The speaker's voice was only fractionally less tinny and metallic without the rat's implant to filter it.

The Doctor stepped forward and folded his arms across his chest. "I am reminded," he said formally, glancing around slowly and deliberately, "of someone I met once, a long time ago. This delightful setting and your openhanded demeanour remind me of him."

"Indeed. Should I be honoured or amused by this comparison?" the thin voice asked.

"Oh, honored assuredly." Dee stared at the unseen figure. "He was indeed a great man. With a great reputation."

Something about Dee's tone held the hidden man's attention. "You wouldn't be attempting to shit me, Doctor, would you?"

"I most assuredly would not defecate on you!" Dee said shocked; he sensed that the illustrious leader whose company he had come among wasn't entirely sure what defecate was or meant, and was not entirely sure that he wanted to find out.

In the confused silence that followed, Dee's host inquired, "Is that a Limey accent?"

"Doctor Dee hails from England originally," Morgan d'Winter said quickly.

This satisfied the figure in the shadows. "Why have you come to me, Doctor Dee?"

The Doctor looked around the room. "Do you usually conduct your business in such goodly company?" he asked. "With rats for companions?"

The rat-faced guards looked at one another, unsure if they had been offended. Dee, whose eyes had grown accustomed to the shadowy darkness, could see that there had indeed been some cosmetic and surgical attempts to make them more ratlike, their chins and noses length-ened, teeth sharpened. Or at least he hoped it was cosmetics and surgery that had rendered the changes.

"I knew a leader once who conducted her business in the open like this," Dee remarked. "Eventually some of the listeners thought they might conduct the business themselves, and at profit to themselves, rather than to their mistress."

"I take it this leader discovered her listeners' plans?"

"Most assuredly. Discovered it and cut off their heads for their thoughts; then spiked their two-faced smiles on the route to her pal—stronghold." Dee cleared his throat, not at all sure the man believed him. "They served as a timely reminder to anyone else who might be tempted to try the same tactic: The heads did."

"But the difference, Doctor Dee," the man said with a snigger, "is that none of my men would dare think that way. Because they know that there is no place to hide from my small electronically enhanced friends. My followers know I have ears everywhere. The little beasties get into everything. However, I do take your point." He stood up suddenly, and Dee, who was not a tall man, was startled to discover that, even standing on the raised step, the speaker was smaller than he was. In this future time the Elizabethan Doctor had gotten used to having others tower over him. He was kindly inclined towards the little fellow immediately.

The man came down the step and into the light. Dee decided that the ratlike features were undoubtedly a surgical creation, narrow slanted eyes, hair-tipped ears, pointed chin and nose, but it was the long leathery tail which caught and held Dee's horrified attention. Morgan d'Winter's hand fell on the doctor's shoulder, urging him to silence, and together they followed the small man through the sullen guards and down a series of damp, rat-laden steps into a subterranean corridor, the leathery tail twitching on the stones. Dee tried to concentrate on his mission, but the tail intruded upon his every thought. He had adjusted to Dyckon's having one, but he could not adjust to a man being endowed with one. Surely, God had put his curse on this man.

Once in the corridor, the small man pressed a tiny hand onto a stone, which glowed briefly red, then yellow. A heavy metal and ceramic door irised out of the wall, ceiling the corridor, and abruptly fresh air, scented with something like olives, blew down the corridor. The flickering smoky sconces abruptly snuffed out, and then lights appeared in the ceiling, racing towards them like the dawn.

"You must excuse the charade, Doctor," the small man said, "but it is a useful fiction to keep the rabble in order."

With d'Winter's fingers still pinching his shoulder to silence, Dee watched in astonishment as the little man shrugged out of the heavy brown leather coat he wore to reveal a cumbersome harness strapped across his chest and ending in the leather tail. He hit a release and it fell off, curling like a dead snake on the floor. Dee was so very relieved. Stepping out of his harness, Dee's host stuck out his hand.

"I'm Piper. And I think you'll agree that the Lord of the Rats should have a tail that befits his title."

"Most assuredly," the Doctor replied and then added, "It becomes you."

"Sometimes, Doctor," Piper said softly, a little of the metallic whine gone from his voice, "it is necessary to use what gifts the good Lord has given us."

"Amen to that," Dee said.

They were in Piper's inner sanctum, a bomb-proof circular chamber deep under ground, accessible only on a series of retinal and voice-password activated locks. The room, Dee had been delighted to discover, was filled with books. Real books. While Piper had prepared drinks, Dee had wandered down the bookshelves, idly trailing his fingers across the spines, touching paper and boards, leather and wood. For a moment, he forgot about his purpose and drank in the presence of all that accumulated and preserved wisdom. Just the smell of them was wonderful, and he promised himself to read more as soon as he had the opportunity, for there must have been several thousand books published since his age. How heartening to be in a real library again.

Piper took a peculiar-shaped seat in the center of the floor. He sat into the curved back of the chair so that he was, in effect, lying forward. He smiled pleasantly, with a hint of self-satisfaction.

"This," Dee said, in genuine admiration, "is a very fine library."

"Coming from an obviously cultured man such as yourself, I will take that as a real compliment." Piper did his best to bow from his seat.

Dee pulled out a book, *The Complete Works of William Shakespeare*, opened it to look at the illustration on the title page, then silently closed it again and returned it to the shelf. In his own time, he had known several Shakespeares, none of them in the chancy world of theatre. This one looked nothing like any of those he knew, though it did resemble a man he had known as Shaxper, who was an occasional scribbler of dramas as well as a performer in Burbage's troupe. But he'd never be a fine dramatist—too flowery.

"Perhaps you think that, like my followers, I have purposefully altered myself to look like this," Piper continued.

Dee accepted a glass of milk from d'Winter and turned to face the reclining man. "I'm not entirely sure what to think." Dee tasted the milk, puzzled that d'Winter had known where to find it, and was at liberty to fetch it. "I have seen some strange sights in this city."

"Well, this"—Piper indicated his face—"I'm afraid, is what my genes have given me. And, to my credit, if I say so myself, I've accepted it. My father looked like me, and my mother, poor dear, made my father look handsome. I've three brothers and two sisters; we all look a little—um—ratlike." He grinned, showing tiny sharp teeth. "Maybe it was something in the water, or maybe it was just a little too much inbreeding where we come from. My folks originally hail from Mammouth Springs; they were one of the few who struck it rich in the New Gold Rush of '66 just before the Crash. Even after the Great Quake, gold still held value. I suppose if I wanted to, I could have had some surgery done, got myself a real face, added a few inches to my height. But do you know something, Doctor Dee? I've grown rather used to my appearance, and, obviously, it has been my fortune. I've learned what a blessing it is. I am Piper, the Lord of the Rats, controller of most of Angel City's underworld. People now have surgery to look like me; I even know of a couple who've had prosthetic tails grafted onto their spines."

"Imitation is the sincerest form of flattery, they say," Dee began politely, "but, with all due respect—"

Piper smiled again. "You must forgive me, Doctor, I

don't get many visitors here, and those I do . . . well, they tend not to be cultured men such as yourself. You're, of course, here for a reason. I'd appreciate it if you would tell me now what your purpose is. Please begin. "

"I do indeed have a mission." Dee sat down on the top rung of a set of tall library steps and rested his elbows on his knees. "I have come to you because Morgan d'Winter recommended you highly. I have need of your special talents and skills."

"What has Morgan d'Winter told you about me?" Piper asked.

"He told me that you were a man of honour. That you could be trusted. That you had access to a vast and unusual source of information, that you always uphold your end of a bargain, and that you dealt in drugs."

Piper shrugged. "All of this is true. Which particular skill do you wish to employ?"

"All of them, Mr. Piper. You see, I am searching for a most unusual drug dealer, dispensing a most unusual drug. He may have an accomplice, which means that there will be more to do than simply stop this one caitiff. And if I do not find him, then the world as you know it will shortly cease to exist."

The little mouse-man roared with laughter. Dee couldn't help but smile at his disbelief.

CHAPTER

18

SECOND COMING OR SECOND CONNING, the head-lines blared on the newsboards and on the displays on street corners. There were endless variations on this question bruited about in all media. Strategy Brooks smiled every time she saw a headline, knowing that it was all her doing, and she reveled in it.

Is he or isn't he? That was the question on everyone's lips, and Strategy was delighted. Since his dramatic appearance at a local man's funeral two days ago, Yeshua Ben David has gone to the ground and was unavailable for interview. So long as Yeshua was unavailable, the speculation about him was free to flourish.

Is he who he claims he is? Strategy Brooks, the GNN anchor seems to think so. She has lent her weight to the campaign. However, GNN itself has issued a formal statement advising caution and suggesting that Strategy was acting in a personal, rather than professional, capacity when she announced her support for Yeshua. However, the fact that she and a GNN camera crew were on hand to witness the appar-

ent miracle would seem to suggest that GNN are, in fact, endorsing this particular messiah.

Angel City Times.com news on the hour:

VATICAN DENIES MESSIAH

Officials at the Vatican moved quickly today to cast doubts on the authenticity of the self-proclaimed messiah, reminding the public that there is no reason to suppose that this man is any more the Second Coming than any other man making such a claim. Pope Paul VII stated in his Sunday address to the Faithful that there was no reason for good Catholics to be taken in by cheap magicians' tricks, such as the supposed demonstration of raising from the dead. The Pontiff insisted that the media frenzy over this man is nothing more than a ploy aimed at gaining publicity for this Yeshua Ben David, remarking that he would have expected him to use Bar Joseph as his patronymic. His Holiness concluded his remarks by saying that discoveries made by the Vatican-sponsored archeological digs in the Sinai have led him to believe that Christ cannot return to Earth sooner than 3451 A.D.

Even the Pope-in-Exile Constantine IV issued a strong warning against believing in false prophets and against accepting the claims of madmen. Pope-in-Exile Constantine, who claimed only yesterday to be in direct communication with the genuine Messiah, said, as he addressed a crowd in Barcelona, "Accept no substitutes."

Vatican Times.com
Osservator Romano

DISTURBING REVELATIONS

*Our members can only view this latest development
with the utmost concern. A person once dead should
stay dead. The Morticians Union cannot be seen to be
endorsing the raising of the dead. Pretty soon it will go
from raising the dead, to not dying at all, and then
where will we be?*

Extracted from The Slab,

The Journal of the Morticians & Sundry
Trades.com

WIDOW NO LONGER, SUES

*In a bizarre twist to yesterday's extraordinary story
about the man claiming to be Jesus Christ bringing a
dead man back to life, Leeta O'Connor, erstwhile widow
of the recently dead Romulas O'Connor, is bringing a
case against Yeshua Ben David, for trauma, suffered
when her husband stepped out of the coffin. "It gave me
quite a turn, I can tell you, when Rommie just stepped
out of that coffin." Mrs O'Connor's solicitor claimed that
his client had suffered trauma, and that he intended to
bring a case against Yeshua Ben David for raising her
dead husband from the dead, the cemetery for allowing
the event to take place, also GNN for publicly transmit-
ting his client's trauma to the rest of the world, and
Romulas O'Connor, for "not staying dead." "This case is
worth billions," Leo Geffner of Geffner, Alter, and Bush,
the premier entertainment law firm, announced. "I
mean you can't just go around raising people from the
dead. It's not natural!" The newly risen Mr O'Connor
was unavailable for comment, and was said to be "resting comfortable" after the traumatic events. He, too, is
said to be considering legal alternatives.*

*In Angel City six other self-proclaimed Jesus Christs
are also bringing suit against Yeshua Ben David, for
"infringement of their copyright." The six messiahs are
also bringing suit against one another.*

Variety & Life.com
All the News That's Fit to Be News

GNN EXCLUSIVE

*At 9:00 P.M. Eastern, GNN reporter, Strategy Brooks
will have the first live on-air interview with Yeshua Ben
David. Is he the new messiah? Find out tonight on
GNN Nightly with Strategy Brooks.*

TV Guide

This was more than everything Strategy had hoped for.
She put her Omninet searcher on Gather mode, and continued to round up all the material she could on what
was being said about Yeshua. She wasn't surprised that
both Popes were being snippy about him—after all, he
directly impacted their business—and she was delighted
that they were willing to say so much, bringing Yeshua to
the fore in the minds of Catholics everywhere, no matter
which Pope they followed.

Rising, she walked around her study, her mind so ac-
tive she jumped from thought to thought too rapidly for
anything more than quick images to form in her
thoughts. She walked through her flat, bristling with
plans, and how she would use this God-sent opportunity
to make her career—and Yeshua's as well, if that's what
he wanted. He was a good-looking man in a kind of
Mediterranean way, and she wouldn't mind having him
around for a while.

The sudden buzzing of her phone surprised her as

much as a gunshot would have done, and it took two more hums for her to compose herself to answer. "Strategy Brooks," she said as she toggled the headset.

"Miss Brooks," said Mother O'Conner, "I think you should know I've had other offers."

Inwardly Strategy cursed. "I thought we talked about this, Mother O'Conner," she said in her best patient voice.

"Oh, we did. But things have changed; they're more fluid now." She paused. "Do you understand what I'm saying?"

Strategy sighed, and asked the question she dreaded. "How much more?"

CHAPTER

19

HAMIL AZZAHZI DIDN'T LIKE the look of the new tenant—there was something not right about the way in which the old man walked, almost as if he were under remote control, and his smell was dry, reminiscent of snakes. Still, the man had paid in cash and hadn't balked at the enormous deposit Azzahzi required for such an irregular arrangement.

"No drugs, not using them or making them. No pets. No visitors after eleven. No cooking on anything but the oven provided. No roommates without prior arrangement. No crimes. No illegal scanners. All deposits forfeit if you break any of the rules or move out with less than twenty days' notice." He pointed to the framed copy of the rules on the back of the apartment door. "I have reasonable right of inspection, with one day's notice, and immediate access in an emergency: *Emergency* is defined on the third page of your rental agreement."

"Fire, flood, earthquake, military attack, weather catastrophe, health crisis, civil disturbance, and imminent danger to me; any other condition must be defined in a court order," said the old man in a voice that sounded unused. "I understand and I've already said I agree."

"Water's included in the rent, but nothing else. You have to contract for power, waste disposal, recycling, and communications. That's separate. So's all food but morning muffins. Do you understand?"

"You've explained it twice," said the old man, who had introduced himself as Corwin Tarlton at Hamil Azzahzi's office, some three hours ago. "I get it. I'll take care of it."

"If you're on a pension, you can get a discount on recycling," Azzahzi told him helpfully; he lingered because he wanted so much to escape. "There's a cleaning service included, but laundry is separate. You can use the basement facilities, or you can arrange for a service to take care of it for you."

"I'll keep that in mind," said Tarlton.

"No modifications of the space unless agreed to in advance in writing. The furniture belongs to the unit and is registered as such, so don't think about removing it." He watched Tarlton warily. "That goes for everything in the unit."

"You made that clear before." Tarlton sounded almost bored. "I won't steal the sheets, either."

"Um," said Azzahzi, and handed over the code-pad. "Welcome to the Waco Palms." With that, he turned away and hurried down the corridor, telling himself he needed to rent the unit; it had stood empty for three months and had cost him money with every passing day. Still, he was uneasy about the tenant. He left the building—one of a series running the length of the block, built in the 2040s, and showing their age—and headed for the mosque, knowing he had some serious praying to do.

Left alone, the old man closed the door and engaged all the locks by attaching a highly illegal electronic bolt. Then he went into the rear room where the bed waited, dropped his two suitcases, and stood still, his form shimmering like a mirage on the desert air. A few seconds later the Roc sighed and lay down on the bed, relaxing into his own shape, contented with his success. He stared up at the ceiling, nothing in particular on his mind except what he had sworn with Fawg set-ut to do. That would not begin for seventy-two hours. He would sleep for a day and a night, and then he would be ready to begin the next stage of his plan.

"You must not malign your fellow men," said the Imam to Azzahzi. "But neither must you bring their enemies among them."

Azzahzi sat across the small room from Daoud Birhan, listening intently to what the Imam had to say. "But how am I to know which this Mr. Tarlton is? So far as I can tell, he's just one of those old men, long out of a job, living on a little pension and his government investment fund, and by himself."

"Yet you say you are uneasy in his presence," said Imam Daoud.

"I am. But that may be nothing." He slapped his palms together. "I cannot decide if I am being fearful— the Arab Riots happened when I was a kid, and I saw how bad it got—or if there really is something off about the guy."

"Hamil," said the Imam, "I don't want you to exhaust yourself about this. Take a day or two, meditate upon it, and come back to see me then. Remember we are Sunni, not Shiite, and vengeance is not our way." He smoothed his well-kept beard as if it were a treasured pet. "In the meantime, try not to fret about this Mr. Tarlton. If you have cause for concern, you'll realize it. Thought comes in the stillness of quiet water."

"Yes," said Azzahzi, happy to have an excuse to do as he wished.

"And if you are truly tranquil of mind, you will also be serene in your soul, and you will know what you must do." He reached out his hand to Azzahzi. "You were born here, Hamil, and you know your neighbors as well as someone named Houston or Campos. They, too, know you, and have from kindergarten. You need only employ what you have learned, and you will be able to make up your mind."

"You're right, Imam," said Azzahzi, getting to his feet and extending his hand to shake Daoud's. "Thanks. It really helps me to talk to you."

"That's what I'm here for." Imam Daoud rose. "If you like, I'll speak with Mr. Tarlton for you."

"Oh, I don't think that's necessary," said Azzahzi. "But thanks for the offer. If anything changes, I may come to you."

"Excellent," said the Imam. "Go in peace, Hamil."

"And you, Imam Daoud."

CHAPTER

20

"THAT MAN YOU RAISED from the dead . . ." Strategy began.

"What of him?" Yeshua turned his back on the city and looked at the newswoman. They were standing on the roof of the GNN West Coast Headquarters, watching the night rolling from the east, the lights of the city appearing in patches, reflecting up against the sulphurous miasma that perpetually hung over the surviving streets of Angel City. In the centre of what had once been Los Angeles, the blackened hole that was the Pit, where the Great Quake had collapsed and swallowed the heart of the city as subways, sewers, basements, and water mains fell in; now tiny lights winked and darted and multicolored gaseous eruptions belched into the poisonous air. In places the yellow fungi that was slowing claiming the Pit pulsed a dull bronze, and as night advanced, the entire area would glimmer with an amber nacreous glow.

Strategy moved through the warren of laser, radar, micro- and macrowave transmitter towers and aerials to lean against the pitted rail and stare towards the Pacific

Ocean. This close to shore the waters glowed phosphorescent green and radioactive silver in the fading light.

"Turns out he's still dead," Strategy said, without looking at Yeshua, her voice vaguely muffled by the microspore face mask she wore over her mouth and nose. "Oh, he's moving, and walking and talking—though not making much sense, as it happens—but he's still clinically dead. No heartbeat, no brain-wave activity." Strategy turned to Yeshua and found herself looking at her own distorted reflection in his Ray-Bans. She wondered what his eyes looked like, and then wondered why he choose to hide them.

"It was even so when I raised Lazarus," Yeshua said. "What point are you making?"

"O'Connor," Strategy said bluntly. "Is he dead or alive?"

"Alive. Well, generally living. Is that not what you wanted? You agreed it would make a good story."

"Oh, it's made a good story—a great story, believe me. Though I'm not sure that the recently widowed Mrs. O'Connor would agree with you. I think she'd prefer him dead. However, I've just spent the past few hours attempting to record an interview with Romulus O'Connor for the six o'clock news. Believe me, an interview like that would be Pulitzer stuff—if I'd gotten it. Which I didn't. I got nothing out of O'Connor. He can talk, but it's utter gibberish. I didn't know what to do with him—I had to fill twenty minutes and he was useless. There are words, strung together into what sounded like sentences but completely unintelligible. God, it was awful! And when he looks at you, his eyes are dead in his head, like pebbles, not eyes. And he sweats, Yeshua, shiny, with a skunkish odour."

Yeshua was unconcerned. "That happens. He was dead for a while. When I raised Lazarus, people told me that he had been dead and would have started to smell before I pulled him out of the tomb."

"This is not the smell of putrefaction, though I kept thinking I get that, too. This is something else. Something swamplike and fetid. We had the doctors on hand; they wired up Rommie to a wall of computer readouts, and they all showed a flat line. We changed the equipment, and it still showed a flat line. And while all this was going on, Romulas O'Connor was sitting up and showing a healthy interest in the proceedings. Though, and here's something I noticed when I was watching him from the monitors, when there are no people around, he lies back, and, for all the world, you'd think he was dead again."

"I would imagine he's tired." Yeshua said. "He's been through an ordeal."

"The man should be dead," Strategy said urgently. "The man is, to all intents and purposes, dead."

"And yet he walks, he talks. What further proof do you want?" Yeshua demanded.

The woman took a step closer to the tall man in white, and watched as he automatically took a step back. He didn't like people coming too close to him. "This is a dead man walking. You brought him back from the dead, but only his physical body is moving. I don't think you brought his spirit, his soul—call it what you will—back. Romulas O'Connor is starting to frighten people. The staff here are calling him 'the zombie.' "

"Not an inappropriate word, all things considered," Yeshua allowed.

Strategy turned away, heading for the stairs. "Until I

can get some sort of coherent interview with the dead man and talk to him about the afterlife, I'm afraid there's not a whole lot I can do. Raising a man from the dead is interesting—medicine can keep a body going for years after it's technically dead, but what makes this event newsworthy is if Romulas himself gives us a report from the other side. Otherwise I might as well talk to a package of ground meat." The door slammed and Strategy disappeared.

Fawg set-ut listened until the clicking footsteps disappeared, then he pulled off the sunglasses and blinked in the dull light, the nictitating membrane sliding across his slit-pupiled eyes, cleansing the gritty pollutants from the sensitive surface. He was beginning to think that perhaps this hadn't been such a good idea. His research had indicated that the humani should have fallen for the returned-messiah ruse, and risen up to follow him without a second thought. A few minor miracles should have authenticated his case and ensured his following, and then he could have marched on the seats of authority with his followers behind him. After all, it had worked for the other fellow. Admittedly, that was a couple of thousand years ago, but the humani hadn't changed that much in such a short space of time, had they? Dyckon ab-ack na Khar had always claimed that the humani advanced at an unusually accelerated rate and that to them a hundred years was a long time indeed. Perhaps there was something to his notion. But it wasn't enough to change any plans, or to contact his disciple.

Had he misjudged? It was an unnerving thought.

Fawg shook his head, blinking furiously; he was Fawg set-ut of the Clan set-ut. He did not admit to a mistake, for that would imply that his data was in error. And he was never wrong. All that these people needed was a few more miracles. That would bring them around. Alternatively, if he could make that stupid dead man talk coherently, and praise the Lord, then that might do the trick.

Fawg slipped the glasses back on, and his fingers fumbled over the tiny pager keypad Strategy had given him. Her blurry face appeared in the palm of his hand.

"What?" she snapped.

"That is no was to talk to your messiah." Even with the poor resolution, Fawg could see the look of disgust on Strategy's face.

"Look, this is turning out all wrong, okay? I've got the world's press gathering down here, and all I've got to bring before them is a dribbling idiot. You've animated a corpse. Big deal. I can do the same by ramming a battery up a frog's ass. It'll hop, but it won't be a frog."

Choosing to ignore this last sarcastic remark, Fawg asked, "Where is O'Connor now?"

Strategy blinked. "I don't know. Gone home. Why?"

"I will go and talk to him. He will listen to me."

"And then?" Strategy didn't allow herself the luxury of hope.

"And then you can talk to the world's press. With Romulas O'Connor. You will have your Pulitzer yet."

"And you, Yeshua Ben David. What will you have?" Strategy asked suddenly.

The man smiled, but without opening his mouth. "Why, my child, I will have the world."

CHAPTER

21

"DO YOU KNOW HOW I started out in business, Doctor Dee?"

"Tell me," Dee asked politely. He had chosen to sit behind an antique wooden desk that resembled his own walnut desk back home. A solid slab of highly polished and much-battered wood—real wood, not the pressed paper-fibre construct that passed for wood in this time—it bore countless scratches and indentations, faded carved names, barely legible dates, and scores of circles and half-moons of too many too-hot cups. Dee ran his long fingers across the scratches, allowing the sensitive tips to trace the lines of names and bygone times, and permitted a wave of nostalgia to sweep over him for a minute or two.

Piper, noting his interest in the desk, smiled. "That desk has been in my family for generations. My father used to say that Hamlyns had been born on that table, eaten at it, been taught at it, loved at it, and died at it."

"It has been privy to much," Dee agreed.

Misunderstanding, the rat-king corrected, "Can't say

that it has. To my knowledge, it's never been in the privy. It's too large." The corners of d'Winter's mouth smiled at the miscommunication. "When the Snow-Snap claimed the Appalachians, and wiped out many of the isolated communities, we were cut off, like the rest of them. For the best part of six months we were snowed in. Luckily, my pa, who'd learned his lesson in the Gold Rush years, had laid in a supply of food and blankets, and we weren't as worse off as some of the others. But towards the end there, we started to burn the furniture, rip up the floor-boards, burn anything that could give us a little heat. But never, not once, did anyone ever suggest that we burn the Hamlyn table. When the Black Death came and took the survivors of the Snow-Snap, I moved out West and took the table with me. Looking at it makes me feel that I'm still in touch with kin."

"I take it from your tone and words that many of your own were lost to the sickness."

"Eventually, I lost them all, Doctor," Piper said evenly. "And I suppose that is how I ended up here, as the King of the Rats, running the underworld and smuggling drugs." There was a moment of introspection, then a jubilant, "Hey, I know my mother would be mighty proud of me." Piper abruptly tucked his legs beneath him and curled up tightly, the movement peculiarly feral and almost foetal. "Do you believe in chance, Doctor?"

Dee nodded. "In chance and synchronicity and what a later age than mine called serendipity. Though I'll warrant that I do not believe, not a cat's whisker, in chance as random happenstance. I am of the firm mind that there is a predetermined order to the universe, an energy which can be effected and affected not a little by our thoughts. As Our Gracious Lord commands, 'His will be done.' Yea,

I've on occasion seen thought manifest itself into substance. In my time, I was oft quoted as saying that Faith lends Substance."

"Faith lends Substance," the Piper whispered. "I think I kinda like that, Doc. I can find little to disagree with any of that, Doctor. It was my faith in this place which brought it into being. It was my faith in myself which made me do all that I have done."

"I've see the sick cured by the power of prayer and what is prayer, but an act of faith." Dee smiled tightly. "The prayers were not always pious, but somehow they worked. In opposition, I've see the hale and well sicken and die for they thought they had been cursed—and a curse is naught else but an act of faith and belief."

"I can find little to disagree with any of that, Doctor. Well then, think about this if you will. I originally came here in order to find drugs to send back home to combat the Black Death. You know what the Death is, Doctor?"

"Aye, more's the pity. Know it full too well, and lost by it, too," Dee said feelingly.

"I'm sorry for your loss, Doc," the Piper said with genuine sympathy. He let a heartbeat of time slip by in remembrance, then continued on with his history. "I'd learned that you could buy anything in Angel City, provided you had the cash. That began back in L.A. Basin, before the Quake, and only increased afterward. Cash my people had aplenty, gold, too, but no food and no drugs. Why, Doctor, at one stage, we even took to eating rats, if you can believe it."

Dee nodded. "I am acquainted with many a handsome inn that has a reputation for serving rat in its meat pie. It savors much like chicken."

"I arrived here, nearly ten years ago, naïve and innocent with a trunk full of cash on one hand and a couple of contacts on the other. Well, those contacts managed to sell me the medicine I needed, at hugely inflated prices of course, and I managed to get them back home—too late for many, but in time for a precious few. Some of those who survived came out here with me and formed the nucleus of my army, and in the interim, I had hooked up with people like d'Winter." Piper's lips twisted, showing tiny pointed teeth. "Men of principle in an unprincipled world. Can you credit it, Doc?"

"Any man who has been about the world a little will know that you speak truly." He glanced at d'Winter.

"You are fortunate, if you're right," said Piper, following Dee's gaze.

"I care to think of it as being discerning. There are always such Men, of a high and noble mind in ignoble times faced with the unthinkable to make decisions that are repugnant to them. I count myself one of Fortune's favorites to have encountered several of these matchless men in my life." With that, Doctor Dee purposefully looked at d'Winter for a second time. No other words were needed.

"I share your sentiments, Doctor. It was d'Winter who pointed out to me that while I was going to great trouble and effort to smuggle drugs out of the city, there were people here, in the very heart of Angel City, in equally dire need. I set up a separate division, if you will, to service these people. Prices were lower, but the demand was much higher."

This was finally what Dee had come for. "Morgan d'Winter tells me that you specialise in medicinal drugs, and do not meddle in soporifics or hallucinogens."

"No, I leave that to some of my competitors." Piper

shrugged. "Hey, that niche is there if I want it. And there may come a day when I might choose to traffic in it."

Morgan d'Winter moved, leather clothing and metal accouterments squeaking ominously. "And that is when you and I must part company," he said slowly, "and, man, you will find me one ugly enemy."

Piper swivelled in the chair to look at d'Winter. "It is one of the reasons I reckon I never chose to go down that particular stretch of road. I would hate to have you, or guys like you, move against me."

"This rat guise?" Dee interrupted. "What prompted you to adopt it?"

Piper smiled, showing feral teeth. "It began as a ruse to cover up my identity from the authorities. It was also a stratagem to keep my competitors at bay." Piper Hamlyn spread his arms wide. "I am not the most prepossessing of men, and I needed something to compensate for that."

"Size isn't everything," Dee remarked. "Is it not a universal truth that women prefer a compact man?"

D'Winter grunted. "You've just only brushed up against women that liked compact men. There ain't anything universal about it."

Dee smiled. "Allow me my tiny vanities."

Piper looked at the two and went on. "So the rat guise took form. In time it grew, as did the legend and the mythology that came to surrounded it, helped, in no small part by our mutual friend d'Winter, who put out the word that this half-human half-verminuous gang lord had appeared. It was one of my own people, a brilliant biomechanician, who perfected the technique of implanting either tool, weapons, or security devices into the rats. Then word of mouth, rumor, and Chinese whispers conspired to create a myth that even I had no control of. The final piece of the puzzle fell in place when the first of the followers began to appear. Men and women who had actually had themselves surgically altered to resemble rodents so that they could serve me. Originally, I was kinda embarrassed by them, and I was going to send them away, but I quickly realized that they, too, had their uses. Now they are some of my most loyal followers."

"I'm not sure what they see in you," d'Winter said sarcastically.

"They see themselves, of course, writ large in spirit if not in flesh," Piper said seriously. "Many of them, either by an accident of birth or circumstances, have survived upon the margins of Angel City. Their twisted bodies or lives caused them to be social outcasts. They barely survived and had nothing to live for. Now their imperfections make them eligible to be part of my lucrative community. The fact that we only deal in medicines is an added bonus. It makes them feel even better about themselves."

"Which, I do believe, has brought us full circle," Dee interjected. "In councils with the good Morgan d'Winter, I did ask him for the most skilled pharmacist in this benighted city. He chiefly recommended me to you."

"I am flattered." The ratman sensed that the English Doctor had come to the reason for his visit—the stated desire and the inevitable negotiation. He casually sat up straight on the couch and planted his feet firm on the floor. Friends or no friends and no matter how congenial the company—a deal is a deal is a deal. The muscles in his pointed face tightened in expectation. He purposefully relaxed back into the cushions, an arm stretched along the top of the couch. The posture—a practiced one—was the picture of a magnanimous man in charge. Piper Hamlyn readied himself for the give and take of swapping.

Dee leaned both arms across the desk and locked his fingers together. "Don't be; flattery is the tool of the assassin. Do not believe my compliment. At least not yet. It occurs to me that if you dispense medicines, it must follow as the Autumn doth the Summer that you would be in the know of where the worst outbreak of diseases occurs."

Piper frowned. "I would, I suppose—"

"I am certain you must be at pains to acquire such information. That surmise begot the next: that you would most assuredly be more aware of the existence of outbreaks than those in authority."

Piper achieved a smug smile. "True. Though you will find, Doctor, that the authorities care little or nothing about what will happen in Angel City. We can all go to Hell in a handbasket for all that they care."

"Undeniably," John Dee concluded, in a hurry to wrap up his logistic formula, "Then, if a new disease were to beset Angel City, you would hear of it first."

There was a subtle change in Piper's demeanor; he grew still and gave Dee his utmost attention. "Absolutely."

"How quickly could you possess the intelligence?" Dee blinked in innocence. "Do you think you would know in a full day?"

"Within hours, maybe less than that. Depends how virulent the outbreak, the nature of the disease. When Viral-Two Ebola hit Encino and wiped out a third of the population practically overnight, my people were there in the early hours of the morning with the vaccine. If they hadn't, hell, we might have lost another thousand or so before the authorities got their act together." Piper uneasily leaned forward and stuck his hands under his thin legs. "You suspect that some new disease is going to decimate Angel City, don't you."

"No," Dee said simply, "I do not suspect. I know. A horseman cometh, Mr. Hamlyn, and he passeth by; his name is Pestilence. And unless we can unseat this apocalyptic rider, then, by all that is holy, I do believe that Angel City itself will cease to exist, for this disease is like nothing you have ever beheld before. It leaves the body intact, but wastes the mind. What remains is less than human but living. And the damage is done not in weeks, but days."

"From the little I know," d'Winter interrupted, "I'll bet the farm that the authorities will take the tack to nuke Angel City just to bottle the disease. Give them just the excuse they've always wanted."

Piper slipped his pointed chin into his thin hands. "You're serious, aren't you?"

"Deadly," said Dee.

CHAPTER

22

ON A DEEP, VERY DEEP, and almost instinctual level, Romulas O'Connor knew he was dead. He remembered dying, he supposed. Or was that a dream? Had he dreamt that he had died? Or had he died? The memories were faded, woolly, as if they were not his memories, but something he had been told, or something he had seen, or perhaps read. Perhaps it had been in a vid, or on a newspot. Now, sitting on the edge of a bed which he dimly remembered as his—in fact he had died in this bed!—in a house which he definitely knew was his, because he had an intimate memory of the geography of the rooms. Snippets of memory came sliding away as he reached for them. Half-formed thoughts and fragments slithered and slid from his grasp, and all he was left with were bits and pieces, but he was unsure in his present state whether he was actually remembering real events or simply recalling other images or ideas.

Romulas O'Connor lay back on the bed. It took him two attempts because he could not make his legs respond and swing themselves up onto the coverlet, and he was eventually forced to physically lift his legs up. But once he was lying supine, his face towards the ceiling or the coffin lid, his eyes closed, a sequence of events locked into place, and he had a brief flash of what he was fairly sure was a real memory. One of his *own* memories. Something that had really happened.

It was night. Dark, but the room was illuminated by the sulphurous acid rain etching itself down the iron-glass windows. He remembered thinking that he would soon have to have the windows replaced; the lifespan of the glass was becoming shorter and shorter as the acid grew ever more corrosive. He had dined well and perhaps not too wisely. The meal—imported lamb from Ireland, chicken eggs from an independent Russian state, wild rice from a Chinese backwater province, and potatoes from a State Farm somewhere in Canada—had been absolutely delicious. Every morsel radiation and hormone free—not like that shit he served up to his customers. Some of the stuff that his fishermen were pulling up out of the ocean looked like a Bosch-inspired nightmare or, even more disturbingly, was beginning to display ever more humanoid features. There were species of squid down there that were beginning to resemble human foetuses, and only last week they had pulled up a five-hundred-pound tuna that had a distinctly human face. Complete with wispy beard. There was no way he was going to eat anything pulled out of that open sewer that was calling itself the Pacific Ocean. He had even heard of whales that were so diseased that they were officially declared as toxic waste.

After the meal there had been—what?—a bottle of— he remembered the taste, because it has been one of the last things he had tasted before the . . . the confusion. But he could not remember the name. A bottle of something dark and bitter, tainted in his memory with the faintest must of a too-dry and brittle cork. Then, afterwards, he had come up the stairs and found . . . and found . . . what was her name? She was his wife, he thought, young and pretty, but he could not remember her name.

She had been in bed—this bed. Waiting for him. Not naked, no, but wearing clothes that made her all the more appealing, all the more exciting.

He had . . . he had . . . gone to the next room, the bathroom, and had looked at himself in the mirror, and he remembered wondering how a very beautiful woman—what was her name?—could find him attractive. In his mind's eye he could recall his own reflection. He was too old, too fat, too bald, too jowly, his cheeks and nose flushed mottled red. It took a tremendous effort to roll from the bed. Arms and legs seemed to work independently, and he found himself sitting in the one position for possibly a long time because he had forgotten what he was going to do next. Once he got to his feet, he directed himself towards the bathroom door, but when he got there, he found he had quite forgotten how to turn the handle to open it. He knew what he should do; knew that his fingers should close around the handle and turn, but he simply could not make himself do it.

Finally he leaned against the door, and it moved gently inwards. Romulas O'Connor stepped into the bathroom and was immediately presented with multiple images of himself from the mirrored walls. He thought he looked very good. Better than he was before—before the blackout. His skin was pink and healthy, looking firm and taut and a little of the flab seemed to have disappeared from around his gut. He tried—and failed—to remember when he had last eaten. Earlier that evening he had sat down to a meal, he thought. Or he should have.

Only his eyes bothered him.

They looked like the dead orbs of something that would turn up in his nets. Under the too-bright bathroom lights, his skin shone with an oily sweat, and he raised trembling fingers to his brow. It took two attempts to touch his forehead. Romulas O'Connor brushed his fingers across his brow. In the mirror the movements were erratic, and his thumb kept waving independently of the other fingers. His hand came away from his forehead covered with an oily sweat. Under the lights it ran with a shimmering luminescence, rainbowlike tendrils of oil on water. Maurice watched it, fascinated. He brought his palm to his nose and tried to smell . . . but he couldn't draw breath into his lungs. . . .

Absently wiping his fingers on a pristine towel, leaving a shimmering tendril of slime clinging to the cotton, Romulas pressed both hands to his chest. There was no movement beneath his sternum—because his lungs weren't working, not filling with air—which meant . . . Romulas struggled for the concept.

Which meant that he wasn't breathing. He pressed fumbling fingers to his wrists, but he couldn't hold both hands steady enough, so he gripped the side of his wrist, seeking a pulse. There was nothing. For some reason that bothered him.

He tried, and failed, to open the mirrored cabinet and finally simply closed his hand into a fist and slammed it into the glass door. The cabinet lurched and swung off the wall, dangling precariously on one screw, tumbling ointments, razors, creams, toothbrushes and pastes, and scores of many-coloured pills into the sink beneath.

There was glass in his hand. Glass from the mirrored doors of the cabinet. Two long ragged pieces protruding from between his knuckles, two smaller pieces stuck into the soft flesh on the back of his hand.

Romulas frowned.

There should be some . . . sensation, a response. There should be pain.

And blood.

He managed to find a purchase on one of the pieces of glass and pulled it out of his flesh. It came out with a slight sucking sound, and for a single instant Romulas thought he saw the wound shimmer with iridescent oil.

Then, as he watched, the cut closed and sealed itself. This was wrong, and he dimly knew it. So wrong. So . . . wrong.

At the back of the cabinet Romulas O'Connor found the cutthroat razor. This he knew. His great-grandfather had brought it with him from the Old Country. Or was it his great-great-grandfather? No matter. Romulas remembered clearly and distinctly his father using this very razor when he showed him how to shave. His father had told him then that his father had also used the razor when he had been a boy. Romulas had hoped that one day he would show his own son how to shave using this heirloom that had been used by generations of O'Connors.

The stainless-steel blade parted the flesh of his wrist with a sound of tearing paper.

The shimmering iridescent sweat appeared in the gaping cut and sealed it up again.

But there was no blood.

Romulas O'Connor knew then that his was no dream and that he was dead, but moving.

And if he had had tears to cry, he would have wept then.

Later, much later that night, Mother O'Connor found her son slumped in the bathroom, eyes wide and unblinking, the open razor on the floor by his side, dark bruises on his left wrist, another on his cheek. It didn't take a genius to work out what had happened. She stared, not wanting to believe what she knew was true.

"Ah, my poor wee boy." There was no way she would give that bleached bitch the satisfaction of this discovery. She would tend to her son, never mind that hussy. Pulling the towel off the rail, she patted at the bruises on her dead son's wrists, then, bringing the towel to her lips, licked the corner and used it to scrub at the mark on Romulas' cheek.

Rainbow colors glowed briefly on her lips, then faded.

CHAPTER

23

BENEATH A CANOPY of clouds Angel City glowed in a sulphurous light, steam rising up from fissures, looking like the smoke from infernal fires. Amid the eerie luminosity there was darkness, lying like scabs on the bright parts of the night. A haze clung to the sky, sparkling where the lurid illumination struck it. The moist Pacific fog no longer routinely burned off in the early afternoon, but hung around through the afternoon, snuggling against the low-lying California hills during the night.

Doctor John Dee emerged with Kelly and d'Winter from Piper's underworld realm into the furtive celebrations carried on by Pitside revelers along a stretch of ruined roadway that long ago had been the westernmost part of Santa Monica Boulevard that dead-ended at the water's edge. The majesty of the ocean lay spread out beyond, stirring his memories of Portsmouth. There, on a caravel to Aquitaine, he had first encountered the formidable grace of the Atlantic, and had heard for the first time the hypnotic tempo of the crashing waves. He had always found peace at the harbors of the world. In his mind he revisited Antwerp, Calais, Brugge, Lisbon, and beautiful Palermo as he had seen them in his own age. But here in Angel City the sea breeze was polluted with the stink from the Pit, resulting in a queasy mix of rotten eggs and open sewers. This is the rankest compound of villainous smells that ever offended nostril, thought the Doctor. Dee turned his face towards the sky, but could not make out more than the gibbous moon; the glistening particles in the air obscured the stars. He felt cut off from Heaven's ministering eye, and the malefic influence of the moon was only too familiar to him.

"What do you think?" Kelly asked.

"I think I need an ephemeris," said Dee.

"No," Kelly said impatiently. "About Piper. Do you think he really will help?"

"I hope so," said Dee. "Ask d'Winter. He best knows the fellow." He was feeling restless, eager to be on the trail of the shape-shifting virus, but still not certain how to begin. He tried movement, taking a turn about the small flat area where Piper's escort had brought them. But pacing only made his edginess worse, so he stopped doing it and brought all his concentration to bear on their predicament. Action would bring him peace, for action was eloquent. The difficulty was in deciding which way to turn.

"I think he meant what he said," d'Winter told her without waiting for her to ask. "He's kept his word in the past."

"Then I hope he keeps it now," said Kelly with feeling.

"Why wouldn't he?" D'Winter was indignant on Piper's behalf. "He risks losing his empire if he does not support us. He may be as much rat as man, but he has everything to loose and his position to retain if he cooperates."

"Aye," said Dee. "I cannot but think he will see the rightness of our cause. Nature teaches beasts to know their friends. The truth is nakedly obvious that any pur-blind eye may yet discern it. Let's have no more doubts on that head."

D'Winter was uneasy at their being out at this hour, when only the most determined revelers remained on the streets. He pointed to the suspension walkways arching above them, providing a means of foot traffic for the denizens of Angel City and the inhabitants of L.A. Basin; they also provided an illusion of safety, being so far away from the contamination on the ground. "We should get up there."

"How?" Dee asked. "There are walls along this swath all the way to the water. Naught but Piper's mice might find scaling easy here. "

"I'll show you," said d'Winter, and moved off the rubble that once was a roadway.

Kelly drew a thin stiletto from her long vest and slipped it into the spring mechanism in her sleeve. "Just in case," she said as she nudged Dee's shoulder.

Dee allowed her to guide him over the hummocks that had been buildings, into a region of darkness. "What should I—"

"Shush!" she warned him, her hand tightening on his shoulder.

This was too much for Dee, who had been containing himself for longer than he liked. "S'Blood!" he exclaimed. "What are we? Pidgeon-livered miscreants, that we must seek safety in shadows? Has not Providence seen fit to deliver us from the bowels of the earth? Now must we cringe when we are once again in the realms of men?" He drew himself up to his full height and was about to raise his voice when d'Winter came up behind him and clapped a hand over his mouth. Dee sputtered in protest and did his best to bite.

"Because we're not in the world of men—not yet," said d'Winter, not quite whispering.

"Then what is this?" Dee was losing his composure; he wanted answers now, clear answers he could comprehend and would be able to deal with. Answers that would lead to actions. The Doctor stopped struggling with the larger man. He used the tone of his voice to oppose him. "Have we got out of one netherworld only to enter another?"

"We're being watched!" d'Winter hissed. "So shut up, and we may get out of here."

"How do you know?" Dee demanded as d'Winter released his hold on him. They were out in an open space and the thin fog hadn't obscured their immediate surroundings. Dee turned his head, scanning their surroundings for any threat. He saw none. He heard only the tide and the wind as they raked at the distant beach.

D'Winter tapped his helmet. "Heat patterns. There are about eight of them, but more are coming." There was an uneasiness in his demeanour. Then, aware of something new he saw on his visor monitors, he froze. "More are coming. Eight in front, more behind."

"Eight what?" Dee was disquieted by d'Winter's fear, for the large black man rarely shrank from anyone. This unseen enemy must be formidable indeed, Dee thought. His next question was if there were more, how many was that?

"They're called Untouchables," said Kelly.

"Something else you elected naught to tell me?" Dee asked, but in a lowered voice. He turned to face her. "Is't possible? More fiends whom your Sodomite city vomits forth that are still unknown to me?" He tried to make light of their predicament, chuckling richly. "Tut, tut. You've slacked in your duties." Glancing around again, he lowered his voice. "Well?" After all, he told himself, he had no desire to risk his mission or the lives of his friends.

D'Winter gave him a withering look. "This isn't the time."

"And when would be, pray?" He held up an admonishing finger. "Define, define, well-schooled Ethiope. Recount their qualities and characters."

"You'll know soon enough," said d'Winter, pulling out a pistol, a thin, short-range Colt Defender.

"How many have you of those?" Dee inquired, indicating the truncated barrel of the pistol. Thinking that d'Winter was more prepared than usual, he added, "What mischiefs do you expect, that you are so diversely armed?"

"I have enough to protect us, I hope," d'Winter replied, waving Dee to silence as he turned in a full circle. "Another three, there on the left."

"Not good," said Kelly.

"Did Piper arrange this?" Dee asked suspiciously, peering into the dark and seeing nothing, though he could now hear a peculiar, slithering sound that was like a snake moving over dry leaves.

"No. Untouchables are as much his enemies as ours," d'Winter said. "Look. There's an old side street on your left. It wasn't too chewed up last time I was here. We need to move closer to it. I think it could get us out of here. We can get out if we can run up the road."

"Won't the Untouchables chase us?" Dee wanted to know.

"They will," said d'Winter. "But we have an advantage once we start running."

"And wherefore is that?" Dee asked.

D'Winter turned and looked at him, and even in the gloom Dee could see the look of repugnance that appeared behind d'Winter's visor. "Because we have feet."

CHAPTER

24

CORWIN TARLTON SHUFFLED OUT of Hamil Azzahzi's apartment house and made his way to the commuter station on the Dallas-Houston line. Anyone looking at him in bright daylight would have seen an odd iridescence to his forehead, and would probably assumed he hadn't bathed. There were about a hundred people on the platform, most at pains to notice none of the others, although a few were traveling together, and they talked in an overly animated manner as if to make up for the self-imposed isolation of the rest.

The commuter liner arrived and those waiting for it surged aboard, making an eager grab for seats. The rest, including Tarlton, took hold of the slings hanging from the ceiling and prepared for the high-speed run into Dallas. Thirty minutes later they left the liner at the Market Center, and Tarlton joined the rest in taking the moving sidewalks to Dealy Plaza.

For the rest of the morning Tarlton wandered the halls of public buildings, visited schools, shops, and restaurants, then took the moving sidewalks back to the commuter-liner platform, where he boarded the next southbound liner, leaving it at Waco, and from there, walking back to Hamil Azzahzi's apartment house. When he reached his own quarters, he let himself inside and sighed as he finally reassumed his Roc shape. He was exhausted and famished, but he was also jubilant, for he now knew it would work. He could fulfill the mission Fawg set-ut had given him. Today had been practice—he would rest for two days, prepare his phials, and then, on the third day, he would make the journey again, but not as he had done today: In three days he would release the virus.

"Mr. Tarlton! Mr. Tarlton!" Hamil Azzahzi was pounding on the door, his insistent drumming penetrating the Roc's stupor.

Grumbling at the inconvenience, he assumed the Tarlton shape and made his way to the front door. "What is it?" he muttered as he released all but the proximity lock.

"We got a problem, Mr. Tarlton. I wish you had a number I could call—I wouldn't have to disturb you like this." Azzahzi had the consideration to look abashed as he leaned on the doorsill.

"And what would that be?" Tarlton asked, getting ready to close the door again.

"It would be the plumbing. In many of these older buildings, there is trouble with the plumbing. I will have to have a plumber come in and scan the walls for leaks. There are two on the floor below, and we have to make sure there are no more."

"Is it urgent?" Tarlton didn't have to work at sounding ill-used.

"It is," Azzahzi apologised. "Part of the wall in the apartment below is soaked and the sheeting is falling in."

"I have nothing like that in my apartment," said Tarlton, preparing to close the door.

"No, but you could have leaks inside the walls that are contributing to the mess downstairs." Azzahzi slapped the wall in frustration. "If you'll let the plumber come in tomorrow, it shouldn't take any longer than half a day. The scanning is done very quickly. You'll see. If there is any more inconvenience, I'll make an adjustment in the rent."

Tarlton realized that refusing to agree would draw more attention to him than he wanted, and so he nodded grudgingly. "All right. It's very inconvenient."

"Believe me, having the wall fall in would be a lot more inconvenient," Azzzahzi said. "Thank you, Mr. Tarlton. The plumber will be here by ten." With the last five apartments the landlord had found that by announcing the appointment time he could quash any tenant's reservations. Mr. Tarlton had not been a nuisance or unreasonable, at least not so far.

"Very well," said Tarlton, shaking a little with the effort of retaining his shape. He was more fatigued from his journey than he had expected to be, and his concentration was suffering for it.

"Good," said Azzahzi. "Thanks, Mr. Tarlton. We'll make this as unintrusive as possible. If you want to stick around and see that nothing's done that you don't like, that nothing's touched—"

"I will," said Tarlton, because it was expected of him.

"Great. Fine." Azzahzi stepped back and let the door close without protest. What was it about the man? he asked himself, trying to remind himself of what Imam Daoud had told him. Did Tarlton really need to wear sunglasses inside?

Behind the door, Tarlton listened until he couldn't

hear Azzahzi's footsteps any longer. Then he let his shape slip back to his own. It was a great relief to be at his own height, his own form again. He arched his back to loosen his knotted muscles. His head almost bumped the ceiling. As he returned to the bedroom, he consoled himself with the thought that it would only be one day that was lost. The world had been given a twenty-four hour stay of execution; it would be four days more, just four.

CHAPTER

25

SCRAMBLING OVER THE ROUGH terrain toward the imposing, powered fence, d'Winter shoved Dee and Kelly into the lead so he could deal with the Untouchables crowding in behind them. The slope increased and it was harder to keep moving. No one spoke, saving their breath for their escape.

Suddenly d'Winter fired, and there was a stridulation that raised the hair on Dee's arms. The sound was unmistakable: locustlike—only louder, larger. They bolted the last few meters to the powered fence, Kelly making sure that Dee didn't touch the shining metal. D'Winter let off another dozen shots, then came up beside Kelly and Dee. "They'll regroup and start up again in a moment. We've got to get out now!"

Kelly slipped between Dee and whatever was behind them. She crouched low, to fend off a ground-hugging foe.

"Stand aside," d'Winter said as he reached into his protective suit and made an adjustment. "It won't last more than a couple of seconds," he warned. "You'll have to go as soon as I say."

Kelly took hold of Dee's arm as she drew the Colt Defender. "We're ready. Give me your hand."

Dee tried to pull his arm away. "I can manage for myself."

"No, you can't. This isn't the time for misplaced pride," said Kelly, who with her helmet's infra-vision was scanning the area behind them. "We have Untouchables approaching. Three hundred meters." Then, never looking at her employer, she added, "Doctor, you pay us to protect you. Let us do our job."

D'Winter stared at Dee. "This is going to have to be quick."

"Fine," said Dee, and with that took Kelly's hand, abdicating. "Will this do?"

"Yes," she said, and pulled him down to the ground.

Not missing a beat, D'Winter pulled out an instrument that looked like a bale hook. He slammed the point into the joint in the metal and was immediately surrounded by coruscating light that crackled as he repeatedly slammed the hook into the four remaining joints. He worked fast as the sound of the Untouchables closing on them grew louder.

Dee saw them now: Creatures more scorpion than human were scuttling toward them, their stumpy limbs obscene as they thrust out toward them. Watching these beasts, Dee didn't see d'Winter peel the section of metal fencing back.

"Now!"

Dee didn't need any more encouragement; he launched himself at the breach in the fence, feeling an unpleasant tingle as he passed through the edge of the energized field. The next thing he knew, he was tucked into a ball and rolling down the slope toward the access

path leading to the nearest fly-over. He tensed in anticipation of rolling onto the uneven paving stones, and in
the same instant was stopped by Kelly, who had somehow moved to block him and was slowly getting to her
feet.

A small group of passers-by stared at them, then were
startled by the sizzling sound of the gap in the fence sealing itself, shutting out the horrors on the other side.
D'Winter came hustling down the hill.

"Oh, well done!" Dee approved, his face alight with
enthusiasm and the thrill of the danger. He held out his
hand to the large black man.

D'Winter made no attempt to take it, but, rather, he
pointedly whispered, "We have to get out of here."

"Absolutely," said Kelly. "The Patrol'll be along any
minute, and we don't want to be detained for breaching
the wall. There'll be hell to pay." Night was just beginning to fade into dawn, and the whole of the city had
taken on a second luminescence. The rosy beginning of a
new day glowed on the edge of the eastern mountains. It
was a welcome sight.

"Right," said d'Winter as he removed his helmet.
"We'll be a bit less conspicuous without these." He
shoved his into the supply sack hanging on his back.
"Not much of a disguise, but it should help."

Kelly had removed her less imposing headgear and
tucked it away as well. "Which way?"

"North, I think. It's away from the media colony in the
desert and the industrial wastes to the south. And we'll be
out of L.A. Basin more quickly going that direction. Come
on." D'Winter lifted his head. "Skimmers. Let's go."

Dee had been listening to this exchange with growing
frustration. "Hold there," he said. "We're beyond that

fence, we're free of the tunnels, why this need for flight? Are we not safe?"

"No," said Kelly. "We're not."

"But why not?" Dee demanded, misliking another retreat.

"We've probably been spotted at least once, and that means we're being hunted," said Kelly. "As you've pointed out, you have enemies. And cities are good places for viruses to spread. With all the public monitoring, we're vulnerable while we're in Angel City, and we could be detained, which would immobilize us completely. If we put some distance between this place and ourselves, we can work out how to stop the infection, and then we can put our plans to work. If we remain here, we'll be dodging trouble every minute. It's your call, Doctor." She motioned to him to follow her, and after a brief consideration, he did.

They turned away from the suspended walkways, turning toward the rising Santa Monica mountains. D'Winter set a brisk pace, and they all moved along steadily, moving just a bit more quickly than most of the people on the road, but not so fast as to be conspicuous. Sometimes they jogged—it was still a popular sport. Finally, after about forty minutes, as they reached the Mulholland Rift, they paused and looked back on the wreckage of the city.

"What on earth were those . . . those things?" Dee asked, giving voice to the question that had been plaguing him for the last hour.

"Untouchables?" D'Winter's laughter was harsh. "They're what became of what was called the Homeless during the Quake, when all the underground structures fell in. The Homeless had been cordoned off into underground centers, to keep them off the streets. The Quake buried many of them alive; the rest weren't so lucky. They had no protection, and most of them were exposed to the Santa Monica Power Plant slag when the shielding failed. Most of them died, but those who didn't had a pattern of genetic problems they passed on to their offspring."

Dee had learned something about the theories of genetics. "I see. The sins of the fathers are visited upon the sons, even unto the seventh generation."

Kelly nodded. "There aren't a lot of them left—too much genetic damage; their infant mortality is above sixty percent—but they're dangerous, no matter how few they are. They're capable of inflicting all manner of disease, including what's called Untouchable Epidermal Lesion Syndrome. It sloughs the skin, and then muscle, and then bone. By the time their children are ten, if they live that long, they've lost their hands and feet."

Dee had seen a few lepers in his travels, and he suppressed a shudder. "Poor wretches," he said sincerely. "Can nothing be done for them?"

"No," said d'Winter a little more harshly than Dee thought necessary; their kind disgusted him. "Not that anyone's ever found. Piper tries every now and then, which is why they leave him and his people alone. Anyone else in the Pit is fair game."

"Why did they give us chase?" Dee asked.

"For food. Meat is scarce in the Pit. Their young who still have hands are trained to slaughter. They're cannibals; they're said to feed on their own when times are really hard." D'Winter grimaced. "That sound they make is hypnotic. It can stop you in your tracks."

Kelly nodded and added, "If they touch you, you're going to have trouble. Considering the subsequent pain, if they kill you, they're being nice."

Dee rubbed his grizzled chin. "Scurvy, pestilent, skain-mates. My teeth still itch from the sight and sound of them." Then he smiled grimly. "Poor worms, they are blighted by no fault of their own. This virus we're seeking—might it not help them? It could change their shapes to wholesome ones."

"Yes," said d'Winter, "I suppose it could. But they'd still be Untouchables and very dangerous, all the more so because they couldn't be identified. And no one could be sure if they had been exposed to UELS, which could mean an epidemic of that as well."

"It was just a thought," said Dee with a sigh. "I'd like to think this pernicious stuff could do some good—other than benefit the Roc."

"It may, but not for our species, and not on this planet. Or the moon, for that matter," said d'Winter at his most blunt. He turned away from the Pit. "Let's get going. We can pick up a Coast Liner and ride up to Pismo Beach."

"And wherefore there?" Dee asked. "Cannot we be safe in—"

"I have a small stronghold there. We can be safe for a few hours, and if we're being scanned—and I am convinced we are—we might be able to identify who is doing it. I have equipment for that." He was walking already, expecting his companions to fall in with him; the first long rays of sunlight struck him, giving him the look of a bronze statue.

Kelly cocked her head to the north. "He's right, you know. There's a lot we have to do, and we can't do it out here in the open, or in your hideout."

Dee stared at the remains of the city and tried to think what London—his London, the city of Good Queen Bess and Burghley and Walsingham—would have done faced with such a catastrophe as had overtaken the L.A. Basin; surely, white and red crosses on the house doors of the diseased; those who could flee would have escaped to the country. The followers of John Calvin would have shrugged their shoulders and said it was the Will of God. To some extent, Doctor Dee agreed with them, for he could read portents in the stars, put there by Providence. The Divine had visited punishment on Angel City, sending it all manner of afflictions for sins known everywhere and transgressions known only to God. Dee himself had witnessed England's earthquake in what for him was a few years ago. He had marveled at the bells of St. Clement and St. Anne's ringing of their own accord. The bells told Londoners they had been forgiven; there were no such signs of mercy here. This destruction belonged to this age, as the Black Plague and Smallpox had belonged to his. Man's pestilences were endurable, but these modern horrors were a living hell. He still wasn't wholly certain that Kelly's insistence that the Plague was caused by rats' fleas was anything more than an obscure joke, for everyone knew that Plague was the result of a miasma and planetary influences, as was all disease, but there were many things he had had to accept about this time and place, and, after seeing those hideous Untouchables, he reckoned that the physicians of this period might have discovered things his contemporaries had not.

Hell or not, there were many things in this age that commanded his respect. All that they called technology had gone far beyond anything he had seen, or even dreamed at Mortlake. Mankind had solved the mystery of light and its properties; it had learned to manage travel, food, and information. Men flew, ventured far beneath the sea and out into the aetheric realms. Medicine had ceased to be an art and was now a skill so exact that bodies could be repaired and kept young in ways that the Queen's Grace would have killed to achieve.

Sadly, philosophy, rhetoric, and theology had lost the esteem they had once commanded. Even mathematics, Dee's own passion, had progressed to levels far beyond his comprehension. What was commonplace for the meanest utility worker could still amaze Dee. For John Dee, these advances in understanding Nature were more awe-inspiring than any cathedral. Surely, amid all these blessings of the mind, God's Grace was present, also. Divine Wisdom had graced this era to an almost incomprehensible degree. But as many gifts as Heaven bestowed, it seemed a curse came with it. For every wonder, there was a horror, for every advance, a commensurate atavism. How to reconcile these inequities? The stars taught that celestial balance governed all Nature, but how could it be that such extremes must exist side by side? Could not a cure be found for the Untouchables? Could not the poisons of the Pit be turned to healthful substances? And if it could be done, why had it not been? These issues jostled in his thoughts as he and his companions made their way over to the Encino Terminus of the Coast Liner. It was a steep walk most of the way, over the fractured remnants of old roads, and as he kept on, he began to hum *And Oh, My Heart*, a sad lament penned by Elizabeth's father, the mercurial, demanding Henry VIII.

"What's that song?" Kelly asked as they neared the terminus.

"It was a popular air in my day," said Dee, and sang the lyrics to her. "*And oh, my heart, my heart it is so sore, since I must needs from my love depart and know no cause wherefore.*" He didn't bother with the various flourishes and repeats, for the simple, plaintive melody conveyed his point, and those ornaments called for other singers in any case.

"Same old lament," said d'Winter, who had stopped to listen.

"Yes," said Dee thoughtfully. "I think it is." Then he shook off his pensiveness. "But we have work to do."

"That we do," said d'Winter, and pointed to the waiting Coast Liner. "Let's get aboard."

26

"HEY, YESHUA! Open up!" Strategy Brooks pounded on the door of the dressing room that had been set aside for Yeshua Ben David's use. The thumping echoed loudly down the corridors of the enormous building. "We've got to talk!"

Fawg shook his heavy, squamous head and pulled himself to his feet. "Just a moment," he called in a muffled approximation of Yeshua's voice. "I dozed off. I'm not decent."

"Who cares!" Strategy was running out of patience with her temperamental messiah. "We've got a problem!"

"Yes, yes," Fawg soothed, in that butter-wouldn't-melt-in-my-mouth ingratiating tone of voice of his.

The newswoman could hear his sofa inside the room creaking with his getting up. She snickered at her image of him hurriedly trying to get his clothes on; she couldn't conceive of the struggle he was having to bring his shape into the form Strategy expected.

"Hey, come on," she prompted.

"Your Savior feels your urgency. I'm almost ready."

"You'd better be, or I'm coming in on my own!" She gave the door another hearty slap just to make her point.

A twentyish, bearded vid-editor stuck his head out of a recording studio down the hall and gave her a withering look; she made an obscene gesture and he retreated.

Ready to deal with her, Yeshua opened the door, smiling seraphically. "Good morning, my child." He was fully what she anticipated, and that made him particularly cordial.

The star of *The GNN Nightly Report* brusquely pushed past him and took over the middle of the small room. Her perfume hid the lingering trace of reptilian musk. "I'm not so sure about that," said Strategy, unmoved by the ministerial unctuousness and determined to get his full attention; his ubiquitous dark glasses made eye contact difficult, but she was undeterred. She turned her nose up at the heavy musk scent in the room; she fanned it away with her hand as she plopped herself down on the sofa where Yeshua had been sleeping. She touched something slightly viscous and pulled her hand away, rubbing her fingers together and seeing a faint iridescence on her hand. The Messiah drool? she wondered. She made a face and wiped it away on the sofa cushion. "I had a call from Mother O'Conner this morning," she announced.

"I see," said Yeshua politely.

"She was calling to tell me that Romulas—you remember him, don't you? The one you raised from the dead?—well, it seems that he's killed himself." Strategy gave Yeshua a hard stare. She waited for a response but none came. "Shouldn't a messiah be able to read minds, to anticipate such behavior?"

"He couldn't do that," said Yeshua. "He was dead—"

"Already," Strategy matter-of-factly finished for him. "So he was. And he finally figured it out."

"Which was going to happen eventually," said Yeshua. "Why does this trouble you?"

"Tell me you didn't set this up," Strategy challenged him.

"But how could I?" Yeshua asked, opening his hands to show his innocence.

"That's what I want to know," said Strategy. "You brought him back to life—okay. I can go along with that and so can the public. Medicine can do a lot of that now. Admittedly, they can't do this once someone's been embalmed, which means this is a genuine miracle. I don't doubt that." She affected a Southern drawl, so that *genuine* rhymed with *entwine*.

"But if you didn't you wouldn't be here now," said Yeshua benignly. "Wasn't a miracle what you wanted? Isn't this what you've been working toward? You must have faith, Strategy."

She glared at him. "I'm grateful for the story, I'll give you that much. But I don't think this latest wrinkle is going to sit well with my viewers. I'm sure it isn't going to play with the suits upstairs." She surged off the suede-covered sofa and moved toward the craft-service table. "Call me cynical, but it strikes me as bad press to have your first big tele-vided miracle turn out to be such a curse that the man has to kill himself all over again." Annoyed, she thrust a grape from the fruit platter into her mouth. "If I'm up on my catechism, suicide is a mortal sin." She threw her hands into the air to frame an invisible headline. "Corpse chooses Hell over Heaven. How're you going to fix this?"

He seemed at a loss; she was secretly delighted that Yeshua was finding this new development disturbing. Up until now he had always been so bloodless, so on top of it all. His constant smug superiority was just a little patronizing. He was so content being the Savior and allowing her to do his bidding. Just like any other man. They were all Princes—or so they thought. This one was divine, but no different. What miracle could he pull out of his bag of tricks to resurrect her slipping ratings? This suicide of the new Lazarus man had ruined her story; the network would surely downplay it. What was this self-proclaimed godhead compared to her lost Tele-VidQ?

Fawg was becoming upset. These people should be overjoyed to follow him, to accept him as their Savior, and to do his bidding, yet here was Strategy Brooks behaving as if he had taken away her greatest prize, and angry with him because of it. She wasn't awed by his powers, rather, she was irritated because Romulas O'Conner's suicide had ruined her story. Her ratings were more important to her than his divinity. He was growing tired of humani and their willful ignorance. "Do you want me to bring him back to life again?"

"I don't think that would be such a good idea," she said, the sarcasm heavy in her voice, "considering."

"Then what?" Yeshua asked, trying to conceal his growing irritation, his voice getting testy. "You must want me to do something or you wouldn't be here."

"Then we have to make this right," said Strategy, as if it were obvious.

"And how do we do this? What is right?" Yeshua asked, his sanctimony returning. Realizing he was coming off a bit cranky, he tried to modify his tone, "If Romulas O'Conner wants to be dead, so be it. He is welcome to the rigors of damnation. There are unreckoned multitudes in my Father's House, yet the loss of a single soul is painful, but it is only one soul. What else do you think I could do that would convince people that I am who I claim to be?"

"Something spectacular," said the blond newswoman bluntly. "But nothing that can go bad the way this did. And it has to make up for his suicide, somehow." With that, she fell back onto the couch, one hand raised dramatically. "Healing the sick, if it's big enough and dramatic enough, might count for something. Loaves and fishes are out—they'd just say you had a new kind of Frankenfood."

Fawg looked at her in confusion. He wasn't sure what Frankenfood was, but he though it best to keep his ignorance to himself. The Savior improvised. "I could restore the blind to sight," he said.

"Anyone can get that done if they have the money," said Strategy, dismissing the notion. "Though the optic nerve grafts don't always turn out perfect. Medicine makes the lame walk, the deaf hear, the mad sane, so long as it's paid for."

"That sounds—"

"Leery? Derisive? We've already agreed that I'm cynical." She got up, running her hand through her hair. "We've got to do something, and quickly. And we have to go extend our condolences to that rapacious old harridan."

"Mother O'Conner?" Yeshua asked.

"That's the one," said Strategy. "She's the bitch that held me up for double her agreed-upon fee for her interview. That's money down the drain. I've got a reputation to maintain. I can't go wasting money like that, I'll be in real trouble."

"You'll really have to lower your voice, Strategy, my child. You'll raise the dead." He smiled at his witticism, then reached out to the fruit tray. "More grapes?" He held a bunch up to the light. Yeshua was hoping to diffuse Strategy's irritation, but it hadn't worked. Did she understand the severity of the situation? He appeared so rapt in savoring the grapes while his thoughts tumbled.

Strategy had a momentary inclination to grab the bunch out of his fingers, to deprive him of something as he was about to deprive her of all she had labored so long to achieve.

Then, as if to prove that he hadn't heard a word she had said, or rather, that he was only now comprehending, he disbelievingly asked, "Aren't you going to talk to her?" Yeshua was incredulous, as if all his reputation had vanished.

"What for? Her resurrected son just killed himself. That pretty much says it all. End of story. Move on." Strategy wondered what she was going to tell daRocelli when he called her—and there was no doubt he would call her—and demanded an explanation of what had just happened.

"But a dead man was returned to life," said Yeshua, exasperated. He was so rattled that for a moment he almost lost control of his shape. "That's a miracle Earth hasn't seen in twenty-one hundred years. Isn't that enough?" It ought to have been, given all he knew about the humani. Why weren't they responding as he expected them to? Hadn't Scripture recorded the previous event in glowing terms, describing the multitude that followed him? Where was that multitude now?

She stood watching the world get the better of him. What an ego, she thought. She could almost feel sorry for him, if she weren't so angry at him for putting her career in jeopardy. "Apparently not," said Strategy.

Yeshua found himself totally at a loss by this. As if on some faraway world, he quietly entoned, "Where are the multitudes? Why aren't they following me? Don't they know that I am their Redeemer? Those who believe in me shall have life everlasting. What more do they require?" He tried to make some kind of sense out of it.

The question stunned her and filled the room, as real as furniture. She saw him try to regain his faltering authority, saw him refocus and come back to the here-and-now. "The most glorious thing we can experience is the mysterious. He who did not stand rapt in awe at the sight of God's Majesty is as good as dead. I don't know what more I can do," he stammered in his Yeshua voice.

"Well, think of something!" Strategy exclaimed. "I'll be back in half an hour, and you better have something to offer me besides platitudes and pronouncements, or I warn you, we're both in deep shit!"

"My child—"

"And by the way, you'd better lay off those grapes. You're looking a little green around the gills." With that for a parting shot, she slammed out of the dressing room, leaving Fawg set-ut to ponder the inconsistencies of humani.

27

D'WINTER'S STRONGHOLD WAS TEN years old, built at the top of a crag overlooking a narrow strip of beach that now had a thick coat of algae over the sand as well as the large, broken boulders at the edge of the beach. The Coast Liner had taken them within a mile of the stronghold, and they had walked the rest of the distance; d'Winter had a number of gates and locks to deal with, which he did with the ease of habit.

"From the air, this place looks like the ruin of one of those hundred-year-old villas that were built to have maximal views, back when the Pacific was still something you wanted to look at. There's a scan-buster in the cellar that scrambles almost anything that can be aimed at it."

"A goodly aerie for defense," Dee approved.

"They can still damage us from the air," said d'Winter. "Land assaults aren't used very often anymore, Doctor. They aren't necessary. There are scans and targeted weapons. That's what we have to be careful of—a weapon that has our DNA signature."

"DNA again," scoffed Dee. " 'Tis the wonder of your

age, less than an atomie, but governor of much of your so-called technology, and religious in your idolatry, you venerate it in the temples of your laboratories."

Kelly laughed. "When we have time, I'll show you why we feel 'reverent' about DNA." She went into the door d'Winter indicated. "I haven't been here before, but I've heard about it. Quite a view."

"It's not a place to entertain," said d'Winter, his face set along hard lines. "I know you don't expect luxury, but it isn't too spartan. I don't believe in asceticism; if I have to hide out, I don't intend to be austere about it."

"In that, my people would concur. Our battlements and houses were oft adorned with jeweled plate and rich-appointed carpets. Cold comfort was not a style to our liking. We had the Italian to thank for that."

D'Winter gestured acknowledgment to his employer as he went to open the thick steel door that led to the elevator shaft. "Come on." He secured the door again.

"Thinkst thou we are going to be besieged?" Dee asked.

"I hope not. It'd be a waste of time. If they really want us, they'll probably sluice us out. Though they may try to use a targeted bomb, if they get the chance, and they're sure they can get the government to okay it," said d'Winter.

"Have you any reasonable knowledge of whom 'they' might be?" Dee inquired energetically as they rode the elevator down into the hillside.

"That's what we're here to discover, with a little skulduggery. When—and if—we find out, we can stop them," said d'Winter. "You have the wherewithal to put half the world out of business if you choose to."

Dee chuckled. "So I'm told." How odd it was to have so much wealth at his disposal—bank account balances that would have been incomprehensible in his own time, but now was seen as lavish but not fabulous. The de' Medicis, the Hanseatic League and Venetian merchants, the Bourbons and their peers, though they had smaller sums to their credit, could have purchased as much, perhaps even more. There was great wealth—and great poverty. If he ever returned to Mortlake with but a fragment of his new-got fortune, Dee thought he could easily eradicate all his life-long, persistent financial headaches and embarrassments. And with the huge sum that remained, he would pay off England's debt as well— no more suing to the Queen for sinecures, she would be grateful beyond reckoning, and it would be she asking for occasional monetary favors, which he would be honored to grant.

Kelly had been looking about with a great deal of curiosity; she stood in the elevator as the door opened. "I'm getting tired of being underground," she said as she peered into the comfortable room beyond.

"We won't have to do this much longer; we'll get the information we need and then turn the tables," said d'Winter. "I've got rooms for both of you; if I were you, I'd take advantage of this time to rest up. Once we go on the offensive, we'll have to keep going until this is settled, one way or another."

"You may be right," said Kelly, yawning suddenly. "It's been a busy fifteen hours."

"That it has. Time passes with diverse speeds in diverse situations," said Dee. "And you're right, Morgan. We have to be prepared to act quickly and decisively if we are to prevail."

"We've already determined there are men looking for you, Doctor," said d'Winter. "Your old hideout—at the railroad?—its location had been sent to security forces all through the L.A. Basin. I found it on my routine scans of security bases. So you must be careful, or we'll be stopped before we can get our tasks completed."

"It is diversionary. If I waste my time fleeing from them, whoever they may be, I will not be able to find the Roc with the virus," said Dee at his most decisive. "Put your machines to work to that end, and deal with my pursuers later." He had taken such a stance before, in the Queen's service, and thus far, he had survived.

"Very well. If that's what you want, I'm going to start my machines working to identify the men behind spreading the virus. It's not just a rogue Roc that needs to concern us—he has human allies, and they must be stopped or the danger will still be with us." D'Winter went and opened a tall wooden panel on the far side of the room; behind it machines were humming. D'Winter dictated new instructions and watched while displays showed the activities of the powerful computers.

"What do you think?" Kelly asked d'Winter. "Who could want this to happen to his own species?"

"It could be that Fawg se-ut has more agents here than we know: After all, they can take any form they like, and that means they can walk among us undetected by anything less than a DNA scanner." D'Winter laughed aloud. "Think what that would mean. Think of the potential for governmental and industrial security breaches."

"I'd rather not," said Kelly.

"If only we could turn away from it, but I cannot, not and return to mine own age," said Dee.

"Do you think any humans would actually help them?" Kelly asked, appalled at the notion in spite of her long experience.

"Aye, verily. Promise them advancement, promise favor, and glass-faced flatterers would flay their grandfathers, and eat the skin. Sadly, the basest parasite would do it for nothing." Dee flung up his hand. "I have attended at court, and know what the promise of patronage will do: You cannot imagine anyone more willing to compromise all, save his ambition, than a smiling knave needing patronage. Commerce and influence are their gods, and their gods confound them." He sat down in a puffy chair that adapted to his frame at once. But his tirade wasn't over. "In the words of the old adage, 'They all have been touched and found base metal.' "

Kelly studied him. "You had the Queen's patronage."

"Was I impervious?" Dee asked, unsure why Kelly had posed it. "No, by the fangs of Timon, but you're right. I, too, danced to that tune." Suddenly he repositioned himself in his chair so that he could command her full attention. He leaned forward to make his point. "Much as I was grateful to the Queen's Grace for liberality, tightfisted as she could be, I didn't succumb to the extent that I gave up what snippet of honour I could claim for myself. There are precious few who could boast the same. That bright quality in me prompted the Queen to trust in me and to employ me with missions—she knew that once my word was pledged to her as her intelligencer, I would not spy for another Prince as many did. And by the Queen's Royal Seal, she trusted in me on many occasions, which honour I loved as I loved England. I served her at Antwerp, at Trebona in Poland, Constantinople, Bohemia, Rome, and more. She put her trust in me as she did in Burghley, Walsingham, Northumberland, and Sydney. More, she relied upon me to interpret the stars for her, and I did that as faithfully as I spied. If you will, I did naught for myself but all in honour of my Queen and country. "

"So slippery deals are nothing new to you," said Kelly.

"You've remarked on that before," Dee told her. "I grant that when it comes to double-dealing, misleading, obfuscating activities, I have done all, and I have taken it upon myself to keep to the course I have sworn to maintain." He folded his hands in his lap. "You don't expect this age of yours to be so much different than mine own. Villainy is native to every time."

Kelly's smile was slightly predatory. 'You may have a point there."

D'Winter closed the panel in the wall. "In an hour or two we'll be a little closer to the answers we're looking for. There's nothing we can do to rush the processing— I've got it on priority already." He strolled over to the huge display that showed a vastly improved vista of the coast, based on the vids and photographs from a century ago. The light was that of early afternoon, the sky a glorious blue that hadn't been seen along the central California coast for more than fifty years. "Enjoy it," d'Winter recommended. "I'll get us something to eat."

"How very good of you to take us in," said Dee, following the codes he had learned so long ago. "It is more than we have any right to expect."

"It is, isn't it? And here I thought you were picking up the tab on all our expenses," said d'Winter. He waved away any response from the Doctor. "Then make yourself at home and we can all get some rest."

"What about a shower?" Kelly asked. "I think I need to get clean."

"There're showers and baths, even a steam room, if you want it," said d'Winter as he strolled into the kitchen off to the left. "I'm not doing anything fancy: just proti-meat and phyto-nutrients. What about a chicken salad? That doesn't take much work."

"Sounds good to me," said Kelly.

Dee rubbed his suit as if stroking an animal. "I'd like to use the steam room." He had been in the baths of the Sultan in Constantinople, a guest of the recently established Turkish regime, and remembered how pleasant the experience had been, a bright spot in an otherwise gloomy and thankless journey. Constantinople had been in Christian hands since the third century; the loss of it was a blow to the stability of Europe. But the soothing delights of the Oriental bath were pleasures of this time that he had to admit he enjoyed. Perhaps he could recapture some of the contentment he had felt there, or at least, get some of the stench out of his hair.

"Down the hall on your right; you'll see it," said d'Winter, the sound of kitchen food assembly accompanying him.

Dee went down the hall, testing doors. The third proved to be the one he sought, and he stepped into the dressing room, securing it behind him. Then he skinned out of his remarkable suit, feeling unaccountably cold as he put it in the cleaning unit. He grabbed a towel that seemed large enough to be a bedsheet, and, wrapping it firmly around him, stepped into the steam room.

The chamber was large enough to accommodate four or five men easily. It had genuine wooden walls and benches, and two brass showerheads affixed in the ceiling. Dee chose one of the higher benches and went to sit down on it. As he did, a puff of steam came from vents in the walls; it smelled of pine and leather, aromas that reminded Dee of his travels in Scotland and the Swiss Cantons. Without his suit he felt terribly vulnerable, but he reminded himself that he was in a stronghold that would resist everything short of bombs. If he couldn't bathe here, where could he? Whether from that realization or from the moist heat, John Dee's shoulders relaxed. He filled his lungs and felt the tension fall away from him.

A display on the wall offered various cleaning substances; Dee inspected them all, reading the labels with care, although most of the ingredients seemed so foreign, so unpronounceable, that he wondered if they were in an unknown language. He decided it must be more of the specific language of technology instead of Latin or Greek. So he selected a washing product that smelled of apples, looked about for a flannel or brush, and a moment later jets of warm water sprayed over him. Startled, Dee almost bolted from the room, then he relaxed and let the soapy water rush over him in an undulating pattern that washed him without ever damaging his skin. Then the water flowed clean and carried away the last, lingering reek of the sewers.

By the time he emerged from the steam room, his skin was rosy and his hair was hanging in damp tendrils. He had donned a robe, and although it dragged a bit on the floor, it was soft and absorbent. As he made his way back to the main room, he heard Morgan say, "But how much should we tell him?"

"God, don't ask me," Kelly said.

"We have an obligation to speak to him," d'Winter reminded her.

"Yeah," she said, sighing. "We do."

Dee stopped still, the buoyant delight of his bath gone. He listened intently, determined to learn what it was that Kelly didn't want him to know.

28

MOTHER O'CONNER RUBBED HER lips, thinking they had felt strange since she kissed Rommy farewell. The flesh felt peculiar under her fingers, as if they didn't quite belong to her, rather like the sensation of wearing the most sheer gloves. She rallied herself, muttering, "Well, you lost him twice, what did you think you'd feel about it?" She was going through his closets, taking away all the garments she had just ordered for him, setting aside one handsome suit for the second burial. It was hard to do this again, and she reminded herself that he had been lost to her from the first time he went into the ground. "That wasn't really him, that thing walking around in his skin. It wasn't. It wasn't." The more she said it, the more she doubted.

The shades were drawn and the lighting kept low, in accord with this somber occasion. Nursing all manner of complicated emotions, Mother O'Conner mentally reviewed all the dreadful events of the last few days, all of which had culminated in the intolerable, final loss of her boy; the pain was enough to shatter lesser creatures, but it could not topple her. She would remain firm for Romulas, and protect his fortune and his memory any way she could. Finally Mother O'Conner sat down on the side of the bed. "The slut has got to go," she announced to the air. There was no word of protest, no hint of objection, and Mother O'Conner smiled, although it hurt to spread her mouth so far. She would be rid of Leeta at last. A few million new dollars and then she would be gone, leaving Romulas' empire to Mother O'Conner to run, without worrying about any interference from the silly wife. She smiled in anticipation of that happy day. There were many things she wanted to do with the business, things that Romulas had been too squeamish to do.

A noise in the hallway broke into her reverie. Mother O'Conner got up and made her way to the door, her body unwieldy. She opened the door, expecting to see Leeta peering in at her. Instead she saw Yeshua ben David, the one who said he was Jesus come again. "How'd you get in here?" she demanded, the stage-Irish accent all but gone in her shock. She wanted to shut the door in his face but was unable to bring herself to do it.

"Does it matter?" He did his best benign smile. "What is important is—"

"You damn well bet it matters," Mother O'Conner interrupted. "I pay a pretty penny to the Domestic Security Network to keep the doors shut to riffraff."

"I walked," said Yeshua, thrown off his pace. He took a deep breath and began again. "When your son decided to return the gift I gave him, I thought I should come to offer you comfort in your time of loss."

"Fine comfort!" Mother O'Conner exclaimed. "The poor boy was miserable, and it's all your fault!"

Yeshua cocked his head as if listening to a distant chorus. "His misery was of his making. He didn't know how to—"

"You're a fraud!" Mother O'Conner cut him short. "You have no idea what he went through on your account. You didn't do it for him, you did it for you!"

"I did it because it could be done," said Yeshua. "I wanted to show him, and the world, that no one need accept the end." He wasn't prepared to justify his actions, and he realised he sounded weak. He made a second attempt. "All life is filled with illusion, a fragile skein spun by ephemeral fingers; you must see that death and life are part of the illusions. I was able to part the curtain enough for your son to assume life again."

"He *wasn't* alive!" Mother O'Conner screamed, poking a plump hand at Yeshua's chest. "He was nothing more than a walking corpse."

"What else did you expect?" Yeshua held out his hand in a gesture of sympathy even as he backed away from her, but Mother O'Conner batted his hand away.

"To me, back to life means alive!" She had taken hold of the door and was ready to slam it closed.

"Mother O'Conner," said Yeshua so authoritatively that he held her attention completely, "you have been put upon, and I apologize for any pain I might have caused you. It wasn't my intention to make you, or anyone, unhappy. I am the Resurrection. I am the lamp unto your feet."

"Well, you fucked up!" She swung the door closed.

Fawg sighed, and made one more attempt. "I think you ought to know, Mother O'Conner," he said in Yeshua's voice, increasingly aware that he was doing this wrong, "that your son was able to live again because of something I did. If you've touched him after he . . . he killed himself, you need to be prepared, because you might have contracted some of what brought about his reanimation—" Fawg was stymied, looking for the right phrase. "The efflux." He was satisfied with that word, and repeated it. "The efflux of his return to life was—"

"Get out of here!" she yelled from behind the door. "You ruined everything!"

"Let me comfort you at least!" Yeshua intoned, but was met only with a drubbing on the other side of the closed door.

"Get out! Get out! Get out!" she shrieked, but the words didn't come out clearly, sounding as if her mouth was stiff, that pronouncing the sounds was difficult.

Fawg's Yeshua-shape shimmered as he took in the shock. Could it be that the damage had already been done, that this fool had been contaminated by her son? Why should the mother be at risk and not the wife? Fawg didn't like the way this was going, and he knew that Strategy would be furious if she found out about this. Reluctantly he made up his mind. It wasn't time to put the virus into the world. His acolyte was going to wait three days and so should he. They couldn't alter their plans now, for that would surely mean exposure without success, or very limited success. He brought his human appearance back into focus and said, "Mother O'Conner, if something is wrong, if your pain is too great, if your grief is too overwhelming, I can help you. Believe me. I don't want to do you any harm."

"I'm calling the cops!" Mother O'Conner shrieked.

"That wouldn't be wise," he warned, and noticed Leeta O'Conner looking up at him from the floor below. He had to contain his aggravation. These humani were so endlessly curious. They got into everything, even those things they knew they should not. Sometimes especially those things they knew they should not. Now he would have to do something about her, just as soon as he took care of Mother O'Conner.

"Leave!" Mother O'Conner was too furious to pay much attention to what Yeshua was doing, and as the door—very stout and made of real wood—buckled inward, she bellowed, "You're *dead*, buster!"

The pistol in her hand didn't look very threatening, but Fawg knew such impressions could be deceiving. He was much more impressed with the patch of vaguely reptilian skin that had taken over her mouth, shining a little where the light struck it. So she had *kissed* her dead son! That would mean the virus was in her system, moving slowly just now, but on its inevitable course. He held up his hands, aware this was a human gesture of harmlessness. "You don't want to do that, Mother O'Conner. Think of Pontius Pilate. You know the story, don't you?" he said gently. "You know what fate awaits those who do not worship the Messiah."

"Blasphemy," she said grimly, and fired twice.

CHAPTER

29

ON THE LOWER FLOOR Leeta heard the door break in, and she stopped still, listening to Mother O'Conner yelling and Yeshua soothing. Then there came two shots, and Leeta panicked. She dropped the vase of silk flowers, paying no heed to its breaking. She grabbed her purse and ran for the back door, pulling it open and stepping out into the grounds of Romulas's fine house. Ordinarily she took great satisfaction in the vast lawn—maintained at fabulous expense—but now all she cared about was that it was easy to run on. Something hideous was happening in the house and she had to get away from it. Fortunately she had a lot of money with her, hidden in the lining of her clothes and in the false bottom of her purse, funds she had squirreled away from Mother O'Conner when Romulas died the first time, money the old harpy couldn't touch. It was not a huge amount, but enough to cushion the blow of the loss of her husband. She had no hesitation in taking it—she had earned it, every single bit of it, and a lot more, but she wouldn't be greedy just now. There were also her jewels, slipped into a hidden pocket in her underwear—rings, necklaces, two watches, four brooches—some of them enough to keep her in comfort if not luxury for a year or more.

At the fence she used her code to get out of the gate, not bothering to check if the grounds camera saw her on its two-minute sweeps of the perimeter. She slid out and slammed the gate, then started down the slope to the road below, taking care not to tangle her clothes in the brush that filled the hillside.

Reaching the roadway, she began to walk toward the largest thoroughfare, knowing she could summon a run-about from any one of a number of call boxes. She tried to make herself think what she could do beyond getting away, but nothing occurred to her. For now, getting away from the house and the confrontation was achievement enough; she would work out the details later, when she had the chance. She set her purse on Adhere, then, satisfied that no one could take it from her, she stepped across the safety bridge over the roadway and put her old life irrevocably behind her.

At the air terminal she took the first flight out, a one-hour hop to North Central Texas. As she settled into her seat, she began to think of what she should do next. She was torn between watching the news and ignoring it. She decided to use the hop time to make a list of what she needed to buy once she arrived. She hadn't been in Texas in a long time, and she didn't think she wanted to stay. It had taken her years to escape—she had no desire to return.

The man in the seat across from hers was busy preparing and sending reports to someone named Steve. She dimmed her area, set the chair on recline, and closed her eyes, only to open them again as images of Romulas as he had been after he had come back from the dead crowded into her imagination. "Never mind the nap," she murmured, and began to make mental lists of clothing she would need, and where she wanted to live.

By the time they set down on the huge flyway, Leeta had most of her decisions made, and she told herself they were good ones that would give her all the opportunities she craved: After she found a place that was safe, she would go to Iceland, set up her funds in one of those super-safe Icelandic banks, then find a place there for the six months their law required for banking, and funnel funds to wherever she was going to stay afterwards. That would give her time to plan and find out how to make the most of what she had. Feeling confident at last, she left the plane and headed for the front of the terminal, hoping to catch a run-about quickly. She ended up waiting for almost half an hour, and during that time, she saw banner headlines declaring that there was an enormous fire raging in the hills of Angel City, and that already three dozen homes had been destroyed. She shook her head, more pleased than ever that she had got out of the place. Then she stared as Yeshua ben David filled up the display, promising to bring rain to stop the fire. How the hell had he got out of the house? Hadn't Mother O'Conner shot him in the chest? she asked herself. How could he have survived? Unless he had contrived to leave right behind her. Which meant he was looking for her. And that she would have to change her plans again. She hissed a curse her mother would have envied, and stared blankly at the huge departure display on the far wall.

The satisfaction she had felt for over an hour evaporated. Yeshua might be just what he claimed to be, but someone like that was hard to deal with, and she didn't want to have to deal with him any longer. She scowled, her face no longer pretty. How could she get away from him? He was more of an opponent to her now than Mother O'Conner was. He was dangerous, no matter how nice he pretended to be. Whatever it was he did to Mother O'Conner proved that—that, and walking away from a deadly chest wound. Just the thought of it made Leeta feel slightly sick.

On the display, Yeshua was telling Strategy Brooks, "I had hoped to console the mother and widow—the whole event turned out so tragically—but by the time I arrived, there was fire everywhere, and though I searched through the conflagration, I couldn't reach them. I only pray they both got out before the house collapsed."

"Then you couldn't rescue them?" Strategy asked sharply.

"Alas, no. The fire was too relentless, and the women, quite sensibly, fled. Reluctantly I gave up my search for them and was forced to join them in flight." Yeshua rolled his eyes heavenward. "If only I had had more time to deal with the fire, none of this need have happened."

Those words struck a sinister chord in Leeta's mind, and she gave the display her whole attention.

"And you say you can bring rain to stop the fire?" Strategy asked.

"Yes," said Yeshua with a limpid smile. "And I will do so as soon as I am allowed to find a quiet place . . . to pray."

Leeta heard the word as *prey* and she had to force herself to stand still, uncaring, as she fought the urge to flee. Never mind clothing, she told herself. Never mind any of it. Get out of here now. Never mind Iceland—Yeshua would probably be watching for her there in any case. Take a flight anywhere away from here. Any country is better than this.

So it was that forty minutes later she was in the air, bound for Lake Bakal International Terminal.

CHAPTER

30

"WHAT CAN WE TELL him?" d'Winter countered. "We have nothing to tell; that's the problem."

Dee moved closer to the wall, lessening the chance of accidental discovery. He suspected there were a great many surveillance devices in this stronghold, but he hoped none would give him away. His fear of betrayal heightened his sense of curiosity, as if he were still acting for Walsingham on Elizabeth's behalf.

"Surely you've found out something," Kelly said, exasperated. "You always find a way."

"That's what has me worried. If you want to give it a try, you go right ahead." He laughed sardonically. "I wish you better luck than I've had."

Kelly hesitated. "You don't think it's your equipment, or maybe the programs?"

Dee lost the next few words as he did his best to get a little nearer to them and still remain hiding.

"—and it was upgraded automatically two days ago; there shouldn't be any trouble. Besides, this is the best snooping equipment in the world, Kel," d'Winter was saying. "The reason we aren't getting what we want is that someone's keeping us out on purpose."

"Why?" Kelly persisted.

"I can think of a couple reasons," said d'Winter in that same hard, amused voice Dee had come to rely upon.

"You mean Dee?" Kelly clapped her hands together. "Most people out there don't know anything about him. Not his legend, and certainly not the truth. If they did . . ."

"Yeah. Things could get dicey." He went silent.

"So what are we going to tell him?" Kelly asked a short bit later.

"Naught but the truth, I pray," said Dee, emerging from his concealment; his reprimand was stern, as he intended it to be. "Oh, I know full well why you might prefer not to do it, but think about the calamity such reticence could cause. If, by some unforseen chance, or by a trick of fortune, we should come upon some unlooked-for peril or miscreant, I would have no knowledge of what to be vigilant against, or what dangers we faced, and so, by my ignorance, I could, wholly preadventure, lead us to the very mischief you seek to avoid. Ignorance is rarely bliss and often perilous."

Kelly looked down at her hands; her face flushed, clashing with the fire-red of her hair. "Sorry, Doctor," she said, abashed. She tried to leave the room for the kitchen, seeking to avoid further reproof, because she knew she deserved this chastisement.

Dee waved her apology away and prevented her departure by taking her arm. "Not yet. We have more to discuss."

She protested. "We didn't mean to put you in danger—just the opposite. We didn't want you to be sidetracked by all—"

Dee didn't let her finish. "That my enemies have discovered I am still very much alive and with them, and not dead on the moon, is to be expected. Tush! You knew that would out. Their machinations are their own. Let them mull over their intelligences and do as they wish. I will not be deterred from my purpose. They are gnats, nothing more." This was more a wish than the truth, but he kept gamely on. "What other nettlesome truth are you keeping from me?"

"You make it sound like we're working against you," Kelly muttered.

He took her face in one hand and looked intently at her, forcing her to raise her downcast eyes. "Sweet, my child, I am not angry with you." He beckoned to d'Winter with his other hand. "I am not angry with either of you." Looking back at Kelly, he released her chin. "What a crusty botch of Nature I should be if I were to fault you for caring for my especial safety. But we are friends, did we not agree? And friendship is constant amid all tribulations." He paused and saw that they were not upset with him. "Fear not. I have imparted my faith to you and fully believe that you will master any hindrances others may have put in your way." He touched Kelly's face again, this time softly, almost caressingly. "I count myself in nothing else so happy as the love we three have found."

Impulsively Kelly hugged him, and he returned it ferociously. He rested his head on her shoulder, trying to convey the reassurance he wished they could feel. "Doctor, you're unique," said Kelly, letting him go and making an effort to return to a more professional demeanor.

"I will thank you, for I suppose you mean that," said Dee, and decided to aid her in her efforts to restore the tone of their dealings. "What are the means possible to accomplish this blocking you speak of?" He cleared his throat, amazed at the complexity of emotions still welling within him. This was not what he wanted, or needed, for any of them. He promised himself he would delve into these sensations at another time, when they were not so put-upon by circumstances.

"Nanoprograms," said d'Winter. "They're very hard to use, but they do block the use by certain parties—such as us—of highly sensitive material."

"I see," said Dee, who wasn't sure he saw at all. "You think you might circumnavigate these . . . these nanoprograms? When I was on missions for the Queen, I often found my work thwarted, and that compelled me to achieve my ends by other means."

"I'm going to try," said d'Winter, "but it's going to mean a little sleight-of-hand, and that takes time to set up. Once it's operative, I'll only have about thirty seconds to accomplish my ends before I'm shut out." He gestured helplessness. "That's the best I can do."

"Makes sense to me," said Kelly, adding her support to d'Winter's scheme.

" 'Tis your metier, d'Winter, my friend; I am willing to abide by your decisions in this regard." Dee nodded his approval, then devilishly cocked his head at the security man. "So long as you always inform me of your decisions and strive to educate me on their whys and wherefores no matter how thick or blockheaded I seem to be, no matter how incomprehensible your methods are, then I will be most satisfied." With that, he went and sat down in the lowest chair and tucked the trailing robe in around himself, hoping to regain some of the relaxation he had just enjoyed. "You have wonderful facilities." Little as he wanted to admit it, he found this age more filled with creature comforts than his own, from the steam room to clean clothing. As rough and ill-mannered as most of these people were, they had found a way to live quite well in this regard if no other.

"Thank you," said d'Winter. "I'm going to work on this for a while. Why don't you go have a nap? We'll have a lot to do later today."

Dee considered the suggestion. "Is there any manner of thing I can do here? Or matter I can learn?"

"Probably not," said d'Winter. "If there is, I'll wake you. My word on it."

There it was, thought Dee. If he didn't go rest, he would give d'Winter an intolerable slight. "Well, since you have offered your word, what a churlish lout I would be not to take it. Very well, I will retire, on the assurance that you will waken me as soon as there is anything that requires my attention or is instructive to me." With that he waved his hand as he had seen his Queen do, then started toward the door, humming *Salva Festa Dies* as he went.

"Fine, fine," said d'Winter, his concentration on the display in front of him. "I'll wake you."

"And what of Kelly?" Dee asked as he gathered the robe around him, resisting the urge to flick the hem at her.

"I think I'll stay here a while, Doctor." She was uncomfortably aware of the subtle change in the atmosphere between them and knew she had to be on her guard or familiarity could compromise her ability to protect him. "Maybe I'll stretch out on the sofa." She waved at him, turning the gesture into a bow, which he answered with a courtly one of his own. "Sleep well; you'll need it."

"We'll all need it," said d'Winter, and continued his work on the display as Dee marched off down the hall, still humming, but this time choosing *Robyn, Gentle Robyn* as his tune.

CHAPTER

31

"SO WHERE'S THE RAIN?" Strategy demanded as she burst in on Yeshua's dressing room, which had a more distinctly reptilian smell than usual.

"My child, you must learn to honour my privacy. Do not come bolting into my presence as if I were nothing more than an employee of yours." He ignored her withering look and gestured concession. "As to the rain, it will be here within the hour," said Yeshua in his grandest demeanour. "Plenty of time for you to get your cameras into position and arrange for overhead coverage from those communication satellites your company uses. A little patience now will be amply rewarded later." He smiled at her. It had been a near thing, for Fawg had been about to let go of his human form; fortunately he had heard her coming and had braced himself for her arrival. He was feeling the strain of maintaining his form, and he deliberately kept to the shadows of his dressing room. He indicated the direction of the door. "You'll need to get out there and prepare."

Instead of leaving, she slammed the door shut. "Oh,

yes! Get ready for the rain, and try to be grateful for it while another twenty houses go up in smoke! Just great!" she reminded him, her wrath increasing with every word. "How do you think the people losing their homes will feel? How are you going to explain to them how you couldn't help them?"

He was exhausted. He'd been giving interviews since early that morning, and had kept at it until he had gone to the O'Conner house. All during the interviews there had been bright lights everywhere, and in the O'Conner house he had been at pains to keep his humani form. His whole being cried out for the chance to return to his rightful shape. His head started to ache from the exertion of meticulous body control. "If they are alive at all, they ought to be grateful," said Yeshua. "I will need some time to myself in order to accomplish the change in the weather."

She went on as if she hadn't heard this last, pointed remark. "Right, right. Just because you intervene, you expect the adulation of the whole world. Well, it doesn't work that way." Flinging up her hands impatiently, she said, "This had better work, Yeshua, that's all I—"

"Manipulating the weather takes time," he said tranquilly. "I can't do it in the snap of a finger, no matter what powers I have. You know enough about physics to know that, I hope."

"You're sure there's going to be rain?" Strategy was skeptical and made no excuses for it.

"Positive," he said. He moved to turn the dimmer switch. "It's very bright in here. My eyes, you know. I'm just going to lower the lights a bit. Bear with me." He took the level down as far as he dared but not as far as he liked.

"You were positive about Romulas O'Conner, too, and look what happened! What a fiasco." She sat down in the Spanish leather chair across from his bed where he had seated himself, yogi-fashion, his white clothes pristine in contrast to the smuts and ashes on her garments. "His mother is going to sue everyone from here to Canada for what happened."

"That was unfortunate; the results were not what was expected," he agreed as he took a deep, meditative breath. "But he had been embalmed." He exhaled, counting inwardly.

"People aren't interested in your excuses. They want you to get it right." She sank her head into her hands. "This was supposed to be so easy."

"My child—" he began, but his mind was more intent on holding his disguise together than in consoling Strategy. Why didn't she just leave him alone for a while?

"Don't you patronize me, you condescending bastard," she said. She moved back in the chair as if determined to increase the distance between them; her nostrils flared. "If you screw this up for me—This was supposed to be the big story, the one that got me to the top!"

"It will," Yeshua reassured her, giving her the benefit of his full attention. "Thomas doubted, and you must, too. It is all part of the Divine Plan."

"God, you make me sick!" She shoved out of the chair and paced down the small amount of room to the bathroom.

"I won't reprimand you for your profanity, since we aren't in church," Yeshua said, adding, "*Pro*—'before, in front of, supporting'; *fanus*—'a temple.'"

"So you know Latin," said Strategy. "Big fucking deal."

"I know all languages," said Yeshua. "Those still spoken and those long-lost." This boast wasn't entirely accurate, but he was fairly sure she wouldn't put him to the test. Perhaps she'd use the bathroom, he thought, and give him a little opportunity to revitalize himself.

"Tell me," Strategy said in a flat voice. "Do you really believe all this crap or is it a scam? I can't figure it out."

"More doubts," said Yeshua. "Yet you saw. You told me it would take a miracle, so I provided one: I raised Romulas from the dead, no matter how it turned out. I did raise him up. You saw him, and you showed the world. He was dead and then he lived again. So you have every reason to put your faith in me, and be of calm mind. How often can one be assured by reason for their faith? You are among the fortunate few. I will do as I say I will: I will bring the rain, enough to drown the fires. As was done for Noah, but, of course, not as much as with Noah. But, my child, it takes time to manipulate the molecules in the air and change the isobars. Still, I can do it." He gave her a fixed look. "If I am allowed to work in peace. I must have time alone—to pray."

"And how can I know it's your doing, and not just a change in the weather?" Strategy asked.

He pointed to the window. Behind his antique Ray-Bans his eyes were steely. "The wind has shifted around to the southwest and it will increase steadily. Within the half hour you'll see more clouds gathering, if you bother to look. They will continue to mass until the rain begins."

"And you say you're doing this," said Strategy.

"Yes. Yes. I say I am taking the weather off the Pacific and bringing the part you need—the rain—to this part of the continent, specifically to Angel City. Where it is needed to put out the wildfire. I've told you and told you. Why won't you have faith?" There was an unmistakable note of hostility in his messiah voice. Fawg had been surprised at how much of his explanation she could understand, but he was running out of patience. "This is beginning now. In an hour you will see, for it will be raining, and the fires will die within ten minutes of the rain coming."

"If you say so," she said, sounding tired. Her fatigue gave him hope that she would leave soon.

"I will find you in thirty minutes, and you can witness what I have brought to pass. Then you will see that I have done what I have promised to do." Yeshua nodded slowly twice. "But for now, I must ask you to leave me alone. So that I can—"

"So you can manipulate molecules and isobars," Strategy finished for him. "Okay. If you're going to try to pull this off, I'll go along one more time." She tugged the door open and stepped out into the corridor. "But this better turn out better than the last time, or you're gone. You got that? And cut back on whatever cologne you're wearing; it's too much."

"Of course, my child," said Yeshua benignly. "Will you lock the door behind you as you leave, my child?"

Strategy slammed the door.

Fawg fell back on his bed, enervated, as his Roc body filled the room.

SLEEP ELUDED DEE, though the bed was comfortable enough, with a mattress that adjusted to his every movement, in spite of the fact that he was fully a foot shorter than the body the bed was designed to accommodate. He stared at the ceiling and concentrated on all manner of things—his precarious situation, the danger that loomed over all humankind, his recollections of his travels so long ago and his travels now, the chance of ever returning to the age to which he belonged—none of them leading to very useful insights. He coughed once and glanced down at his suit, which he had retrieved from the cleaning unit, trying to puzzle out what it could be made of that allowed it to protect him so thoroughly. Leicester would have conquered half the Low Lands for such magical drapery. He longed for his Day Book, so that he could record his thoughts and insights, but it was back at Dee's railroad house, for he had not wanted to risk taking it into Piper's underworld. Now he was without it, and missed it as much as he would miss a finger or an ear.

Stretching, he luxuriated in the cleanliness of his

body—in his own time, he rarely bathed oftener than once a month, and that was considered excessive by many, who sewed on their winter drawers in October and didn't remove them until May. The Queen—God save her—was changing that practice, washing as many as ten times a year. By contrast, the people of this age were positively Roman about washing, as Dee had discovered since his arrival here, especially as they were truly convinced that disease was inoculated by unseen atomies. His stock in trade—purgatives, clysters, blisters, bloodletting, watercastings, and leeching—he was told, were pointless quackeries, even harmful to the patient. He shook his head, trying to make sense of that, and supposed it could be possible that such motes might travel in the miasma of pestilence. At least, he had to admit, there was no trace of Smallpox, the sweating sickness, swine fever, tetters, and suchlike that marked a man for life. But there were also the Untouchables, showing that the Hand of God could still strike down these modern savages.

But this virus they sought, that was something more than a cloud of infection to be remedied by soakings and pokings, and it would engender that mind-destroying plague that no Doctor could hope to arrest once it began to spread. Dee wished he could talk to Dyckon, to seek his advice. But d'Winter would not allow it, for it could lead to their enemies finding them and destroying them: That would never do.

"Therefore," he told himself aloud, "you must needs untangle this hard knot for yourself, John Dee." His stern order didn't bring about any more response within himself than he had summoned forth before, but it did help him to get his feet back on the ground. His attention needed to be here and now, not anything later. If he botched the now, there might never be a later, or, more important to him, a return to his own age and Mortlake. The vision of his lost life tightened his throat. He would not be stuck here, in this time of marvelous, dangerous toys, among people who did not fear God or know His Mercy, or mind the stars, a populace without courtesy or taste! He sat up, and the bed adjusted to support him sitting. "Alas, I am a man whom Fortune hath cruelly used," he whispered. Then he rose, sighing. Never one to dwell on defeat, he reminded himself. "Saith Pandulphus: 'When Fortune means to do a man most good, she looked upon him with a threatening eye.' And so she does." He scratched his chin. "I will find the way by perseverence, one step, another step, and so to the end of my journey."

Dee went to the plank desk hanging from the wall. There was a display board mounted in the plank, and he sighed again, wishing for a quill and a standish of ink and a sheet of vellum or paper upon which to write. He shook his head in frustration. "Blast! For want of a nail a war was lost." He put his hand on the display and it hummed to life. "Barren practitioners. Where be the grace of writing? This era hath eschewed such things, having no eye for the elegance of it, or hand for its art. They prefer their machines." Dee pulled up the one chair in the room, tossed a pillow from the bed onto the seat, and climbed onto it, bracing his elbows on the plank as he began to work the arch of the keyboard. "D'Winter display," he said, as he had been instructed to do, "on."

Obediently the display brightened, and Dee set to work.

He began by listing Roc with virus, and enclosed this

in a box entitled "Roc with Virus". Then he made a box for himself, d'Winter, and Kelly, another for Dyckon, another for Piper, and three empty boxes. In Dyckon's box he wrote *information*; in Piper's box he wrote *action*; in his own box he wrote *investigation*. He struggled with putting functions into the other boxes, although *quarantine* was obvious enough, and *public warning*, although he wasn't sure that was a good idea, given the human tendency to panic. The last box niggled at him, but finally he put *lieutenant*, for there was always the possibility that there was more than one Roc with the virus, and that would mean two, or more, places where the disease would appear. He was more certain than ever that there was more than one culprit involved. Probably a Roc, but perhaps another alien species. Dyckon insisted that the Roc would not do this, that they were essentially a peace-loving group. But Dee had known Irishmen who didn't drink, and Italians who couldn't cook. Such prejudices could serve to underestimate an enemy as to overestimate one. Roc were clanfolk, as testy as the Scots, and Dee knew they often worked in pairs or trios, so it seemed likely that if the original bearer of the virus was a Roc, there would be a partner with him. And both of them would be shape-changers.

Roc or some other species, Dee had to assume that Fawg was not acting alone. In his long years as a spy, Dee had discovered that it was only when he was completely on his own that he got into trouble, and remembered that his successes always came when he had had Kelly or some other man to back him up. It couldn't be so dissimilar now, and the Roc could not be so unlike men in that respect. "Life and death makes all living souls kin," he murmured. So, he decided, one was too precarious, too easily foiled. But two, or three . . . "Ah, that is more reasonable." If one were stopped, the damage would still be done. In a precarious mission like this one, there had to be at least two. "Tell me," he said to the air.

For an instant it seemed as if the display would have an answer, but then it began to shriek, the siren-blast nearly knocking Dee off his chair. Over the communicators came d'Winter's voice. "Get under something. We've been targeted!"

CHAPTER

33

STRATEGY WAS DRENCHED AND the crew working on the edge of the fire were scrambling for shelter. Water pelted down from massed clouds that seemed solid as granite. The hillside was soaked, and the first trickles of mud warned that a landslip was coming. "Jesus Christ!" Strategy yelled at Yeshua.

"So you *do* believe," he said, his arms extended in a modified crucifix position, his hair matted and sticking to his skull in dripping ringlets; his smile was beatific. "I am grateful."

"You needn't be," she snapped. "Don't you know what this is going to do to the hillside? It'll be a disaster. All the ground cover's burned off—there's nothing to hold the mud."

"But you wanted rain," said Yeshua, bewildered by her outburst. This was just what she had been asking for, and now. . . .

"Yeah. Enough to put the fire out. But not like this—I didn't want a downpour." She was trudging down the fire-line toward the road where their production vehicles were parked. Her boots were caked with mud, and the weight was tiring her out. Already she could feel her legs shaking a little. "Look at this! We must be getting two inches an hour." The downpour was so deafening she could barely make herself heard by shouting. At least, she consoled herself, it wasn't windy, so she wasn't chilled through.

"Closer to three, I'd say," Yeshua said proudly. "I wanted to be sure."

Strategy shook her head, her hair whipping about her face like a nest of tiny serpents, her umbrella having gone to her technical support man to keep his expensive equipment dry. "You idiot! Some miracle!" She thought about everything daRocelli would say to her, hoping it wouldn't include "You're fired." As she slowly made her way through the storm, she watched in disbelief as the Spanish tiles of a nearby roof began to slide away, clattering and breaking against the house. An unwelcome thought struck her: On top of everything else, some shyster with a greedy client might try to sue her for aiding and abetting an Act of God. If that was possible, it would be possible here, in Angel City, the L.A. Basin.

Yeshua tried to console her. "It'll stop in a couple of hours if I don't do anything more to keep it going. That wouldn't be too bad, would it? Look how the fires went out, just as I told you they would."

"It depends on the mudslides," said Strategy bluntly, trying not to swallow the rain, for in Angel City, anything could be toxic. Her hairdresser would no doubt take her to task for letting so much rain fall on her hair.

"Are you certain they'll happen? Mightn't the hillside hold?" Yeshua was at his most persuasive, his words coming with warmth and compassion. "Can't you believe in me at all?"

"No, I can't, not right now," said Strategy. "I don't see how anyone could." She motioned to her crew to get a move-on. Their van was just ahead of them now. Twenty paces at the most. "There are fracture lines up the hill. Get out of here. I don't know how much mud is coming down, but it'll be a lot."

Luis, her usual driver, ducked his head nervously. "I've been watching the hill for the last twenty minutes. We gotta get out of here." He went to gather up a sealed portable power pack and tossed it into the GNN van. "Pakki and I want to get clear of here as soon as we can."

"Where is Pakki?" Strategy asked.

"Over by the fire-control post, trying to get pictures of the men working the bots on the hillside. They say they're running low on retardant. Not that it matters now, in all this rain." Luis put his hands together in a brief gesture of ironic prayer. "Pakki likes to push to the limit."

"That he does. Do you think they'll move the post back?" Strategy asked. "They could get buried if the slope gives way."

"They sure could. They got enough displays to show them how risky it is," said Luis.

"There's nothing to worry about," said Yeshua, and did his best to calm these two excited humani. "If the hillside starts to move, I'll stop it."

"Sure you will," said Luis, making no excuse for his sarcasm. He had almost everything packed up; the cameraman was still missing. He slammed the rear door shut and wandered to the middle of the road, hands around his eyes, looking for Pakki. "Where the fuck is he?"

Strategy stuck her hands into the pockets of the all-weather duster, feeling for her set of the van's cards. "What more can happen in Angel City?" Strategy asked of the air. "The Quake, the Pit, the fighting, the fires, and now this."

"You forgot the resurrection of Romulas O'Conner," said Yeshua, his features shining with beneficence and water that in certain lights had a sheen to it not wholly from the rain.

"No, I didn't," said Strategy. She looked at Luis and shouted, "No cards!"

Luis came over and yanked the panel open, then hopped into the driver's seat, pulling the joystick into position. "I never lock it. Better get in." He thumbed the exterior speakers to life. "Hey! Pakki! Get bonging back here!"

Strategy took the seat immediately behind Luis. "You ready to leave?"

"As soon as Pakki gets in," said Luis, glowering at Yeshua, who had taken the seat next to him. "I'm putting us on the beam now."

"Better go to manual," said Strategy. "You may want it if the hill starts to give. No tower, no signal."

"You got a point," said Luis, and bellowed into the speaker, "PAKKI! NOW!"

The rain was making so much noise that it was difficult to hear anything, let alone Pakki shouting back at them. But Yeshua heard enough to say, "He's going with the men to the firefighting post. They're bringing the bots down now."

"Do you expect me to take your word for that?" Luis challenged, his head resting on the driving console out of exhaustion and impatience.

"You're worse than Thomas," said Yeshua with a sad shake of his head. "Signal the fire post and find out."

"I can't reach them from here, and you know it," said Luis. "News facilities are blocked from all such contact during crises, and you know that, too. Or you ought to know it." He lifted his head and pushed on the power with the heel of his hand. "I'll swing by the post. We can pick up Pakki and then get the hell out of here."

"Sounds good to me," said Strategy, settling into the shape of her passenger chair.

In the next instant the van started moving, bound for the post that was on the edge of the ridge. The street was slick, and in spite of the guiding signal, the van sloughed about on the thick film of mud and ash, once or twice veering near the edge of the roadway. Luis flipped the van to manual and took a tighter hold on the joystick. "Shit!" Luis expostulated as a charred tree branch came rolling down the hill towards them.

"You have nothing to fear," Yeshua announced, holding up his hand and making a series of gestures that froze the branch in place. "You may go on without fear." He closed his eyes in order to concentrate on keeping the branch where it was. His face shifted its shape a little because of the effort this took.

"That's what you say," Luis muttered. "You're not driving."

"Would you rather I did?" Yeshua asked, his eagerness overriding his concentration and bringing the branch down behind them with a resounding crash.

"No!" Luis burst out, hanging on to the joystick for all he was worth. "This is hard enough without you getting into it!"

"Why do you refuse to trust me?" Yeshua inquired in his most rational tone. "I am the Lord, your God. I died for your sins."

"And you could do it again if you keep up this crap!" Luis exclaimed.

"If I must, then I suppose I must," said Yeshua. "If it is the only way to show you that I am who I say I am."

"Stop it! Both of you!" Strategy ordered.

"But I was only—" Yeshua began, only to be interrupted by a shuddering moan that went through the hillside as if through an injured giant. Then the hillside began to slide, fissures appearing near the crest, then calving and widening as the saturated, trembling earth increased its separation from the bedrock. Mud and rock mixed with charred vegetation and flowed like a sluggish stream, bringing down everything in its path. Trees that still smoked from the fire tilted and then collapsed in the growing avalanche.

"Hit the rise!" Strategy screamed.

Luis was already doing it, putting the van into hover mode. The van slithered and bucked as the landslide passed beneath it, picking up speed as it went. "I don't know if I can hold it!"

"Try!" Strategy shrieked as the van started to cant, its stabilizers howling.

Luis dragged the joystick and kicked the directional jets to put them down the slope. "What about Pakki?" he asked as he brought the van under a degree of control.

"Can you see the firefighter post?" Strategy asked, her breath coming too fast.

"No," said Luis somberly.

"It is under the mudslide," said Yeshua. "It is quite deep, but it's moving along. It may reach the foot of the ridge in an hour or so."

"Pakki will be dead long before then," said Strategy, as if speaking to a foolish child. "Unless he made it out alive?" This last was more a desperate hope than a possibility.

"I can bring him back to life, if you—" Yeshua began.

"*No!*" Strategy and Luis protested in unison.

CHAPTER

34

THE SUN WAS HANGING over the ocean, its brilliant shine off the polluted water turning the whole world bronze. The flyers circling the crater that had been d'Winter's stronghold continued to cross and recross the area, their engines making a persistent snarl that followed Dee down the slope like a swarm of bees; he could see d'Winter far ahead of him, and he thought he could hear Kelly scrambling through the brush, but his ears were still ringing from the explosion, and he couldn't find any way to separate those sounds from all the others around him. Even his own panting sounded alien to him.

D'Winter veered suddenly and dove away from the downward turn of the slope. A moment later Dee saw the reason why: Two combat crawlers were churning up the hill, spewing and pulverizing plants in their wakes. One of the crawlers went in pursuit of d'Winter, the other continued upward toward Dee, as determined as a rhinoceros, which Dee thought it resembled in bulk and temperament.

"Doctor!" Kelly shouted, her red hair revealing her position in the brush. "Over here!"

Dee sprinted toward her just as a furrow of bullets sliced up the hillside to the place he had been standing half a second ago. He flung himself forward onto his face, twigs, thorns, and brambles ripping at his skin although his miraculous suit remained unmarred. "What is going on?" he demanded as he fetched up beside Kelly.

She had drawn the Viper d'Winter had given her, and had taken a stance to fire. "Whoever they are, they're in trouble."

"Yea, verily," said Dee sardonically. "And so are we." His ears still felt as if he were underwater and someone were ringing a gong. He needed a clear head to spot where the shooting came from, for not all of it was from the crawler. "Hang me. This soft, dull-eared, sot-brained infection about my head shall be the death of both of us!" he thought angrily. He managed to stay on his feet, his balance precarious, as Kelly let off a round at the approaching crawler. "What are you aiming at, girl?"

"The steering housing, where the stabilizers are," said Kelly. "That instrument between the treads."

Dee heard her, the words seeming a bit more distinct, their meaning still just so many strange phantasimes. "A difficult target, I should think," said Dee, doing his best to maintain his aplomb in spite of everything happening around him. " 'Beareth a swashing and martial outside, no matter the peril; it is a comfort to our weaker vessels,' saith the text." What carroty-red hair she had, he noticed, and wondered how that should catch his attention in these circumstances.

She nodded. "Difficult, but not impossible." She squeezed off a second round and saw the crawler lurch. "Got it," she said with calm satisfaction as the crawler careened out of control along the narrow pathway, tumbling off the track and into the scrub, its treads roiling at the sky. "Hurry. We've got to get out of here."

"But whither?" Dee asked, falling into step beside her.

"We're off to the rendevous place. D'Winter will join us there unless he gets caught, and if that happens, we'll be on our own." She spoke without dismay, and despite the combat they had come through, she maintained her practiced air of confident certainty. She'd come a long way from the rather naïve business and entertainment agent of their first meeting who was looking for a wealthy client to the professional she was now. Though a green girl not so long ago, she had impressed him with her manly forwardness. Too kindly a father makes an unruly daughter, he reminded himself. But, then, women who treasure themselves make their bodies more rich. She was a second Portia, and like the Roman Brutus, Dee decided to try it her way.

"Is it likely? That he'll be caught?"

"Oh, I don't think so," said Kelly, hunching over to conceal herself from any overhead surveillance as well as to avoid the worst of the branches. "He's not that kind of man."

Dee nodded in agreement, thinking, and you are not that kind of woman. He followed her lead, ducking down as they continued through the manzanita and scrub. He had to force his way through the stiff, low-hanging branches. "Have you any plan to follow if he is unable to join us?"

"Oh, yes," she said, keeping the Viper pointed upward; her stride increased and she urged Dee to move more quickly. "Don't let them get a fix on you. Good thing they didn't bring their DNA scanners, or we'd be sunk."

"Why should that be any worse than heavy gunfire?" Dee asked.

"Because we couldn't elude anything DNA targeted. Nothing can." She sighed. "Don't worry. We'll manage without d'Winter if we have to."

"That's good," Dee approved, breathing a bit more strenuously as he trotted beside her. His suit was already changing colour, blending with the dark red-brown branches and sage-green leaves of the manzanita, resulting in a pattern that was surprisingly attractive. "Kelly," he began, scrambling more quickly to match her pace. "This DNA, this marvelously precise code of identity, how does one retrieve it?"

"Retrieve it?" She looked over at him, confused by the word and his question. "We all have DNA signatures in every single cell. We're born with the code in place; you don't retrieve them."

"Yes. Yes. I am aware of that. My meaning is—how do they"—he indicated the flyers buzzing overhead—"obtain our DNA signatures? Is it not a private matter? Surely they cannot set upon you and cut off a finger, or some such?" Some loose soil and gravel gave way, throwing Dee forward; Kelly reached out to grab his hand. He righted himself, panting a little.

"Very private. But our DNA codes are imprinted on our biochips—"

"Which are sited in the left shoulder," he interrupted.

"Right." She was surprised that he knew that. She glanced back over her shoulder—no crawlers, and the flyers were moving away from them. "And biochips are the exclusive property of police departments and world government."

"Then either the authorities are attacking us," Dee said, continuing relentlessly when Kelly tried to object, "or"—looking up nervously as he heard a high whine from a passing engine—"private interests sufficiently powerful to suborn the law to their own purpose."

"Duck!" Kelly barked, dropping onto her face and huddling; a sharp sizzle from a lazer pistol started the dry scrub burning. "Oh, great!" she said as she got to her feet. "This is all we need!"

"Fires are dangerous in hills like these," said Dee, smelling the first hint of smoke.

"They've had a fire burning in Angel City for days, up on the ridges. We could have the same thing here." She looked southward. "Those clouds aren't sending any rain this way."

"How can you be so sure?" Dee asked. "The wind could shift to the south, and then—"

"Not now, Doctor, please." They were almost to the access road, and Kelly motioned him to stillness. "Is anything coming?"

"Just the fire," said Dee, his attention on the flames behind them, already spreading out its bright fingers and leaning on the breeze off the water. "We must flee this place."

"No argument, Doctor," Kelly said. "How do you recommend we do it? They'll be waiting for us at the edge of the burn, and—"

Dee gave her a grim smile. "My suit. It should stretch enough to accommodate us both. And if it can keep me safe on the moon, surely it can protect us enough to walk through fire." He gave her an arch look, and tugged open the front closure. "Join me, Kelly."

Kelly Edwards regarded him steadily. "What about breathing? We could scorch our lungs, and that would be as deadly as—"

"The near-breathless climes of the moon should have

harmed me far worse, yet this suit, by what powers I know not, prevented all. There's not time to prate. The fire spreads apace." Dee cocked his head toward the advancing fire. "The best way to safety is to creep into the suit with me."

She glanced over her shoulder once more, then looked back at Dee. "I see your point," she said, and came up to him. "How do you want to do this?"

"I am no gelding palfrey, best bestride me. A-pillion."

"A-pillion?" she repeated.

"No matter. Climb in behind me facing front!" he exclaimed. "We'll work it out from there."

CHAPTER

35

YESHUA STOOD AT THE edge of the destruction wrought by the mudslide; the rain had tapered off to a shower and the sky was beginning to lighten as the clouds broke up, freed from the compulsion of Yeshua's will. He was exhausted, and his shape was wavering as he strove to keep his human form. A short distance away Strategy and Luis were caught in discussion with a half dozen firemen, now bent over their screens while scanners drifted over the slide, probing for what lay under the mud.

"How much longer?" Strategy was asking, her pretty features distorted by worry and fatigue.

"We've only found six bodies," said the firefighter working the scanners on the part of the slide nearest their position. "There's going to be a lot more."

Strategy. She began to pace, going a dozen strides away and coming back as if this was enough to spur the scanners to greater activity.

"What do you think?" Luis whispered. "Will we get him back?"

"His body, you mean?" Strategy asked sharply. "Yes, I

think we will, or daRocelli will have our heads, and we'll deserve it."

"You going to cover this for the news? Should I get the other camera?" Luis was nervous, his pinched expression eloquent.

"Of course," Strategy said, sounding worn out. "I'll have to report as is, and daRocelli won't like that, but what else can I do? I look like a refugee."

"It might work better without cosmetics," said Luis. "You might be more authentic, if you know what I mean."

"You mean I look like I just escaped a landslide that came after a fire?" She made herself laugh once. "Yeah, well, I can't argue with that."

"Good. I'll get on it." Luis hurried off, going to where the van waited, a safe distance from the mud.

"I can find him for you, if that's what you want," said Yeshua, coming up to Strategy. He, too, was bedraggled, but he wore it better than she did, giving the impression that he had become disheveled heroically.

"How? The scanners are set for finding bodies. Let the firemen work them." She was tired of him, of his constant harping on his miracles—miracles which so far had been disastrous—and her need for faith.

"I can do this; all you need do is ask it, and I will," Yeshua said, trying to sound consoling, although he wasn't sure he had got the right tone.

"If you can find Pakki, then do it. If you can't, then leave me alone. I have a story to file." She brushed her damp, limp hair out of her face and coughed to get the roughness out of her voice. "Do you mind if I ask you a few questions for our viewers?"

"Go right ahead," said the fireman without looking up from his screen.

Paying no heed to their talk, Yeshua wandered off, going out onto the unstable landslide, moving carefully and certainly to the place where he could sense Pakki's body lying at some depth below the mud. This time, he said to himself, he would work a miracle that Strategy could not quibble with—Pakki wasn't embalmed, and he should return to life relatively easily. Of course, he would have the virus in him, and his body would not behave quite the way it had before. Perhaps that would bother Strategy, he thought, but it would be a good demonstration of his powers, since the rainstorm hadn't convinced her.

"What are you doing out there?" the firefighter shouted suddenly, looking toward Yeshua and shading his eyes against the returning sunlight. "It isn't safe! Get back!"

"I am looking for Pakki," said Yeshua sedately. "I am going to bring him forth, as I brought Lazarus from the tomb. This mud is Pakki's tomb, and I shall summon him from it." He held up his hands, making ready to work on the mud.

"You can't do that!" The fireman was frightened now, his voice rising as two of his colleagues came to his side and joined their admonitions to his.

Strategy shook her head. "Great," she muttered. "Just great." Then she raised her voice. "Luis, get back here right now! Yeshua's up to something."

Luis obeyed promptly, the camera already in place on his head, the powerpacks hanging from his harness. "I'm running. Start talking."

Gathering her wits, Strategy stood next to the portable displays of the firemen and said, "This is Strategy Brooks in Angel City, at the site of a catastrophic mudslide that

has buried more than fifty houses and killed an unknown number of people here in the hills overlooking
the Pit. The mudslide was the result of a sudden downpour that put out a fast-spreading brushfire that destroyed more than seventy homes and was in danger of
burning twice that number. The deluge that put the fire
out was so intense that it triggered this slide, which you
can see behind me. Among the victims was Pakki Sunderland, longtime cameraman and imagemaker. He was attempting to film the slide when it caught him. Now the
firemen are using scanners to try to locate the bodies of
those buried by the mud. Ironically," she added, "one of
the houses destroyed in the mudslide was the house of
Romulas O'Conner, who had been the subject of much
media attention following his resurrection, which this reporter covered in detail. The firemen haven't located the
ruins of the house yet, but it is assumed that O'Conner's
mother and wife were in the house and are listed among
the missing." She paused to take a deep breath, then
went on, "There will be a report issued within the hour of
any confirmed dead, along with a full account of the extent of the destruction." She signaled to Luis to pan over
the hillside. "As you can see, the slide was more than
three kilometers wide and four long. Three major roads
were ruined, and more than four dozen minor ones."

Luis came up to her, his helmet camera aimed directly
at her. "What next?" he mouthed.

Strategy leaned toward the fireman. "Can you tell me
what you're doing now? This is firefighter"—she read the
name on his badge—"Hal Godoro. Tell me, Fire Officer
Godoro, what is going on here just now?"

"Well," said Godoro, "as you can see, we have scanners
out, and these displays give us a three-dimensional repre-

sentation of what is under the mud to a depth of four
meters. Once we have identified and retrieved all the
bodies we can, then we'll begin to stabilize the hillside
with permaseal." He pointed out onto the slide, and
paused. "Oh, my God!" he exclaimed.

Strategy turned to stare at what Godoro was watching,
and gasped. For a fissure had appeared in the mud and
Pakki Sunderland was just climbing out of it, his body
wholly covered in mud so that he looked like a moving
statue; Yeshua ben David was bending over him, his
hand extended to assist the cameraman. "Shit," she burst
out. "Not again!"

CHAPTER

36

FROM LAKE BAKAL INTERNATIONAL Terminal, rails and air routes fanned out all over Siberia, Mongolia, Manchuria, and west to the Urals. Arriving there shortly after noon, Leeta took a high-speed train to Irkutsk. It was full of students on spring break, many of them from American schools that still boasted campuses and classrooms. The students were enthusiastically rowdy, enjoying the free vodka and Karemma wine provided by the transit authority and the Magistrate of Buryat's office. A few of the bolder young men approached Leeta during the ride, but she gave them no encouragement.

When the train came to a shuddering halt in Irkutsk Station, Leeta stood up and reached for her small bag. Taking advantage of her vulnerability, one brash college upperclassman made an attempt for her attention, and soon regretted it, for she delivered a colorful and pithy summation of his behaviour that made him blush and slink away back to his companions at the end of the car. She was proud of herself for being able to deliver withering ridicule. As Leeta made her way down the aisle, two female passengers applauded her as she slipped past her chastened Romeo.

"I haven't lost my touch," she said to herself as she left the train and took stock of her surroundings.

Irkutsk was an expanding city already showing the dubious badges of progress—pollution, traffic, and a number of displaced people wandering the streets. For a place that was harsh in winter and murky in summer, it had become a success in spite of itself. In Irkutsk, rules weren't written in stone; civic government was inadequate and the state security sqauds allowed what the traffic would bear. Leeta had seen places like it in Texas and New Mexico—except that here the winters were far more hellish than back home—and she knew how such towns worked. It wouldn't be hard to settle in for a time.

She found a restaurant that had signs in Russian, Chinese, English, and Arabic; there was a picture in the window of steaming noodles and rotisserie Siberian pheasant. She peered inside; the booths appeared plush, and the tables were covered in pink cloths. The customers didn't seem rushed: She decided to give it a try. She was seated at a deuce near the kitchen.

A blousey artificially blond Tatar waitress of middle years stopped at the table and deposited a red velveteen menu with Leeta. Her gold teeth gleamed as she smiled in greeting. "I get your order when I come back. No problem. You take your time."

Leeta was mildly surprised to be addressed in English, but supposed that it was probably the first language the waitress used with foreigners. She opened the menu and skimmed the six pages, but her thoughts were elsewhere. She'd need to find a place to stay, and since she was traveling with no real luggage, she knew it wouldn't be prudent to go to one of the first-class hotels, where such a lack would raise eyebrows. So she'd have to ask around to find a place that was good enough, but not so fussy. She raised her hand to recall the waitress and asked her to bring her "something good, but not too heavy."

"You got it," said the waitress, and hurried off to place the order.

After a large bowl of borscht and plimeniy, she was feeling much better. She hadn't realized how famished she was, and how on edge she had become. She had put real distance between herself and that freak Yeshua; she had enough money to hold her until she found someone—that special someone—to take care of her. That might not happen all at once, but in a place like this, who knew what would turn up? She practiced her best smile and determined to make the most of her situation and her assets.

"Good, no? Anything else I can get for you?" asked the waitress.

"Well, yes, maybe you can help me," said Leeta. "Im looking for a place to stay. Not a hole in the wall, and not a fleabag, but not the Hilton Bel-Aire. Something nice and local, if you know the kind of thing I mean." She contemplated her glass of hot tea as it sat in its pewter caddy. She cupped her manicured fingers around it for its warmth. "I've got money, and I can afford a nice hotel, but I don't want to blow it all on brass fixtures and tips— you understand."

The waitress gave Leeta a knowing nod. "Maybe you want is the Majestic. It's on Fedeyov Street, two blocks south of here." She pointed in the direction. "Big place, about eighty years old, kitted out like a Tsarist hunting lodge, stuffed animals in the lobby, antlers on the furniture. Grafdav upholstery and draperies. Private bathrooms in all the suites, and one for every two rooms in the rest of the place. Good, strong coffee. Maybe that's the place for you."

"It sounds nice," said Leeta, wanting to be convinced.

"Priced good, too. Not so small that everyone notices you, but not big that you get lost. You can't miss it." She paused. "Tell Boris that Ludmilla sends you."

"Boris?" Leeta wondered who this might be.

"Boris Shevyenetz. He owns the place. A big guy, gruff on outside, custard on inside." Ludmilla winked. "A sucker for a pretty face. He loves people from U. S. He'll take great care of you."

"Sounds promising," said Leeta sincerely.

"Hey, I'd send my own kids to Boris," said the waitress. "Can't say better than that."

"I guess not," said Leeta, liking what she heard. Her heart warmed toward this stranger's openness. So unlike the Angel City phonies, she thought.

"Then you go when you finish eat, and talk to him. If it isn't what you looking for, you come back here, and I'll try to find you other place. That is, if it's copasetic for you," said Ludmilla, doing her best to look welcoming. She wanted this fine young woman to take her advice and go to Boris, who would know how to make the most of such an opportunity.

"I will; thanks," Leeta said, finally feeling she could let her defences down for the first time since she had left her house. She decided to leave a big tip by way of thanks.

"I think you'll like Majestic." Ludmilla refilled Leeta's half-empty glass with more black, scalding tea. "Use sugar. It's better sweet."

"Okay," said Leeta, and had a sudden vision of Mother O'Conner as she had last seen her. She shuddered, blinked, and felt her stomach churn.

"Anything wrong? Food no good?" Ludmilla asked in a near-whisper so that the patrons at nearby tables couldn't hear her.

"No," said Leeta shakily. She willed the image from her mind, but knew she would see it again in her nightmares. She exhaled raggedly.

"You look real white," said Ludmilla, her concern making her seem more real to Leeta. "Travel-lag, no?"

"Probably that," Leeta said.

"You okay? Travel-lag!" Ludmilla persisted, then went on maternally and with a brisk clapping of her hands. "I can bring you something more to eat."

The thought of food made Leeta distinctly queasy. She reached out for the waitress' puffy sleeve before she could turn on her heel. "No, no food, thanks. It's . . . nothing. Just travel-lag, like you said. It's caught up with me." She saw her hands were shaking and folded them into her lap. The rings on her fingers felt cold and foreign, almost accusing.

"You'll want to get over to Majestic and have a nap. You don't look too well." Ludmilla glanced at the cook. "I'll call over and tell Boris you're coming, to make sure he has room. Yuri—my boss here—won't mind." She waved to another waitress, signaling her to cover her tables for a moment. Then she pointed to the phone, watching Yuri nod wearily from the kitchen.

"You're being real nice to me," said Leeta, tasting the tea and reaching for the sugar.

"We don't want people thinking there's anything wrong with Yuri's food," said Ludmilla. She went over to the side of the counter, punched the communication board, and dialed up a privacy shield. "Boris," she said in Russian to the growl that answered, "this is Ludmilla at the Spotted Cow. Remember that rich fishmonger who was raised from the dead in America? Well, his wife—or his widow, whatever she is—is sitting at table five, looking like she's been hit by the Vladivostok-Kazan express. I've told her to get a room at your place."

"You sure that's who she is?" Boris sounded interested but cautious.

"I'm positive. Unless she has an identical twin, it's her. Light-brown hair, pretty face, breasts like melons, perfect teeth, fine skin, expensive clothes. Who else?" Ludmilla lowered her voice in spite of the privacy shield, determined not to be overheard by anyone. "She looks like she's in way over her head."

"And if she is?"

"Don't be a dunce, stepbrother," Ludmilla admonished him. "A woman like that always looks for a man. Why shouldn't she find you?"

"Um," said Boris. "Is this trouble?"

"It could be. It could also make your fortune. She's alone, and she's running. I'd wager my last kopeck that she has money with her, a lot of money. You should see the rings she's wearing. Your venture could use a fresh infusion of capital, couldn't it? Well, treat her well and you'll get it, and more besides," said Ludmilla, and rang off. She went back to the table where Leeta sat. "It's all arranged. He waits for you."

"Okay. That's great," said Leeta, who was still feeling peculiar.

"Two blocks south and one block east. On the northeast corner. You can't miss it. There's a stuffed bear in a glass case out in front." She paused. "Would you like me to call a taxi for you?"

"I should be able to walk it," said Leeta dubiously.

"Excuse me for saying it, but you look like you need a little help. Let me call you a taxi," said Ludmilla at her most solicitous.

Leeta allowed herself to be persuaded. "All right. I'm sure the cabbie is well paid for a short run." It made her feel a bit less shaky to make this offer. "You can give the address, and that should be okay."

"Very good," Ludmilla approved, her grin showing all her gold teeth. "Just wait a moment and I'll have taxi here. You drink glass of tea. It'll warm you up." With that, the waitress pulled her improbably blond hair back from her face and headed back to the phone.

"Oh. Yeah. Thanks," said Leeta to Ludmilla's retreating figure; Ludmilla never heard her. "Really. Thanks," the recently re-widowed Leeta O'Conner reiterated with no strength at all. She hoped she wouldn't throw up, or if she did, that she would be able to wait until she was in her room at the Majestic. There were too many things pressing on her, and she wasn't feeling as safe now as she had a half hour ago. She drew out two large Siberian banknotes. It was more than enough money to cover the food, the tea, and a generous tip for Ludmilla. Gathering up her single case, she rose from the table and went into the small, many-windowed entryhall, vowing to put her past behind her and make the most of this new place once she rested up. She closed her eyes and waited for the taxi to come.

MAKING PROGRESS DOWN THE hill through the fire proved difficult; coordinating their movements in such confinement made every step an ordeal. The fire stubbornly kept moving ahead of them, erasing their progress. They were having trouble keeping their separate balance in the shared suit. The fire swirled and roared around them, sucking the air away from them so that the suit was forced to function at its utmost limit, growing hot and restrictive. Under other, less arduous circumstances, Dee might have enjoyed the tight proximity that he shared with Kelly, but now it was grim necessity that united them. Knowing that her life literally depended on his every move extinguished any pleasurable impulses he might have had. They found a large outcropping of rock where they paused to get their bearings. The blaze surrounded them on all sides, a sea of flame lapping at their island, kindling every drooping bough, blade of grass, or toppled tree in a kilometer radius. The fire thundered all around them, a roaring beast seeking to devour everything; they stood, exhausted, in the middle of this inferno, struck with terror, too tired to think.

A sudden breeze shifted the thick black smoke and they could see the sky. "Clouds drifting up from the south!" shouted Dee as he peered through the flames.

"What?" She had to yell.

He pointed. "Clouds!" he bellowed, wanting to bolster her hopes.

"That's a long way off," said Kelly. "We won't get anything from them, not soon enough."

Dee exhaled in exhaustion, unable to contemplate taking another step. "This suit is a wondrous hermetic device, but not perfect," he croaked.

"No, it's not." She started to laugh, and sucked in more stinging, hot air than the suit's buffers could handle; she started to convulse with coughing. She turned her head so as not to spray sputum over Dee's head and shoulders; she couldn't cover her mouth since her arms were pinned against her body inside the suit.

Dee could feel her chest against his back, her lungs straining for relief, her hands clenching in frustration and pain. There was nothing he could do to comfort her. He waited patiently, holding still so she could catch her breath. Finally, as her gasps subsided, he asked as gently as the sound of the fire permitted, "Are you all right?"

She blinked back the sooty tears from her eyes, unable to rub them clear, and answered, "I'll live."

"Are you able to go on? We should get out of here while we can." He angled his chin at the shifting fire.

"I'm ready." She took a deep breath to steady herself. "You first."

They followed the slope downhill, over the smoking stubble. Like the double reed of a shawm, they moved as one. Falteringly, and with many stops along the way, he led and she followed. Painstaking minutes slowly became one hour, then two.

Kelly did her best not to stagger and trip. "Sorry," she repeated again and again as she tried to match her pace to his. Dee suddenly stopped as the upper half of a stone pine split and fell away from the lower part of its trunk. The shining canopy of flaming boughs and needles came crashing towards them. It landed amidst a spume of sparks and twisted branches not more than a meter to their left. "Not much farther. Maybe four metres."

"That's yet a distance in this fire," said Dee, moving grimly towards the edge of the burn. He was sweating freely again, more than he had in the steam room; Kelly was sweating, too. From shoulder to thigh they were stuck together, and their coordinated exertions intensified their contact. "Are there any pure wells about, or is all befouled?"

'I don't know, not for certain," said Kelly. "I have a purity gauge somewhere in my things. I can check any water we find."

"Good. I perish for drink, and a want of aqueous humours is perilous to the mind." He managed to take another three steps, lurching with the effort. She hadn't been ready and fell on top of him. He was unable to support her; they tumbled to the ground. Leaning on an elbow, Dee kept his face up and off the ground, avoiding the cinders and sizzling pine sap. A large black beetle escaping from the fire crawled near his nose.

Kelly was too tired to try to keep her weight off his back. She lay on him wanting only to lie there; she felt him breathing, the gentle rocking almost enough to send her to sleep. Whatever reserves of stamina that had driven her before were now exhausted, and she gave herself up to the comfort of the moment.

"We must on, my foreign chatelaine," Dee whispered.

She yelped as flames suddenly spurted up around them, fueled by a stand of tarry creosote bushes. "Yeah. We must on," she echoed, more to herself than to him. She was aware that he needed her full participation if they were to survive. Her first duty was to preserve him, and she knew she had to act. She arched her back, wishing she could use her arms for leverage, and struggled in the confines of the suit to aid him to rise. Together they managed to maneuver themselves upright. "God, I can't wait to get out of here."

The tree line ahead of them was a wall of fire and blackness. He could feel heat coming through his shoes; it was becoming uncomfortable—he didn't want to contend with burned feet. He made himself walk with care, for tired as they were, it would be easy to make fatal mistakes.

"You're doing fine, Doctor," said Kelly hazily, coughing a bit. "This was a great idea."

"Necessity impels invention," said Dee. "I had but to look to the Classics: Like Aeneas and Anchises, we flee the flames of Troy. They escaped unscathed and so shall we."

Kelly nearly stumbled, wishing she could hold out her arm to make sure she wouldn't fall; she almost yanked Dee off balance. "Sorry." Dee barely heard her small voice. His attention was riveted on the fire ahead, searching for a breach. As he scrutinized the fiery curtain, Providence rewarded him with a vision. There, way to the left through a sparse grove of flaming trees, was a rift in the clouds of black smoke. He could make out a distant pasture beyond the direction of the fire. A large bush directly in front of them caught fire, the lozenge-shaped leaves crinkling up and disappearing in flame. Dee changed direction at once.

"So," she ventured, "what happens once we get out of this?"

"We seek protection, then water, and then we hunt for d'Winter." He edged them nearer to the fire line. "I see a way out. Not much farther to go."

"No, probably not, unless the fire flares up again." In his day Dee had seen women accused of witchcraft brutally burnt at the stake, and had dreaded that his investigations into the Black Arts might someday lead to his own undoing. The London rabble had razed his lodgings once already. A foreboding of his own death by fire had always haunted him. Yet this was different, and not entirely due to the suit he wore, but to the certainty that he could escape unharmed. He walked cautiously, trying not to do anything to overtax Kelly's balance. Dee was so weary that he was unaware of how unreliable his own equilibrium had become. "Wisely and slowly. They stumble that run fast," he reminded himself aloud.

"Do you think we can get d'Winter out?" Her voice was raw and sleepy.

"It depends upon where he is, and in what condition," said Dee. "I have walked in dire circumstances in my life ere now, and 'tis well I to tell you that I oft despaired of being loosed from durance vile. Yet here I am."

"Not much of an improvement," said Kelly.

"Not just at present, no," Dee agreed. They were three steps from the edge of the fire now, and the breeze had shifted around to the south, so that they no longer had to keep up with the movement of the burning. "But shortly

we'll be out, and then we can set ourselves to our task."
He could feel her strain to take a wider stride, the pressure of her thighs against the back of his silently eloquent, and he did his best to accommodate her. He was
so tired, the delicious lassitude of d'Winter's steam bath
long gone. Now his legs ached from his exertions, and he
knew fatigue would soon take its toll of him.

Kelly saw a small herd of miniature cattle a short distance beyond the fire; they were running, panicked, from
the fire. "Look! They might have a barn nearby."

To Dee the cattle seemed freakish, their bodies no
larger than Mastiffs. Such aberrations had not existed in
the time he had served Good Queen Bess and England.
He scrutinized them, saying, "You have the right of it. No
farmer will leave his stock to roam at will; it is too dangerous. But mightn't there also be a cowman, set to guard
them? Or a cowherd, if they wander far from the byre?"

"Cowman?" Kelly repeated. "More likely there's a
sheepdog about."

"A sheepdog for cattle?" Dee once again found this
barbarian age perplexing. At another time he would demand answers, but now he wanted to take that last pair
of steps and finally get out of the fire.

Kelly was of like mind. She took an uneven breath.
"Almost done," she declared, preparing to go through the
edge of the burning.

"We'll have to be quick about it," Dee warned, preparing his mind and body for the exertion required. "This
last push frees us from the accursed inferno."

"Very well," said Kelly. "How far past the edge should
we go?"

"Methinks at least half a dozen steps. That way we
should have room to run if the wind changes quarters

again." Inside the suit, Dee took her hand in his. "If you are ready?"

"Just say the word," Kelly replied, her fingers tightening.

"Then—*now!*" He all but threw himself at the burning line of trees, desperately searching above them for falling boughs and tree trunks. They staggered beyond it, Kelly holding on to his hand as they did their best to break away from the fire. Finally they collapsed in an untidy heap on a stretch of flat, dry grass, the declining sun making deep shadows behind them. Dark grey smoke drifted over them. Dee reached for the opening of the suit and sighed as the fabric parted, allowing Kelly to work her way out of it. He had a brief moment of regret as their bodies separated. But there was so much they had to do. Both of them were acutely aware of the nearby wall of fire. Dee prayed that it would maintain the natural firebreak and come no closer to them.

Kelly got to her knees, checked her weapons, and looked about. The flyers were gone; the sky was empty except for the huge columns of pitch-black smoke circling up into space. There was still a chance of land pursuit, but at the moment, there were no crawlers or skimmers in sight. "Okay. I think we're going to make it."

"I hope so," said Dee, closing the suit, and having the satisfaction of seeing it shrink back to fit him. "You were saying about a barn?"

"Let's keep an eye on the cows," Kelly recommended. "They'll have a water trough, and their water has to be certified." She brushed off her clothes in a tired, perfunctory attempt at tidiness. But despite their miraculous synthetics, she, and her clothes, were rumpled and wet. "Come on. The cows'll head for home at sunset."

"Are you certain?" Dee asked, seeing the animals milling some distance from them.

"It's standard," Kelly said. "Most ranchers don't want their animals out at night. Too many rustlers about." With that, she exhaustedly started walking away from the fire towards less open space. She left Dee sitting on the grass, worn out from their ordeal.

With resignation, knowing she was right to take cover, he wearily rose to follow her. He watched her, though she never looked back to see if he was behind her. The gap between them widened. He smiled at his sudden abandonment and began haltingly to move after her. He was reminded of lines from an old play: "A proper woman as one shall see in a summer's day. A most lovely, gentlemanlike woman." He wondered what she would say to that observation, and decided not to put her to the test for now. When he returned to his own age, he knew he would miss her.

CORWIN TARLTON SAT IN his apartment, staring at the small vid display at the foot of his bed. He had spent another afternoon exploring the various transportation centers in the region, and was now fairly sure he could use the trains and skimmers to spread the virus among the people. All he needed now was the signal from his master. He leaned back on the pillows, satisfied that he would help in the glorious work that would transform the humani to the devoted servants of Fawg, so that their restless minds no longer perturbed them, their emotions remote as the most distant stars.

He thought again of the coming pandemic, when every humani the virus touched would be the victim of uncontrollable shape-shifting, when their identities would be destroyed. He made a sound that humani called laughter, although the amusement it expressed was harsh. He and Fawg would be heralded heros to their people, and gods to these humani. Their tremendous achievement would become the stuff of legends among the next generation, a fine example of what Rocs could achieve were others to emulate the Roc of Fawg. The so-called high-minded attitude of most Roc had caused them to lose so many chances. Now they would have to see the possibilities beyond their scholarly curiosity. His thoughts filled with the anticipated adulation and the many favors that would be bestowed on them by their grateful fellow Roc. It was ample reward for all that was demanded of them now—living among this species of irrational, disordered beings. It would be over soon, he reminded himself, and the humani would become tractable and malleable to Roc rule, and all Roc would have to accept their role of leadership. To be part of the glorious transformation of humani was a high honor, he realized, and a tribute to his clan. His reverie was cut short by a knock on the door. He rose and went down the hall to the door. "Who is it?" he asked without bothering to look at the visitor display.

"It's Hamil Azzahzi," said the voice just beyond the door.

"Yes?" Tarlton said warily.

"I need to speak to you," Azzahzi said.

"I'm listening," said Tarlton,

"I need to come into your apartment. I'm sorry, but I've had a complaint, and I have to investigate it." He sounded contrite, and he added, "It's required that I check out all complaints."

"What is the nature of the complaint?" Tarlton asked.

"They say . . . certain of your neighbors say . . . that there is a noxious odor coming from your apartment." He was flustered, and went on too quickly, stumbling over the words as he did. "I th-thought it might be a d-dead lizard in the walls."

"You are fixing the walls," Tarlton reminded him.

"This is something else." Azzahzi said. "I don't want to make this any more unpleasant than necessary, but if I don't inspect, the complaining tenants could move out and sue for a partial return of their rent."

"How strange a custom," said Tarlton under his breath, then cleared his throat. "I have not been aware of any odor."

"Will you let me just check it out?" Azzahzi asked. "Once I do, then if there isn't anything in your apartment, I can arrange to inspect other apartments."

"Why not inspect the others first?" Tarlton was annoyed to be singled out in this way, and made no attempt to conceal his displeasure.

"They are not in during the day. You are," said Azzahzi. "It won't take but a moment. Just let me in, and I'll finish up as quickly as I can."

Tarlton relented. "Oh, very well." He triggered the locks to release and stood back as Hamil Azzahzi entered the small front hall. "Do what you must."

Azzahzi muttered, "Thank you," to Tarlton, then lifted his head and sniffed. There was something odd about the air, a vaguely reptilian aroma, but nothing offensive, as if there were lizards in the walls, or snakes. With this disquieting thought for company, he went down the corridor, sniffing as he went.

Following after him, Tarlton observed this strange behavior, thinking it intrusive and odd. "As you can tell, there is nothing here to—"

"But there is a trace of something," Azzahzi interrupted. "I can't place it exactly, but I do think there is something living in the walls that shouldn't be there. Nothing as extreme as the other tenants describe, but something, nonetheless."

"Perhaps it is in their walls, not mine," Tarlton suggested. He leaned on the doorframe of his bedroom, a mild expression of disgust on his human features. "Have you inspected what is under the floor? Mightn't there be something untowards there?"

"It could be," said Azzahzi uneasily, coming back to Tarlton's side. "I'll have an inspector in to locate the problem." He looked around again, aware that Tarlton had put nothing personal in any of the rooms: no pictures, no vids, no books, no ornaments. "Well, thank you. I'll have to look elsewhere for the trouble. I appreciate your cooperation."

"Glad to do it," said Tarlton without a hint of sincerity.

"You know how it is," Azzahzi went on. "There're laws about these kinds of things, and I have to abide by them."

"No doubt," said Tarlton, eager to have the landlord gone, but unwilling to rouse his suspicions by compelling him to leave: In a few days, he told himself, Azzahzi and all the others would be mindless and devoted to the clan in every way.

Azzahzi made his way back to the entrance of the apartment. "I'll make a little adjustment in your rent, for the inconvenience."

"Much appreciated," said Tarlton, imagining how he would order Azzahzi to serve him. "If there's nothing else?"

"No; nothing," said Azzahzi, and stepped out into the corridor. Only when Tarlton had closed the door behind him did he allow himself to scowl. He could not rid himself of the sensation that there was something very wrong about Corwin Tarlton, and although there was nothing in his apartment that was alarming, the man himself made the hackles rise on Azzahzi's neck whenever he had to deal with his new tenant. He dictated his report to his pocket secretary, and continued down the corridor, fighting off the certainty that he was turning his back on a disaster.

CHAPTER

39

DEE LET THE FEED pellets run through his fingers, then dusted his hands together. "Is this truly fodder for those cattle?" he asked Kelly as they explored the storeroom attached to the cow barn, which he insisted on calling a byre. It was just after sunset, and the sky was still glowing with the hot, metallic shades of early evening; inside the barn it was dark and warm from the presence of the cattle.

"Yes," said Kelly, busy with making a complete circuit of the interior of the barn. They had been there less than half an hour and had just completed their first appraisal of the place.

"How odd." Dee peered into the gathering dusk. "I suppose we could be back in Piper's realm." He saw Kelly frown and elaborated. "This byre is dark, as is Piper's realm. It smells of manure and animal sweat, not unlike the tunnels that Piper's legions inhabit. It is chilly except when animals are near, and then it is hot and cold at once. And, for those who dwell in it, it is a safe and secure haven from the dangers of the broad world."

"You mean this isn't as bad?" Kelly asked, and answered for herself before Dee could speak, "No, of course it's not. For one thing, there aren't guards about who've changed their appearance to look like cattle."

"Does that bother you?" Dee stopped looking over the sacks of feed and gave his attention to Kelly. "This is a spacious byre, larger than those we have where I come from. Handsome in its way." This last admission felt awkward to him.

"I think it does bother me," she said, completing her survey of the perimeter. "It's taking cosmetics to an extreme I . . . don't like."

"Cosmetics. This is a very . . . cosmetic age, is it not? You, yourself, when once you could, did all that you might to disguise the scars that Newton's men had given you. You wrapped yourself in scarves and painted your face an inch thick to preserve the shadow of your beauty. This is expected in this age, more than in mine. The Queen paints . . . painted her face, but not the way those of this age do. She wanted to preserve the face her people knew, but you do much more than that. She had but paint, whilst you have your technology that can belie countless years of age and ripeness and mischief. You worship at the altar of youth."

"Your time had other expectations of age and life's demands. What was done in your time was different than what happens now," Kelly allowed, going to the storeroom and taking up a guard stance by the door.

"Yes." Dee tipped two of the closed sacks over, then climbed atop them. "I've had worse beds than this one," he said with an amused wink.

"You must have had," said Kelly. "Get some rest. We'll head out around midnight, and be able to cover a lot of ground before morning. I'm pretty sure the fire burned itself out. The air seems cleaner."

"I hope so," said Dee. "I mean nothing to your discredit, Kelly, but I should not like to have to make such another walk as we two have done this day."

"I share your sentiments, Doctor," said Kelly, and folded her arms, facing the door.

By midnight Dee was rested again, and ready for a long walk, though his calves, thighs, and back ached with tightened muscles. "You know which way to go?" he asked Kelly as he adjusted his suit. Dee walked back to the water trough and drank with his hands from the artesian well water that provided drink for the herd. Earlier when he had awakened, Kelly had explained the hazards of dehydration to him, so he had been at pains to take several long swallows until he felt seriously refreshed. He'd said, " 'Tis not as good as small beer, but 'twill serve." The Doctor shook the excess water from his hands, looking for something to dry them on.

"East, for now," said Kelly. "When we get to the Coast Liner tracks, we'll find out where d'Winter is and decide where to go."

Dee considered this and nodded. "Is there any way to now employ my resources? I am accounted to be a wealthy man, but of late I have felt myself naught but a pauper." He waited for her to answer.

"If you access anything, you'll give our location away. We need the right machinery to do a multilevel blind withdrawal, and we've got to assume your enemies are monitoring your accounts and all transactions." She judiciously inched the door open and stepped out carefully, her weapon at the ready. "Let's move, Doctor."

"*Après vous*," said Dee, ready to go on.

Kelly then just as carefully slid the barn door closed.

"Keep under the trees as much as you can, in case there're any scanners monitoring this area."

"More of your DNA?" Dee suggested; he, too, looked around and then did as she instructed.

"Or heat, or pulse, or sound, or—" She broke off, holding up her hand. "Stop."

"Why?" Dee came up to her side.

"This is going to be tricky. There's a fence with scanners. It's for rustlers, but it'll display us on the monitors as well as anyone." She muttered an oath under her breath that shocked Dee, not for the strong language, for the court of Elizabeth Rex was not a mealymouthed one, but for the coarse obscenity of it.

"Why would anyone fornicate with a duck?" he demanded in a whisper.

"It's just an expression," said Kelly, more focused on the problem of the fence than on the Doctor's remonstration.

"Um," said Dee, certain that this soulless century had lost much of civilization's poetry and delight in words by letting Aristotelian Rhetoric slip from children's instructions. Vulgar banalities were always the result of a bad education. He held back while Kelly scouted the edge of the camera range along the fence. He reminded himself once again that it was not entirely seemly that he should be so much overmastered by a woman—women were destined to bear children; they were by Nature weaker vessels, except for the Queen herself—and therefore not suited to the hardships of life or the ordeals that men faced every day. "Women should not seek for rule, supremacy, and sway when Heaven hath made them to serve, love, and obey" went the age-old rhyme. He tried to realign his thinking to believing that in this time the expectations of women and their capabilities had radically changed, but it still did not sit well with him to take a backseat to a woman facing dangers for him. Nevertheless, she did know more about those dangers they faced, and it was politic to keep as many options open to him as possible.

"Doctor," Kelly called from a stand of brush not far away. "I think there's a way through."

Relieved, Dee hurried to where she had hunkered down in the brush. "Where?"

"There." She pointed to the heart of the thicket and did her best to sound optimistic. "The scrub doesn't extend very far on the other side of the fence, but perhaps it's enough . . . to cover our escape."

"Why do you say that?" he asked. "How do you mean—enough?"

"I think we can make it appear that we didn't come through from this side, and that the fence and cameras turned us back." She sounded fairly excited. "We'll have to scramble once we're past the fence, but that shouldn't be too difficult."

"And the fence?" Dee inquired at his most civil. He had seen enough of the security of this time to take nothing for granted.

"You're right," she sniggered to herself. "That may be a bit of a problem," she admitted, looking away from him.

"Out with it, girl," he told her. "What hazard do we venture?"

"It's made of razor wire," she said. "And it's electrified."

40

DEE STOOD VERY STILL, trying to recall everything he had been told about electric fences. Razor wire was self-explanatory, and it seemed to him that electrifying such a fence would be redundant. He folded his arms. "Can we roll beneath it?"

"I sure hope so," said Kelly, smiling a bit to encourage him, and herself. "Because that's the plan. There looks to be just enough room to risk it."

"But?" He sensed her reservation, and knew he needed her to tell him everything she knew or suspected in order to act successfully.

"But there may be sensors in the ground, and they would be triggered by weight, or body heat, or both." She looked up at the sky. "They may have overhead surveillance, any number of possibilities."

"None of them to our vantage," said Dee, scowling as he considered the dangers.

"No," said Kelly. "But we can't allow that to stop us."

"Aye, verily," said Dee, who, in spite of their concealed position, was beginning to feel dangerously exposed. He wondered if his suit would allow him to be hurt by razor wire, or any other weapon they might encounter. He didn't want to depend upon it.

"So we'll have to take a chance," said Kelly, moving a little nearer to the wire. "There's at least one thing to our advantage: These fences were meant to keep men out and cattle in. A woman my size, and someone"—she glanced meaningfully at Dee—"someone your size . . . we might be small enough not to trigger any alarms." Hearing this, Dee wasn't sure he was complimented or offended; Kelly continued, "I want you to wait until I'm under. If I'm okay, you come after me. If I'm not, I want you to find a way to the main road and get to the station—"

"But if you fail to escape successfully, how am I to do it?" Dee asked her, dismayed in spite of himself. He had been able to accommodate this world well enough, but he was a man without real friends beyond Kelly and d'Winter, and if they were incapacitated . . .

"You'll think of something," said Kelly, and dropped prone. "Keep an eye on the countryside around us. If anything as much as breathes, warn me."

"Other than cattle," Dee suggested.

"Use your best judgment on that," said Kelly, and began to slide toward the fence. Her stealthy movements brought back to Dee memories of the Untouchables.

Dee huddled in the brush, watching her carefully, and occasionally taking stock of the land around them through the screen of twigs and leaves his hiding place provided. He was disinclined to give much notice to the cows, and after a long five minutes he saw Kelly get to her feet, brush herself off, and signal to him to follow her. Dee stretched out, facedown, and wriggled towards the razor wire. As he neared it, he could hear its hum, and that seemed an especially ominous note. He wondered even if he could fit under the wire, would he be safe from the electricity, which might be able to strike him as lightening could. He continued to move, wishing he could burrow into the ground like a mole. This was worse than his escape from the clutches of the Spanish Duque, who had arrested him in Pamplona, claiming he was an English spy—which, of course, he was—and promising to turn him over to King Philip, which meant the Inquisition. He had had no hopes of English ransom then—Philip of Spain hated Elizabeth of England. So he had had to make his way out through the channels of an old, unused latrine, unpleasant but not so imminently dangerous as his current predicament.

He arrived at the fence, and disputed with himself whether to slip under head first or feet first. Each maneuver had its advantages. Finally he opted for feet first. It was easier to retract an electrified foot than a scorched face. Gingerly he extended his left foot under the band of linked barbed wires. Nothing. Next the other foot. Nothing. Pushing with his hands and careful not to flex his knees, he slowly scooted his body under the gleaming wire.

"Keep still!" Kelly's voice sounded as if she were only inches away from him.

Obediently Dee froze, wishing he dared to raise his head to try to discern what had caused her such alarm. There was nothing in front of him other than a line of black ants, marching along in single file, many of them carrying bits of something in their tiny, sideways jaws. At another time these little creatures might have intrigued him, but now they were intruders, unwelcome and distracting. Time seemed to elongate as he lay, still under electrified the razor wire, listening for all he was worth, and hearing only those noises he expected to hear. Once he heard the fence start to hum to life, he felt an uncomfortable tingle in his chest, as if he had bumped his elbow. But the hum ended as quickly as it had begun.

Finally Kelly spoke again. "Okay. It's safe to move now."

"God be praised," said Dee, a bit testily, for his feet and hands were in danger of falling asleep. He scuttled the rest of the way in a hurry and clambered to his feet as soon as he was clear of the wire. "What was the matter?"

"I thought I heard engines—crawlers or skimmers—but I can't hear them now. We've got to get moving, though," she said, and pointed away towards the low hills. "The main road is just over the rise."

"Are you sure of that?" he asked with forced jocularity.

"Yes, Doctor," she said, sighing. "I'm sure." She began to walk in the direction she had pointed, her pace steady and fast enough to cover the ground in a timely manner.

Dee, who had walked away from any number of sticky situations in his long and checkered career, kept up with her, saying, "What about surveillance? You said we might be observed."

"And I meant it." She frowned. "I don't know what to tell you, Doctor, and that's a fact. There've been too many instances when I should have expected us to be discovered, but"—she gestured—"I thought about it after what happened to you on the moon, and it still bothers me."

"And d'Winter? What about him?" Dee inquired. "In my time all the Great Ones employed intelligencers—you would call them spies—Leicester, Cecil, the Spanish Ambassador at the English court de Spes, all had intelligencers to inform them. After all, it was politic to so behave, for there is less danger in fearing too much than in too little. But our methods were nothing like those you use." A sudden stab of homesickness all but took his breath away. How he longed for that time, subterfuge and all. "For all of my profession are as inconsequential as dust compared to the spirits of machinery that your Great Ones—and even those not so great—employ. They may search out secrets in a nonce and learn a hundred times more than ever I could in a year."

"I know," she said, "and that's what's bothering me." She shook her head. "You'd think someone would have noticed by now."

"Who? What?" Dee asked, growing more baffled. "Whom do you believe should view us?"

"Well, the cops for one," said Kelly reasonably. "There should be state and federal law enforcement swarming all over us, and corporate security groups as well. Instead, nothing worth mentioning. Just some DNA scanners and occasional fly-overs."

"What may have befallen d'Winter is worth the mention," said Dee, his voice sharp.

"Yeah, I suppose so," said Kelly. "But you hired us as security, and that should have lit up a board somewhere. D'Winter and I aren't exactly unknown to the various law enforcement agencies; I'm less well-known than he, being new to the business, but I'm not a complete novice, either. And they usually keep track of us, one way and another. It's part of the game."

"These are spies for your leaders?" Dee guessed.

"Among other things," said Kelly, then remembered. "They didn't have police back in your time, did they?"

"If police be sheriffs, constables, and night-watchmen, aye, most asssuredly, we did," Dee answered brusquely.

"I remember: Bow Street Runners, and then the Peelers, in the nineteenth century, but nothing specifically like our police before then." Kelly laughed. "Yes."

"Yes?" Dee challenged. "What meanst thou?" He was surprised at the emotion she exposed in him, and knew that when he was gone from this age, he would long for her company in his own.

She looked at him, searching his features as if trying to make up her mind. Then she nodded once. "Okay. Let me explain about cops—police. They're appointed officers of the government to provide security to the people, the investigation of crime, and the apprehension of criminals for the courts. Their purpose is maintaining order and enforcing the law. They have official powers and legal authorization to do this, through the courts."

"The security forces of the leader," said Dee. "A guard, or bailiffs."

"More than that. They function at many levels, from protecting the streets to guarding the highest in the land," said Kelly. "The leaders have their own security, and so does the rest of society. The police are not the servants of any patron. They have their authority from the courts."

"Which serve the interests of the leaders," said Dee, thinking back to how many of high rank had been brought low by others whose powers allied with the most puissant in the land.

"Not just for the leader, for the citizens," said Kelly.

"With no patron but the courts?" Dee smiled his doubts.

"At times you may be right." Kelly lengthened her stride. "But they exist at local, state, national, and international levels. And the big corporations have their own security as well, sometimes hundreds of people in a force, just as d'Winter and I serve you."

"And those who attacked us—were they police?" Dee knew how city guards could be, and decided that the men at d'Winter's haven might be the current age's version of them.

"No. They would have had to follow procedure if they were. They were probably military." She frowned.

"That is different from police?" Dee asked, confused once again.

"Yes. The military isn't part of the courts," said Kelly.

"Armed men are hired everywhere," said Dee.

"It's more complicated than that. Private security isn't supposed to supercede the law, and are expected to defer to the courts' police in any question of legality." She stopped, holding out her arm to block Dee's advance; ahead of them a rattlesnake wound across their path, its tongue flicking.

"This is absurd," said Dee, watching the snake.

"Rattlers can poison you," said Kelly.

"I meant what you're telling me," said Dee. "How can I believe this? You cannot have men serve two masters. Inevitably your police, as you call them, would have to choose to protect the leaders or obey the courts. It was ever thus."

"The courts are given more might than the leaders," said Kelly, motioning Dee to move on now that the snake had gone.

Dee chuckled. "Does anyone in this benighted era believe that?"

CHAPTER

41

PIPER STOOD IN FRONT of his rat-faced troops, his eyes shining red. "We have a mission." His voice resonated throughout the large chamber's cavernous stone assembly hall. He strode up and down in front of their ranks. "You cannot falter. This is where we prove ourselves or go down in ignominious failure. A great responsibility is ours, and ours alone. If you will not do this, I must assume you no longer want to serve me."

A sound of unhappy chittering went through his guards, and one of the better-armed spoke up. "What do you need from us?"

"You must go onto the surface. You are looking for an alien, one who can change his shape to that of any living thing. He is carrying a virus that will cause spontaneous shape-changes in anyone exposed to it." Piper folded his scrawny arms. "Changes that no one could control. You will have no say in who you are."

"What kind of shape-changes?" A woman with a rodent's jaw and a pointed nose held up her pistol.

"I don't know. No one does," said Piper. "But they would be uncontrollable and lead to a loss of reason."

"Would it change *us?*" The officer wore a shocked expression, and his voice went up to a dismayed squeak that carried to the very top of the three-story ceiling.

"If you are exposed, it probably would," said Piper. "We can't be sure, but the information I have been given suggests that it's likely." He let them think about this. He allowed them time to turn to their neighbors with questions and fears. The sound in the mousery grew, augmented by flicking tails and twitching feet. Piper went on. "We have an advantage most don't. We have enhanced olfactory capacities, and we can literally sniff out this imposter." There was a pause. "From a distance."

"What does he smell like?" There was a note of purpose in this question that gave Piper hope.

"Not like a human, that's certain. This creature is more reptilian than mammalian, but even then, I would think that he—or she, or it—would not smell like any reptile you have ever encountered." Piper gestured emphatically. "You must find out what disguise this intruder is using. You must stop him. He can be detained and held down here, and his contagion with its lunacy can be isolated."

"Then we will have to expose ourselves to the contagion, whatever it is," said another officer. That observation raised a nasty hubbub that spread quickly throughout the hall. The din grew as the gathered multitude became frightened by their impending danger. Beady, accusatory eyes focused on Piper.

"Yes. This is true enough," said Piper, determined to regain their wholehearted allegiance. "It is a great deal to ask of you. But we can do it better than anyone else, for even if you are exposed, you can stay here, with me, and you need not pass on the contagion to those in the world above us or amongst ourselves. There are many isolated chambers down here. Moreover, I give you my word that I'll do everything in my power to find the right treatment—drugs, shocks, decompression—to take care of those who might be infected. If I can't, their families will be taken care of. They'll never want for anything again. I will work harder than anyone to protect every member of my people."

"So tell me," said a youngster, "why should we do so much for a world, and a species, that rejects us? What do we owe them?" This acknowledgment of their exile was enthusiastically approved by many and mulled over by many more; Piper was prepared for this.

"Nothing," said Piper. "We owe them nothing. We do this for ourselves. Remember, unchecked, this virus will slaughter all of us." That caught everyone's attention; the room's occupants were more attentive. "But if we do this for ourselves, then we will have the certainty that we have done what the beautiful people failed to do. We have sensitivities that give us the unique ability to ferret out this creature and bring him—or her, or it—to account. We will have proved our worth. In fact, we will be proved better than they are. They will have to recognize their ostracization for what it is—racial prejudice. Then, if the rest of humanity continues to despise us, we will know in our hearts that we took the high ground. And though we did all that we could to save ourselves, and all of humanity, they turned their backs on us for no reason other than bigotry." He had achieved in his listeners the utter silence that is the goal of every orator. He went to the end of the line of his troops, then started back the other way. All present held their breaths, waiting for his inspiring words to continue. The only sound in the vast chamber was that of his tail twisting through the sand on the floor. "You can do this, and you can show that we are worthy of respect." He swept the gathering with a look of profound sorrow. "Do this for ourselves, and for no one else, and you will achieve all, for everyone."

A lone voice from the back dared to call out, "And if we fail?"

Piper was unperturbed, answering without hesitation. "We fail?" He laughed as if this were an utter impossibility. Others took up the laughter; he quieted them with a gesture. "Should we falter, all we have done to show your difference from the 'others' will mean less than nothing as all mankind will change shapes without warning. At least we must try. To permit so many changes to be visited upon the world would redound to our discredit. Where would be our pride then?"

"It would be terrible, such a world," said the most ratlike of his soldiers.

"Yes. Exactly," said Piper with an emotion very like paternal pride. "We would lose our unique identity."

The host of ratlike humans made a kind of skittering cry, and one of the youngest exclaimed, "For our honor, we will do this!"

"Yes!" cheered Piper, topping the cry of his followers. "You make me honored to lead you!"

The crowd cried in jubilation, "Piper!"

He let them work. "Time is of the essence, remember. Whoever this villain is, he is willing to inflict a dreadful fate on mankind, and we will have to suffer along with them." He held up his arms again. "Be brave! Be determined! Be victorious!"

"Be brave!" the troops repeated. "Be determined! Be victorious!"

CHAPTER

42

STRATEGY BROOKS SIGHED AND pointed at the display. "I don't know what to say," she told diRocelli. "I tried to get him to stop, but he wouldn't." She stared as if mesmerized at the parade of resurrected bodies who trudged out of camera range.

"I am the Lord, thy God," Yeshua was intoning over the landslide as he pulled another body from the mud. "I bid you live again!"

The latest cadaver tottered off, the man blank-faced, a shine on him like the gloss of slime.

"He's been at it for hours," said Strategy. "He won't stop. He says it is his duty to bring these unfortunates back to life, to prove his identity, and to give glory to his Father." She shrugged.

"How do we stop him? This is getting embarrassing," said diRocelli. "Particularly if he really *is* what he says he is."

"Yeah," said Strategy. "I know." She sat down on the draughting stool with her back to the display. "If he is what—who—he keeps insisting he is, this could be terrible. The Bible-thumpers would tune me out in droves. I could lose my entire southern-hemisphere following."

DiRocelli cocked his head toward the display. "We can't put all this on the air. We'd be laughed out of town, no matter how much of a miracle it all is. It looks phony. Hell, it looks like a cheap stunt. One man brought back to life is newsworthy, an army of reanimated is like something out of a bad, old-fashioned movie."

"I know, I know," said Strategy. "I thought we'd have the scoop of the century, or the millennium, but I didn't count on anything like this. I thought this would be a major story, a blockbuster. Now it's something from the *Enquirer* network."

"Those men are like zombies," said diRocelli. "They might *be* zombies, for all I know."

Strategy sank her head into her hands. "It's a nightmare."

"No kidding," said diRocelli.

A silence fell between them, and then the display faded and Strategy said, "That's all we have."

"It's more than enough," said diRocelli. "They won't like it at MCHVN and R." The very mention of their parent company was uttered in a hushed tone.

"Oh, God," said Strategy, feeling sick.

"Um-hum," said diRocelli. "How can I put a good face on this?"

"I wish I knew," said Strategy. "It gets worse. He's announced his intention to raise everyone who died in the mudslide and the fire. He'll do it, too. He has no concept of timing, or moderation. I can't reason with him. Most of the time he can't even find the lens, like a rank amateur."

"Not good," said diRocelli. He pulled on his thinning hair. "What are we going to do about this?"

"I don't know," said Strategy. "I want to have a chance to fix it, if I can. We have to work out something so that we aren't in court for the next twenty years."

"If we're lucky. MCHVN and R could hang us out to dry, to get out from under any legal complications," said diRocelli.

Her head was beginning to ache. More than anything she wanted to be rid of Yeshua ben David, to forget she had ever seen him. How could she have been so suckered? "I've been in this business long enough that I should have seen this coming."

"How?" DiRocelli didn't rush her to answer. "Given what you were told at the start, I'd have done just what you did. I think you aren't as badly off as I am; after all, I authorized this whole thing."

"On my recommendation," Strategy reminded him miserably. "My career is down the drain. Just gone."

"So we'll face them together," said diRocelli. "If they fire us, they fire us."

"Or send us to Uruguay or the Chukchi Peninsula. That would be worse than firing. I'd rather quit, no matter how that makes me look." Strategy closed her eyes again. "I can't stand it. I've been doing this for fourteen years. I've made covering the news my life. Now I'm up against this."

"I've been in the business nineteen years," said diRocelli. "If we're cooked, we're cooked. But we did our job. We did what they told us to do—found a unique story and gave it full play."

"We can't plead insanity," said Strategy.

DiRocelli clapped his hands. "Maybe we can say that *he's* insane!"

"Who?" Strategy demanded.

"Yeshua!" diRocelli exclaimed. "We can say he's nuts! We can say we found out about the miracles before we found out about the craziness. That should get us a little time to fix things."

"How?" Strategy was interested in spite of herself.

"Well," diRocelli said, becoming a bit more cautious, "this is just off the top of my head, but it could work."

"What kind of nuts do you mean?" Strategy asked.

"You know. Mad as a hatter. Out of his mind. Barmy in the crumpet. Round the bend." DiRocelli rubbed his hands together. "We say we were so amazed by his reanimation talent that we didn't see how insane he was. Now we know that he's loony, and we need to stop covering his exploits."

"Maybe we could make that the story," said Strategy, her buoyancy returning. "Maybe we could do something about the shared lunacy this man represents!"

DiRocelli grinned. "You mean, revealing the danger beneath the wonderful appearance?"

"Yes! If we can talk to some of those resurrected people, we can show just how bad his supposed good has turned out to be." She felt enthusiasm welling in her. "You're right. We can turn this around."

"I think Perry and Natasha are free. Have them work tech for you. They'll cover anything," diRocelli recommended.

"Right. I'll play up the nutsiness of what he's doing," Strategy said, living up to her name.

"Let's look at that display again," said diRocelli.

Strategy took a deep breath. "Let's get to it."

CHAPTER

43

DEE SAW THE TRACKS soaring over the valley, hanging from a line of pylons that stretched to the horizon. Like a ladder across the Heavens, he thought. He pointed to them. "In what manner or by what device can we scale this edifice?"

"We don't. We go along to the next station," said Kelly. She stared up at the tracks that carried the suspended, high-speed trains down the length of the Avila Valley sixteen times a day, every day. "There should be another—"

Holding up his hand, Dee said, "Hark, I hear something."

An instant later there was a keening wail from the rail above, and the pylons quivered as if in anticipation. Far to the north of them, the sun glistened off the speeding train, the windows like brilliant scales on a vast, metal serpent. Dee recalled the rattler and shuddered, wondering if this were an omen, or only his exhaustion catching up to him. If he had had a chance to study the zodiac more closely, he would know.

"We'll catch the next southbound one," said Kelly. "We'll take it all the way to Borderland."

"Why so far?" Dee asked, trying to image that remote place south of Angel City, surrounded, it was said, by high, killing fences, and containing all those who had been caught trying to leave southern California.

"Because I'd bet that's where they've taken d'Winter."

"If he still lives," Dee said morosely.

Kelly paused before responding, but was resolute in her answer when she finally gave it. "He's still alive." There was another pause, a bit shorter than the first. "It's where the army takes all its civilian detainees." Kelly made a face. "It's a pretty strange place, Borderland."

"And Angel City isn't?" Dee responded. A cool sea breeze wafted past them. His suit turned porous and lightweight. He wished he knew how it had been made, and why it was given to him, although he assumed it had something to do with his shift in time. How would he explain it to the Queen and the Privy Council? Would he ever show it to her—assuming he ever saw her again—and how would he account for it? A present from a living gargoyle? The Royal Fool would make much of that. Lacking in fur, ruffless, and barren of any ornamentation, the court would find it sadly plain, more worthy of an Ottomite or a Puritan than any courtier of Albion. But the Queen would recognize its merits if she allowed him to. She was uncommonly brilliant for a woman. Even the French courtier, deMaisse, no friend to England, had allowed that "she was a great Prince whom nothing escapes."

"Doctor," said Kelly, taking him by the arm. "We've got to get out of here." She was looking up at the approaching train, staring at its underside.

"And why, pray tell?" He was annoyed at her brusque manner.

"They've got gun-turrets on the underside of the train, and cameras. We don't want them to know we're here." She tugged him behind an outcropping of rock. "Wait until the train's gone. There's usually a second turret mounted in the rear."

"By the Mass, what is the meaning of such weapons?" Dee asked even as he squeezed himself under a hanging ledge. The ferocious sound of the oncoming train was becoming overwhelming as it came nearer.

"There are rebel groups living in enclaves in the Valley, and from time to time, they like to blow up pylons, to stop the trains running for a while." She said this loudly but so casually that Dee believed her. "The trains maintain security forces to deal with them."

"Police?"

"Private security. Like d'Winter and me. More of them, of course, and in uniform, but still private, for all that." She put her hands over her ears as the train screamed over their hiding place.

He followed her example, but even with his ears shielded, the sound was louder than any he'd ever heard, and it came with a wind that threatened to blow him and Kelly off their hiding place. Dee looked up and to his amazement realised that the massive machine had no wheels, nor did it touch the elevated tracks, but floated a meter or so above the tracks. He was awed by the power and majesty of the miracle above him.

Unaware of Dee's astonishment, Kelly continued, "The army or the police hunt down the rebels, depending on whether people are killed or not." Kelly, realizing that

Dee could not hear her waited until the express passed and the noise abated before going on. "When people die, it means the army takes the case. When the tracks are brought down, the police handle it."

"Why?" Dee demanded, failing to see the sense of this, and wanting clarification.

"Killing people is considered an act of insurrection, an act against the State," said Kelly. "Blowing up pylons is considered industrial sabotage."

Dee still couldn't see the difference, and said so though his ears still rang, which made him speak more loudly than usual. "Mayhap," he allowed, "but is it not reasonable to posit that the action of 'blowing up a pylon,' as you call it, is more intended to harm those riding the trains and is therefore, by your definition, an act of insurrection?"

"No, acts of sabotage are primarily intended to damage the transportation company—collateral loss of life is a secondary feature," said Kelly patiently. She was speaking normally once again as she rose from their hiding place. "I can see how you might find it confusing—many people do."

"But you don't," said Dee.

"It's my business to know these things. When I was doing publicity, I had to explain all the differences." She put her hand out to him. "Come on. We've got a couple hours' walk ahead of us."

He shrugged. "How many miles?"

"Miles?" She converted the distance in her head, "About ten—a little over; not quite eleven. The ground's uneven, and we'll have to shelter from time to time, when the trains pass." She set a good pace—not too fast, but enough to keep them moving steadily—and pointed to the south. "Look for the towers of San Luis Obispo."

"Towers. Is San Luis Obispo a walled city?" Dee asked, wondering if such things existed in this new world: He hadn't seen one.

"No, but it has two towers in the middle of town— one is a government building, the other is a state jail— you can see them for miles," purposefully using his measure of distances. She grinned at him. "It won't be long now. We'll get into town, find something to eat, and get on the train for Borderland."

"Very well," said Dee, keeping his mind open. "I'll prove a faithful follower."

"Of course you will," said Kelly. "You don't know this place, or this time, and I'm the only one who can help you who's on your side."

In his mind's eye he remembered tramping through Poland, behind Edward Kelly, who had been more bosom friend, a persona grata, than an inferior. The Doctor owed his life many times over to the quick-witted, redheaded Irishman. Perhaps one day in this world, if Providence could intervene, he would return to his old friend again. What a night of carousing they would share! A pang of loss went through Dee as the memories of his old companion welled up in him. In Poland, Edward Kelly uncharacteristically had taken the lead, knowing just what cities to make for and what men of right-thinking to inquire about. Edward Kelly's extensive knowledge of the eastern European countryside had been enormously important on that mission. Dee glanced over at Kelly Edwards, who was picking her way through the Avila chaparral, and thought how neatly Fate had contrived to put him in the hands of two such capable, and two such similar guides. Was this what the French meant when they spoke of déjà vu?

"Doctor!" Kelly said, sensing his abstraction. "You're a thousand miles away." He nodded. "True enough—and five hundred years as well," he added in response, and smiled as he continued his steady tread behind her along the gravelly under the elevated train tracks.

CHAPTER

44

A HUGE GLASS CASE at the entrance to the lobby of the Majestic Hotel contained the preserved body of a gigantic bear, standing on its hind legs, front legs raised menacingly. Leeta stopped and stared at it, then took in the brass-and-paneling of the rest of the lobby with its decor of trophy heads. "Shit," she whispered. "This is worse than Texas."

From a corridor off the lobby, a gruff voice called out, "I'm coming. I'm coming," in acceptable English.

"Are you Boris?" Leeta asked, watching the man, who seemed to be a smaller version of the bear as he shambled toward the lobby, a load of folded towels in his up-lifted arms.

"Da. Yes. I am Boris." He put the towels down and ducked behind the registration counter. He was dressed in a dark blue double-breasted jacket; tight around his middle, it was missing buttons on the sleeve. Leeta had a sudden tug of memory of her grandfather in just such a jacket as she climbed on his lap to pat his stubbled chin.

"Ludmilla? Over at the restaurant? She called you

about me," said Leeta, feeling quite peculiar in this place that was so foreign and so familiar at the same time. All of a sudden she wasn't so sure this had been a good idea.

"Yes. I know. I am readying a room for you," he said, shoving the old-fashioned registration book toward her. "Put here your name and passport license." He handed her a pen; she noticed the impeccably shaped nails on his oversized hands. "It is leaking," he warned.

Leeta took the pen, holding it steadily, and signed her name, then pulled out her passport license and read the number off the back of it, copying it down carefully, on the open page of the black, leather-bound book, making sure she made no mistakes. That would draw attention to her and that was the last thing she wanted. She carefully replaced the pen in its holder and swivelled the register back to the hotelier. "Mr. Boris, what kind of rooms do you have here?"

"Boris Michialovich Shevyenetz. For you, a suite. Two rooms, very nice. One with a large bed, one with a . . . a couch and a coffee table, and a satellite pickup display, like all good hotels are having." He smiled and his rough features took on an unexpected friendliness. "There is kitchen here, open twenty-four hours, make you food when you want it, all kinds."

"That sounds wonderful," said Leeta.

"Very reasonable prices. You see." He handed her a sheet of charges in dollars, common-market currency, yen, reals, dinars, rubles, and virtual money. The rates of exchange looked current enough and the amounts didn't seem unusually high. "You will be liking it here"—he glanced at the registry—"Mrs. O'Conner. Yes? Ink blotting here," he said, pointing to the smudged O in *O'Conner*; Leeta nodded, a little ashamedly, and Boris smiled slightly at her discomfort. "Such a nice, traditional name. Mrs. O'Conner."

"I'm a widow," said Leeta, realizing that it was true.

"I am sorry to be hearing this," said Boris, his lugubrious visage sagging with sympathy. His thick eyebrows were like fuzzy caterpillars.

"Don't be. It was time," Leeta said. "But thanks."

"Ah." He laid a finger along his nose. "Long illness is a burden for everyone." He reached around behind him. "I will take you up to your suite. We use keys here, as in the olden times. You will want to keep yours with you except when you go out, and then you will be leaving it here, at the desk."

"Fine. It's just fine, Mr. Shevyenetz," she said, having seen enough old-style hotels in those hard days before she met Romulas. "Why not a DNA scan?"

"Too easy for Security Committee to use. I want my guests not to have to worry about such things." Boris smiled winningly. "Come. I will be showing you up to your suite, Mrs. O'Conner." He once again ducked under the counter and rose in front of her, pulling his long hair back from his broad forehead. He gently but firmly took her one traveling bag from her.

"Call me Leeta," she said impulsively.

"If you call me Boris. It would honour me." He opened the door to another old-fashioned feature: an elevator. He pressed number 3 in an array that said L, 1, 2, 3, 4 and smiled as the ancient machine wheezed to life. "Slow, but it works."

"It seems fine to me," said Leeta, still trying to think about what she was going to do now. The lurching start to the elevator ride made her queasy. Her hand clutched at her stomach through her clothes, as if to stroke it calm again. But in spite of everything, she realised she was feeling distinctly better than she had an hour ago.

"Good. That is very good." He didn't say anything more until they reached the third floor. "On the left, the fourth door. It is a corner suite, a good view of the city."

"Thank you," said Leeta, warming to the man.

"A fine woman like you, it is an honour to have you visiting my hotel," said Boris as he opened the room door and stood aside for Leeta. "Now, you see, a nice couch, a good coffee table, two chairs."

None of them matched, but the effect wasn't unpleasant, not after the rigorously tasteful home where Mother O'Conner held sway. Leeta went to the couch and tried it out—it was firm enough and it didn't creak under her weight. "This is very nice." The manager cum bellman carefully laid Leeta's suitcase on the bed, careful not to disturb the sateen coverlet. She handed him ten new rubles, a handsome tip, and held her hand out for the key. "Thank you, Boris."

"You get a nap, and then you come down to dining room. I will see you have the best dinner we can present: reindeer steaks in cloudberry sauce with mushrooms. You will be liking it." He pocketed the money and started for the door. "There is tea and coffee in the bathroom, and a hot-pot. There is a filter on the faucet to make the water pure. You can make whatever you want."

"Okay, I will," said Leeta, liking the man more and more.

"You can be calm here, Leeta. I will be taking care to see you are not disturbed." He smiled again, looking at her with something more than professional concern.

Leeta found herself flirting a bit, smiling from under her lashes, her lower lip just caught in her teeth. "You're being real nice to me, Boris."

"An easy thing," he assured her, about to leave. "You are a beautiful lady, and well-mannered."

"Oh, Boris," Leeta said, flattered by his attention and not quite willing to let him go yet.

"Yes?" He lingered willingly in the door.

"That bear?" She chose the first thing that came into her mind. "Where did he come from?"

"The one in the lobby?" Boris held himself with pride. "You have nothing to fear from that bear or from anyone else. I'm shooting him."

CHAPTER

45

THEY CAME OUT OF the steep, rocky pass from the Avila Valley to see the city below them. It sat on a hilly landscape that cozied up to the sea. In the midday heat the city seemed to breathe as if a slumbering beast lay sunning on the hills. The fumes of its mass-transit radiated out in all directions. The towers Kelly had mentioned were like two horns on the forehead of the city; they pierced the low-flying clouds coming in off the Pacific.

"Ten more minutes and we could be on the platform. But we don't need to rush. The next train won't be in for more than an hour." Kelly grinned in anticipation.

"How are we going to pay for our transport?" Dee asked, voicing the question that had been bothering him for the last twenty minutes.

"My implant will be charged." She stopped. "You don't have an implant."

"No, and from what you've told me, this could be a problem. The authorities will wonder why I don't have one. Certes, they'll detain us with questions." He looked around, his face showing the ruddy touch of sunburn. The bridge of his nose was absurdly pink.

"You're right. And we don't have d'Winter's scanjammer we used coming north. Damn," she muttered. "This will require a little planning." She went on for more than a dozen steps, her expression distant. Then she looked down at Dee, a speculative light in her eyes. "Do you think you could fit in a back duffel?"

"A what?" Dee asked, mistrusting the sound of this.

"A back duffel. You know, those big packs travelers carry on their backs? You've seen them—I know you have."

"You mean those tinkers' swags?" Dee had indeed seen the objects Kelly mentioned. "The ones containing clothing and other supplies? They attach to a kind of frame that sits on the back and the shoulders?"

He was beginning to understand her drift. "I have not the youthful spring I was wont to in erstwhile times, but I might, like a lawyer's letter, fold myself over for a time—perhaps an hour or two—if it's necessary. I've endured worse."

"I'll find a shop selling duffels," said Kelly.

They had reached the outskirts of San Luis Obispo now, and the spread of abandoned, half-collapsed buildings fanned out around them, a reminder of how extensive the damage from the Quake had been. A few of the buildings had withstood the shaking, and a smaller number had been rebuilt, but for the most part, there was devastation everywhere. The few homes they passed were ramshackle and weathered by the elements. In the front yard of one pale blue residence, rusted gutters drooping from the eaves of the house hung over a middle-aged woman tilling an impoverished garden. Dee found this a nostalgically comforting image, not much different from many he had see in the Cotswolds.

Kelly led the way toward the old university, California Polytechnic State, saying to Dee, "There are always duffels for sale in the students' quarter. I used to date a guy up here."

"Um," said Dee, wondering what a university would look like in this city, and this time. Without doubt, it wouldn't be anything like St. John's College, Cambridge where he had studied in 1542. "What manner of studies does one follow here?"

"Agricultural chemistry, engineering, microcircuitry, for the most part," she said.

"Those teachings savor not of a university," said Dee indignantly. "Why does not the curriculum include theology, natural philosophy, or the measure of the stars?"

"Astrophysics isn't a strong department here. You have to go to Irvine for that, and oceanography." Kelly looked slightly amused at Dee's affronted expression. "I guess you meant astrology. That isn't considered a legitimate academic study anymore."

"But the digging of tunnels is?" Dee exclaimed in dismay, for in his day, engineers worked with miners. "How can engineering, with its colliers and woodcutters and general laborers, be a legitimate study, and astrology, which divines the course of one's life, not be?"

"You can study all that—and almost everything else— electronically. Only about five percent of students attend an actual, physical university anymore. This is one of them, because of its agricultural department."

"I cannot credit that. You flout me. Scholars, studying on their own, is as wild a tale as ever I have heard. Boys at school must be closely watched, or they shall turn their thoughts to naught else but tables, dice, and trifles. The enforcement of the rod, sweet child, is as necessary for the course of learning as a library."

Kelly laughed. "Perhaps you have a point there. I'm sure I wouldn't like being caned, but I could have used a little more discipline during my undergraduate years. But independent study courses are the way it is nowadays." She shrugged. "It seems to work. These students you see are the exception in education, not the rule."

"But do many young men come to university? And it is yet mostly peopled by sons of the titled and the wealthy?" Dee asked, recalling that those youngsters of his era who attended Oxford and Cambridge were fewer in number and percentage of the population. It was an acknowledged embarrassment of Tudor times that a university education—originally meant for poor scholars—had begun to attract scions of the rich and powerful. The high-born, with their privileged position, subverted the studious life of cap and gown, turning it into a shameless excuse for indulgence and debauchery. Needed financial scholarships, which were far from plentiful, had become inaccessible to the needy. Dee, the son of a vintner, had been hard-pressed to find the monies needed to attend St. John's. To a man like John Dee, a university mind, trained in the arts and sciences, it was a perversion of study, making it a revelers' holiday and a crime against education.

"Almost everyone who can read gets some kind of college degree, mostly electronically." Kelly was becoming familiar with Dee's prejudices, so she took real pleasure in what she told him next. "Even women attend the university and receive advanced degrees. I graduated summa cum laude from Trinity College in business and entertainment studies, as well as earning a master's in investment protocols—in other words, economics, media, and advertising."

"Such things are taught at university?" Dee was incredulous now. "Ridiculous!"

"Things change, Doctor. You said it yourself." She saw the kind of shop she was seeking, and headed toward it. "I'll purchase the largest duffel I can carry. And a couple of throws, to pad you in a little. You might as well sit down and wait, over there on the bench. I'll be out shortly, and then we can grab a bite to eat before catching the train."

"Of course," said Dee, his sarcasm lost on Kelly in her general excitement to put her plan in motion. He could only look around and see how much the rigors of monastic life had degenerated. He watched the students with disapproval.

The streets were busy, hundreds of people on foot, others on individual hoverers, making their way around the extensive cluster of buildings that occupied more than ten city blocks. More than half the persons on the street were young—Dee guessed their ages to be between sixteen and twenty—almost all of them carried readers and a collection of plugs the size and shape of fingers that contained texts and instructional material; a few had actual books with them. The sight of the books gave Dee a sharp pang of homesickness. They were tiny and unadorned, but they were still essentially paper and printer's ink, and they were still the portals to new ideas. Words, words, words. How he doted on them! He missed his grand library at Mortlake, the luxury of sitting by the fire of an evening, a branch of candles next to his chair, a book open on his lap! What joy there was in the discovery of an apt phrase, or a revelation on the nature of the triangle. The love of learning and the thrill of immersing himself in the arcane arts had brought him and Dyckon together in the shared delight of scholarship. All that followed stemmed from their mutual love of knowledge. And what sacrifices he had made in this pursuit! It was a bittersweet admission.

Kelly emerged from the shop with a duffel and frame in her hands. "Got it," she said triumphantly. "Food next, and then we'll find a private spot to load you in."

"Not on a full stomach," said Dee firmly. "Whatever meal next we eat, we must not overdo. Despite our present hunger, a well-provisioned repast must be postponed till later. We owe such diligence to d'Winter. When he is with us once again, then we will have right good cause for celebration. We shall feast as well as any sultan. We shall burn moonlight into day in his honour and leave no bottle uncorked."

"Okay, okay," she said, a little wearily, for sometimes Dee got a bit too Shakespearean for her. "A snack now, and real food later. But I better warn you, I get hypoglycemic when I'm hungry." She saw his stare of incomprehension and was startled by it. Then she laughed merrily, her mirth belying all the danger they had recently endured together. "Doesn't your translation device know hypoglycemia? I thought it was infallible." Her tone was at once superior and self-deprecating. "Well, Doctor John Dee, late of the sixteenth century, now you know how I feel half the time when I'm listening to all the gobbledegook that comes out of your mouth. Welcome to my world."

"Touché," he politely acceded. He touched his forefinger to his brow in salute.

Kelly pointed to a sandwich shop a short distance ahead. "I'll split one with you," she offered.

"Satisfactory," said Dee; they made their way down the

block and read the menu in the window. "All right. What choice do we have?" He realized that question could be taken two ways, and both would be correct; he liked the inherent ambiguity.

"Ham and cheese on black bread with mustard, lettuce, tomatoes, pickled ginger, and with olive oil and balsamic vinegar for dressing," Kelly ordered without consulting Dee. A holographic waiter took their order and vanished. A real-life waitress with high-piled pink hair appeared moments later with their food on a platter. Kelly paid for the food with coins and handed half to Dee.

He regarded the sandwich suspiciously—the foods of this time still seemed strange and unpleasant to him: he longed for green goose and meat pies with rampion, for cream bastard and fresh-caught tench in beer, for larks on a spit and beef marrow on Cheshire cheese, for venison in vinegar and honey and mutton with barley, for cabbage with butter and cream and spring hare cooked in whipped plover eggs, for larded partridge and peas porridge, all washed down with pots of sack and ale. . . . He took a bite of his half of the sandwich and found it lacking in savor. "How can you enjoy this? Its flavour is as muddied as a Flemish boot!" he exclaimed as he chewed.

"It's good," Kelly said. "And I'm hungry."

Dee ate steadily, determinedly. "How long until the train docks?"

"We have enough time. We'll get to the platform in half an hour, and that'll put us there with ten minutes to spare, just when things are getting busy, so we won't attract much attention."

Dee finished his half of the sandwich and squared his shoulders. "All right, Kelly. I'm ready," he announced.

"Good," she said, taking a last, lingering bite. "Let's find a place to do this."

"Where do you think is best out of view?" Dee wondered, looking around at the general confusion.

"I noticed a unisex rest room back by the kitchen. I think we should be able to find an unmonitored stall to load you in. If you stand on the bowl, it'll be easier on my back." Kelly rubbed her hands together. "This shouldn't take long."

"Fine," said Dee, wishing he meant it. As he followed Kelly, he said, "Your implants—you all carry them, don't you?"

"Yes, except for a handful of people." Kelly gave him a curious look.

"The aliens we seek—they also don't carry them, do they?" Dee pointed out.

Kelly stopped walking and looked at him. "No. They don't." She began to smile. "We should have thought of this."

"You're accustomed to implants. I'm not. You take them for granted," said Dee, taking the lead at a brisk pace, then gallantly holding the rest room door open for her. "It gives us another tool."

"So it does," Kelly agreed as she hurried past him.

CHAPTER

46

STRATEGY BROOKS FOLDED HER arms and regarded Yeshua with a jaundiced eye; he was muddy, and his manner was exultant. She motioned to her new camera-tech, Willard, indicating he should cover this from a distance. "How many so far?"

"Two hundred ninety-one; there are more to come," Yeshua announced, as if heralding the arrival of the heavenly hosts.

"And you plan to continue this?" She kept the skeptical note loud in her voice.

"Of course. I am the Son of God, come to restore mankind to Grace." He held up his arms. "I must continue. The longer they have lain in the earth, the harder it is to call them forth from their graves."

"Was that what happened with O'Conner?" The challenge was open.

"That, and embalming fluid." Yeshua bent down, thrust his hands into the mud, and called, "Come forth, Gaultiero Wong!"

There was an ominous sucking sound, and a mud-colored figure pulled out of the earth, eyes still closed, limbs moving as if controlled by strings. The man struggled to climb away, face as blank and unresponsive as a wall.

"Two hundred ninety-two," said Yeshua to Strategy.

"What's going to happen to him?" Strategy asked in her most professional manner.

"He will live," said Yeshua. "He will walk the earth, and sing the praises of God and Me." He put his hand to his chest.

"Those people you brought back to life are like stolen property." She was goading him now, deliberately provoking him.

"Stolen property? Hardly." His laughter was a bit wild, just as Strategy hoped it would be. "They are returned to life."

"*Your* life, to be *your* servants, to sing *your* praises, to give *you* glory," Strategy pressed on. "This isn't for them— it's for you."

"No," Yeshua protested. "You make it sound as if I'm doing something wrong, when you, of all people, should know I am doing this to save the dead!" Fawg was feeling uneasy, sensing that something had changed with Strategy, making her mistrusting. This should have filled Strategy with awe and the city with gratitude, not with this annoying distrust. Why were these humani so difficult? he asked himself. "What do you want from me?" He took a moment to realize he had spoken that question aloud. He bent down again. "Lucinda Ford, come forth!"

The woman had been some kind of maid, for she was in a sodden uniform and her hair was confined by a neat, old-fashioned cap. She wandered off, her disjoined movements ungainly and strained.

"Give glory to God!" Yeshua cried aloud, and moved a bit farther out onto the landslide. "Miguel Sanchez, come forth! David Henderson, come forth!"

The two men, gardeners by the look of them, shuffled out of the ground, wandering away from their Savior in a dazed state.

"Are they going to recover more than this?" Strategy pursued Yeshua. "Or will they stay like that?"

"They will clean themselves up, in time," said Yeshua. "And they will praise—"

"God and you," Strategy finished for him.

"Yes. And the praises will be heard on high. It was promised that I would do this on my return, and lo, it has come to pass." He smiled benignly. "How many of you want to have these people live? I would guess that most of them have families and friends who will welcome them back, and celebrate their return, no matter how changed they might be by this experience."

"Then you do admit they are changed," Strategy said emphatically.

"Of course they are changed. It says in Scripture that the dead will be raised incorrupted and that all shall be changed in the twinkling of an eye. Think of Lazarus. He was no longer the same when I brought him back from death." He moved a little farther. "Marie-Louise Koyn, come forth!"

Another muddy figure emerged and stumbled away.

"Manfred Funk, come forth!"

Strategy was growing alarmed, for the risen dead were drifting about the edge of the landslide, aimlessly moseying about, fixing on Yeshua from time to time, their expressions showing no emotion but a kind of doglike devotion. "Why aren't those . . . people you reanimated leaving?"

"They follow me now," said Yeshua, smiling almost merrily.

"Because you saved them?" Strategy said.

"And because I am the Son of God. I am worthy of their regard," said Yeshua. This confidence came off as extremely arrogant, so he tried to modify it. "Any man who saves another is worthy of high regard."

"I see," said Strategy, and added, "So you expect them to remain devoted to you?"

"It is the nature of these people to want to follow me," Yeshua declared. "Leslie Fleming, come forth!"

This summons brought a teenager in outlandish clothing out of the landslide, all cocky defiance gone and only slavish adoration remaining.

"Doesn't that seem a bit self-serving?" Strategy was preparing to skewer Yeshua, to reveal his madness. "Or perhaps even delusional?"

"No, it doesn't. Your species always puts great significance on those who can save others from death. You see such men as heros." He flung his hands toward the milling group of reanimated corpses. "Who has done as much as I?"

"You say that you are doing this altruistically?" The doubt in her voice was so thick that it almost distorted the words.

"I say I am doing this because it is what you want of me," Yeshua countered, and prepared to pull another person from the mudslide. "Petronella 'Maggie' O'Conner, come forth!"

From out of the drying mud there came a terrifying figure, the features all but burned away, her clothes nothing more than scraps, the shape of bones showing through the muscles.

Watching this, Strategy felt the hair rise on her arms and neck. The wrongness of it filled her, and she turned away, repelled but still satisfied that she had done what she set out to do: reveal Yeshua as the demented egomaniacal madman she knew him to be.

The ghastly body struggled out of the earth. She prostrated herself before Yeshua, "My Lord," said the hideous form of Mother O'Conner.

47

THE DUFFEL PACK WAS stuffy and tight, but it proved a successful ruse, for they had passed through the turnstiles without incident. Dee was surprised at Kelly's strength, for she carried him as if he were nothing but a sack of clothes and a sleeping bag. He could hear the approaching rumble of the train, and that gave him real satisfaction, for he was aware that once they were on the train, the close surveillance would be at an end until they reached Borderland.

"You ready?" Kelly murmured as she moved forward on the platform.

"Tally Ho," he whispered, readjusting his head between his knees.

The train arrived with a humming clatter; the doors whipped open, more than a hundred people surged forward into its interior, the doors snicked shut again, and the train was off.

"Relax," said Kelly. "County Line is the next stop, and then Angel City. Then San Onofrio, and Borderlands. Two and a half hours."

To Dee, who was lying on his back with his legs over his head, muffled in two soft throws, relaxing seemed highly unlikely, but he reminded himself he had been in tighter confines than this present situation, which, although uncomfortable, wasn't as hard as what he had endured before; he resigned himself to the journey.

There was a huge influx of passengers at County Line, and many people jammed into the seats and aisles of the train. Now there was standing room only. Dee's duffel was jammed up against Kelly's side, and a male voice hinted loudly that it was rude of certain unnamed passengers not to put her duffel on the floor. Kelly ignored him.

"Angel City, Angel City, next stop," the train announced. "Exit on the east side of the train. The arrival platform is on the east."

"Any ideas?" whispered Kelly.

"Is Piper scheduled to loose his forces today?" Dee said in a measured cadence, finally giving voice to something he had been quietly pondering.

"Yes. Do you think he will actually do it?" Kelly spoke out of the side of her mouth, barely audible.

"I hope so," said Dee, and made up his mind. "Let me off here," he said firmly. "I shall find my way to the Pit. I'll have assurance the ratman has honored his promise, and if he hasn't, I'll do all in my power to bring this scurvy criminal to your justice. Meanwhile, you continue down to Borderland and get d'Winter out of whatever confinement he has been enforced to. Do it speedily, but take care not to trample on too many laws. I am in need of all the help you can provide, not another mare's nest to deal with. Settle the matter. When law can do no right, it is right that law bar no wrong. With d'Winter in your care, return to his Angel City lodging and wait for me there."

"I'll have to get off and take the next train south," said Kelly, standing up as the train began to slow. She slid her arms through the duffel-frame harness. "I don't feel right, leaving you on your own."

"Gramercy, but that you must," said Dee.

"You're probably right," said Kelly uncertainly. "If we had another day—"

"Alas, but we don't," Dee remonstrated ironically. "At present, time is too precious a commodity for us to waste it." He felt other passengers press in around him, and was glad of the padding the throws provided. As the train lurched to a stop, he wished he had something to hang on to other than his haunches.

They were hurried off the platform by the flow of humanity, and riding the moving walkways, Kelly was soon on the street. She ducked into a café and found a booth large enough to allow her to put her duffel on a bench and help Dee out of its confines. "I'm going to order something to eat. Do you want anything?"

"Nay—not at present," Dee said, stretching his cramped neck and shoulders, thinking of the many things he wanted; he could certainly forego another such journey as a folded stowaway. He would much rather be back in his own time and at home at Mortlake, casting charts and studying traingles. The chase was on; there was no time for refreshments. "I'll have something later, when this is all done and I can be at ease again." Recuperating from the uncomfortable ride in the sack, he straightened himself as best he could, running his fingers through his hair to restore a semblance of order. He saw the pattern of his garment begin to unwrinkle and change again, and no longer wondered at the alteration, for the suit had a mind of its own in such matters. He nodded nonchalantly to the couple in the booth across the aisle who had caught him popping out of the bag; Their expressions were priceless.

"Do you know how to get to d'Winter's place?" Kelly asked.

"I have a passing fair notion. I remember the street name and number. The locks should be set to recognise me. A right good invention, such locks." Dee held out his hand to Kelly in the manner these people employed.

Instead she sidled closer to him and hugged him tightly. "Good luck. I'll look forward to seeing you again."

"And to you," he said, breaking their embrace. "I'll number the hours until our next meeting. Be wary, Kelly."

"Are you sure you can do this?" Kelly persisted. "My job is to take care of you. I don't feel right about not holding up my end of the—"

"Right now . . ." He touched her cheek. "You do me the better service by attending d'Winter. I'll hold you blameless for any mistake I make. This is my decision, Kelly, and as long as you are in my employ, you will do as I bid."

"How can you be sure about this?" Kelly asked.

"I can't be," Dee admitted, "but I have been about the world—perhaps not this world, but not so different from it—and I know that to succeed in life, risks must be taken. I cannot remain idle while humanity is faced with the problem of spontaneous loss of oneself. A few may become accustomed to it, but most others would be beyond help in a matter of days, and then all our efforts would be for naught."

Kelly studied him. "No arguing with that," she said, sharing Dee's concerns.

"Then do as I bid you," said Dee, feeling a little pang of regret.

"I will," Kelly said. "But I have to tell you, I'm not comfortable about it."

Dee knew that he shared her apprehension, but he said, "I'll take that as a compliment."

"Um-hum," said Kelly. "Well, I'll hope to meet up with you tonight or tomorrow. At d'Winter's place."

"739 Puerta Nueva," said Dee, pulling the address out of his memory without hesitation.

"Yes," Kelly said, awkward in the parting; she got to her feet.

Dee shimmied out of the booth. His suit felt like silk. "Time to go."

"Do you want the duffel?" she asked.

"I think not," said Dee.

"Then I'll take it," said Kelly, swinging it onto her arm with ease now that it contained only the two throws. "You never know, it might come in handy."

"I'd prefer to travel lightly," said Dee, waving Kelly toward the café door. He watched while she stopped at the counter and ordered a glass of wine. While she waited for the big-eared bartender to serve her, Dee slipped out the side door onto the busy sidewalk, and the sweltering, sulphurous air of Angel City.

STRATEGY BROOKS RETREATED FROM the landslide, trying to make the best of a situation that had turned frightening. She did her best not to make it appear she was running away, walking quickly but not quite breaking into a run. She put her hands around her pickup unit and wished it were a gun instead of a communications device. This was no longer where she wanted to be, but she dared not make a hasty retreat, for fear that she would give the resurrected dead an excuse to pursue her. By the time she reached the van, she was shaking visibly. "I have to sit down," she said as soon as she was sure she was no longer being picked up by camera or microphone.

"They are pretty scarey," said Perry as he gathered up his equipment. "I think we're through here for now."

Natasha, the relief driver, buckled into the driver's seat, kept watch on the crowd behind them. "It's time to get out of here." She had started the engine, and the van hummed, ready to roll.

"Is there something to drink? Not water or tea—something stronger?" Strategy asked as she secured herself into her seat.

"I've got some grappa," said Perry, reaching into his kit bag.

"God! That stuff is horrid—I'll have some!" Strategy held out her hand for the bottle.

"Do you think they'll do anything to us?" Natasha asked as she put the van in motion.

"I don't want to find out," said Strategy as she took a long swig of the thick, alcoholic drink. "Dreadful stuff," she muttered, and drank again.

"They're not coming after us," said Perry with unmistakable relief in his voice. "I don't know what we'd have done if they'd chased us."

"We'd have had to run over them," said Natasha. "That's the rules." She sent the van careening along the narrow roads, its engine whining.

"I don't think that would have turned out well," said Strategy. "We'd be sued from now until 2500." She flung up her free hand. "No, thank you."

Natasha laughed edgily and made the van go faster, no matter how unsafe it was. She was frightened, but she was also enjoying herself. "I'll get us back to the office in ten minutes."

Strategy took another mouthful of grappa. "How did you get this stuff, anyway?"

Perry chuckled. "My grandmother makes it—an old family recipe." He took the bottle back. "It's got quite a kick to it."

"I'll say," Strategy agreed as she felt the alcohol hit her system. "Wow!"

"Have some strong coffee, and you'll be fine. That's what they do in the old country," said Perry.

"Whew!" Strategy exclaimed as the van careened around a steep corner. She grabbed her seat belt and hung on for all she was worth.

"We've got the story ahead of the other services," Natasha crowed, and an instant later slammed on the brakes. "What the hell—?"

Ahead of them on the road was a group of armed men, all of whom had more than a passing resemblance to rats. They were moving steadily, purposefully, in the direction of the landslide.

"Get them on vid. I want them recorded," Strategy said, her words slurring a bit but her thoughts astonishingly clear.

"What are they?" Natasha demanded, pulling the van to the side of the road.

"Beats me," said Strategy, unbuckling herself and preparing to get out of the van to intercept them. "I'm going to find out, though."

"They have weapons," Perry warned even as he reached for his camera, slipping it into his headmount.

"Be careful," Natasha warned. "I don't like the look of them."

"No kidding," said Strategy as she got out of the van.

"Don't get too close if you don't have to," Perry said. He held the door open for her and took a stance suggesting a willingness to fight.

Strategy approached the group of rat-faced soldiers. "Hello. I'm Strategy Brooks, and I'd like to find out a little about you."

The armed troops ignored her.

"Hey!" Strategy was used to a great number of responses, but total indifference wasn't one of them. "Hey!" She matched her pace to them. "You look like serious people. Can you tell me what you intend to do?"

"We will triumph," said the soldier slightly in the lead; he paid no attention to Strategy beyond glancing once in her direction and then resumed the march up the hill.

"What will you triumph over?" Strategy pursued. "What is your purpose?"

"We follow the purpose of our leader, Piper!" exclaimed one of the soldiers.

"Piper?" This was a name out of rumours and myths to Strategy, who prided herself on knowing every important person in the Western Hemisphere. "Who is Piper?"

"Our leader," said the head soldier.

"Yes, I got that," said Strategy. "But who is he? And what are you doing for him? You're carrying major weapons here. Did Piper provide them? What do you carry them for?"

"To save the world," said the lead soldier as he shouldered past Strategy.

"So you said," she persisted, growing impatient. "Tell me what you're doing, and I'll put it on the air, so everyone will know."

The leader turned back to look at her. "We're saving the world," he said, then swung back and trudged on up the slope, leaving Strategy to stare after them, puzzled and sensing a new lead dawning.

CHAPTER

49

DEE SET OUT ALONG the main thoroughfare, walking steadily as he had done many times in the past. He dared not risk taking public transportation for fear his lack of an identification chip might precipitate an arrest. He had walked miles and miles in his beloved England, in France and Poland and Hesse, in the Swiss Cantons, and in Tuscany and Lombardy. Angel City wasn't as mountainous as the Cantons, nor was it as poorly roaded as France had been—he supposed that France was different now. Perhaps prettier, but unfortunately still peopled by the French. It was a warm day, and the heat slowed him down as he trod up the long inclines to the crest of the hills where fires had so recently burned. The air still smelled of charring and the acrid odor of the flame retardant that had been so lavishly sprayed.

By two in the afternoon he had almost reached his goal. He needed to find Piper, to see if he had located the Roc. He wanted to tell the ratman about his ideas concerning the missing chip implant. It was another hour to cross the Hollywood Hills and to descend into Santa

Monica and the Pit. But travelers must be content, he reminded himself. How many times had he trudged the long road from Mortlake to the Queen's Placentia Castle or to the theatres in Southwark? Dee's neighbor, Lord Burghley, often had offered Dee his barge. The Thames was the speediest—and safest—way to get to London. Dee had always refused. The ferrymen hawking rides just down the slope crying "Westward Ho!" were as plentiful as the drifts of swans that clustered on the river. He'd refused them, too. He smiled at his own shortcomings. He had an uncommon dread of boats, especially smaller ones, and for that reason, Dee had turned the wearisome, often damp, trek to the capital city into a favorite pastime. The leisurely ramble allowed him to see his neighbors, experience the change of seasons, view the parade of hopeful travelers bound for London's myriad opportunities. He had watched the village parish beadle sniffing out vagrants, and all of the bustling merchants—from the highest to the lowest—who swarmed around the greatest city in Europe. Important secrets could be acquired if one took the time to hobnob with foreign sailors, country-bound courtiers, and tradesmen. He always felt better after a walk, and attributed his sound health to the time well-spent on his constitutionals.

But he had to put such remembrances aside to keep his mind on his mission. He wished Dyckon were with him, for Dyckon could see so many things Dee could not, and with every minute precious, he longed for all the help Dyckon could provide. He reminded himself that he had to be alert and attentive, and redoubled his efforts to be careful around all the men and women on the streets. A threat could come from anyone at any time. It seemed he had undertaken an impossible task, but he reminded himself that his presence in this place at this time was an impossibility in itself; he could not deny that he had already had several inconceivable experiences—surely this would be no different. He was confident that the Roc must be in Angel City, and that, with Piper's help, he would be found in time. He couldn't go to the authorities about the Roc and the threat, since he was certain no one would believe him. Even if they did, they would either eradicate the Roc or place him in such extreme isolation that Dee would never have the chance to contact him, and he would never gain the time-slip device that had brought him across the centuries. That was not acceptable to Dee, not after all he had been through. There was also the accomplice. Were they together or separated? Questions and fears tumbled through his thoughts like shuffled cards.

If only he had a reliable ephemeris to chart the stars. But that would take time to acquire and then to calculate, and time was the one thing he did not have to spare. He went up the last sharp incline of the crest of the hill that presided over Lake Hollywood Preserve and peered down at the array of canyons and defiles that spread out from the ridge like pleated skirts. Northwest was the San Fernando Valley with its towers of communal apartments. To the southwest spread ashen clouds of smoke still lingering from the recent Hollywood Hills burn. They tarnished the otherwise blue skies that had followed the rains. The most recent mudslide showed like a huge tear against the tawny velvet texture of the hillside. Walking along the crest, Dee found himself studying the swath of slipped land in front of him, thinking it had transformed the hillside as surely as the virus the Roc was carrying would transform the people of this world. If only Angel

City were not such a center of travel! But that, of course, was its attraction to the Roc, that, and its tradition of illusion and deformities. Dee thought of his fortune, and realized it would do him little good just now. If he succeeded in stopping the Roc, he knew he could put some of his money to excellent use by developing a scanner that would reveal the presence of unknown viruses and other animalcules that could harm humankind. There were lunar influences—the mudslide demonstrated those aspects clearly—that he had been unable to calculate, and this bothered him, but not enough to stop him from doing his duty, not in the face of the threat of an intolerable cognitive and physical contagion. He sped up his pace toward the muddied area that lay between him and Piper.

A huge truck lumbered by him on Ventura Boulevard, carrying salvaged goods from the fire and landslide. Someone was profiting from the misfortune of others, but that was not new to this century. He was reminded of Europe after the Plague had struck down more than 18,000 in the 1590s, and the devastation he had seen; this world was not prepared for such ravaging, and Dee knew much of the fabric of humanity would not stand the strain of any epidemic. He watched the multitudes passing him by and appreciated how many good people there were, all deserving of their sanity, their liberty, and a reasonable hope for a meaningful future for themselves and their families. It spurred him to keep going. He was heading toward the mudslide, for he was sure that there he could salvage an abandoned vehicle that would get him more quickly to the Pit where he would have the answers he needed.

He could see the blackened edge of the burn along the

outer edge of the mudslide, and he paused, for the road had slid, leaving no trace of paving behind. He would have to make his way over the unstable earth, and he was apprehensive about how he would manage the crossing. Then, toward the foot of the slide, he saw a gathering of mud-covered figures, many of whom had the same disoriented demeanor that Romulas O'Conner had had after being brought back to life.

"Andre Richie, come forth!" The sound of Yeshua's summons reached Dee far up the slope.

Dee stood very still at the top of an unstable hilltop, watching the earth part to eject Andre Richie, who got up clumsily and wandered off the slide. Dee leaned forward, concentrating on what he saw, and keenly aware that there was a great evil masquerading as great good. Setting his jaw, he started down the slope, his feet slipping on the hardening mud as he went.

CHAPTER

50

"SO WHAT DO WE do now?" Natasha asked Strategy as she came back to the van.

Strategy smiled. "We follow them. I think there may be a fight brewing, and if there is, we're going to cover it." She climbed into the back. "Turn around, and keep about three meters behind that bunch. There's something strange going on, and I think Yeshua is at the heart of it."

"Newsperson's hunch?" Perry asked, hanging on tightly as the van swayed while Natasha dragged on the joystick.

"I don't think Yeshua is as adored as he thinks he is," said Strategy, hoping that she would be in time to show the world how dangerously crazy he was. She had made a beginning, but now she had an opportunity to finish it.

"You mean those odd-looking guys with the guns?" Natasha asked.

"That's who I mean," said Strategy, a grim little smile pulling at her mouth.

The ratlike troops stood across the roadway, facing the mud-covered reanimated corpses, their weapons raised, half-aimed at the walking former-dead, two unlikely armies watching each other, making their presence known.

"Pull over here," Strategy ordered, preparing to get out and resume coverage of Yeshua.

"Okay," said Natasha, doing as she was ordered. "You be careful. This could turn ugly real fast."

"Let's hope it does," said Strategy. "That's what we're here for."

"Don't take chances," Natasha insisted.

"Nothing I can't deal with," Strategy promised, and flung open the rear doors. She jumped out of the van and started towards the group of soldiers. For once she didn't announce her presence, wanting to get as close to the two antagonistic groups without drawing any attention to herself.

"I command you to depart," Yeshua was declaiming. "This is no place for you."

"It is no place for you," the leader of the rat-soldiers said.

"I am the Lord, thy God, the Three in One!" Yeshua cried, pointing his hand at Piper's soldiers.

"You are not!" two of the soldiers countered, their voice rising to furious squeaks. "You are not even human!"

"Of course not!" Yeshua exclaimed. "I am more than human!"

"You have the odor of reptiles about you, and it is on those you have called back from death!" the leader of the troops shouted.

This was better than anything Strategy had hoped for. She crept nearer, her recording unit held up. Her other hand was clutched around the miniature mike at her throat. She hoped Perry was recording a complete display of this; if he got full coverage, she and diRocelli would be out of trouble. In fact, she decided, they could yet be given awards for their work. Her heart fluttered with excitement; her determination drove her onward.

The rat-soldiers moved forward, bringing their weapons up to the ready; Yeshua held out his hands. "Halt! You must halt!"

The rat-soldiers didn't pay any attention, preparing to fire at Yeshua. The leader began to bark out orders. "Aim!"

Strategy was almost abreast of the soldiers now, but she stopped still, anticipating an eruption of violence. "There is conflict looming," she said for her viewers' benefit. "It appears that this militialike group is going to attack Yeshua Ben David. They have already accused him of not being human. The truth is they look less human than he does."

"You must not attempt any action against me," Yeshua ordered, and he pointed toward the resurrected crowd. "They will come to my rescue, if you insist on this unholy assault."

"You are the enemy," said the leader.

Yeshua sighed. "So many have despised the truth, and you are among them." He gestured to the reanimated bodies. "Stop these misguided vermin."

Mother O'Conner was the first to move, launching herself at the troops with a howl that chilled the blood. She jerked as the bullets tore through her, but kept on advancing on the soldiers, her hands clenched and raised above her head.

"All of you! I look for succor! Aid me now!" There was a moment of silence, then the rest of the restored cadavers began to move. They marched in jerky-but-purposeful steps, their lifeless eyes focusing on individual soldiers of Piper's army.

Bits of flesh and mud spattered all over as the rat-soldiers fired on the advancing dead, slowing but not halting their advance. Smearing the smudgy mess on her face to a brown smear, Strategy decided it was time to withdraw, and was backing away from the incipient fray when she saw another figure coming down the mud-slide—a smallish man in an unusual suit of clothing, who was shouting something she couldn't hear—and she crept back to observe this new development.

CHAPTER

51

YESHUA SWUNG AROUND, glaring at this new inter-loper. He pointed at Dee, and in a thunderous voice ordered, *"Stop him!"*

The walking bodies faltered, a few of them changing course and beginning to march in Dee's direction, reaching out to maintain balance as much as to seize him. The figure in the lead was the appalling remnants of Mother O'Conner, who blinked her one remaining eye as she attempted to gauge the distance to her prey.

The rat-soldiers took advantage of this and moved forward, still firing into the corpses, their bullets continuing to tear into flesh and bone, sending them flying so that the air was filled with a reddish haze through which the bodies tottered, fell, and rose again in ever more shattered forms.

"Are we getting this?" Strategy whispered to Perry from her hiding place just across the way from the army of the dead; she was crouched behind a hedge that was still standing in spite of fire and landslides. The char, wet to the consistency of papier-mâché, sat an inch thick on the top of the hedge's rubbery leaves. Through a chink in the foliage, she could—if she dared—spy a limited view of the combatants.

"Yeah! We just went to live feed!" Perry was thrilled, and he made no attempt to hide his delight. His tapping feet sent shivers through the GNN control van where he was monitoring the broadcast controls. The vid feed played out in front of him. "Shit! Just look at it!"

Yeshua's resurrected hosts were a juggernaut of arms, legs, and teeth; they inexhaustibly kept coming. Like mongrel wolves, they clawed and chewed their way through their unlucky victims. The agonized cries from those attacked were horrible. Perry slid the earphones off—the keening screams of unalloyed pain and terror were making him sick.

"I'd rather not look; I'd have to get closer," said Strategy. "No telling what I'd get on me."

"The troops are moving in on the zombies," said Perry. "And that little guy on the hill is still trying to reach Yeshua."

"Who is he, do we know?" Strategy asked, wondering how she might get an interview with him as soon as all this finished up. "What's he saying?"

"Something about viruses, and aliens," Perry told her. "Can't you hear him?"

"Not over the gunfire, no," said Strategy. "I feel half-deaf." She snuggled a little closer to the clustered thin trunks of the hedge. She felt tiny branches and twigs trying to push her away.

"Oh, great," said Perry, adjusting a few settings to get a more complete display of the carnage. "Just stay where you are for now. It's pretty messy out there."

For once Strategy was disinclined to argue. She stayed

in her protected zone, her hands clapped over her ears, her eyes narrowed against the spray of mud, flesh, and bone that continued to fly over her head.

"There's another squad of rat-soldiers coming," said Natasha as if this were of minor interest. "They're moving pretty quickly." Natasha's job at the moment was to maintain the color resolution.

"Oh, great," said Strategy, and ducked lower. "What's happening to Yeshua?"

"Nothing," said Perry, unbelievingly. "Nothing seems to phase him."

"I was afraid of that," said Strategy. "Keep an eye on him. If he tries to get away, follow him. This is just window-dressing. Yeshua is the real story here."

"I guess he is," said Perry, and added, "That other guy seems to think so, too. Yeshua is keeping the fighting between them. He's kind of shining."

"Who?" Strategy demanded. "Yeshua or the other guy?" She hated being unable to see for herself. But she didn't dare risk looking through the hedge.

"Yeshua," said Perry, slightly alarmed now.

"Shining how?" she kept on.

"You know—he's glistening. All over. So are the zombies, the ones that can still walk."

"How many are out of commission?" Strategy wondered aloud.

"Maybe sixty," said Perry, trying to assess the broken limbs and torsos on the ground.

"Out of almost three hundred, that's not enough," said Strategy, beginning to worry again.

"The trouble is, until their legs are blown out from under them, they continue to get up," said Perry.

"That's not good," said Strategy,

"Here come the next wave of soldiers," said Natasha, her voice at its blandest, as if she saw things like this every day.

"It's going to get bad around here," Perry warned. "Maybe you should get back here, and we should blow."

"We've got to keep recording," Strategy insisted. "Right now. We have to keep rolling." This was turning out better than her most outrageous hopes. She hunkered down and listened to the gunfire, happy to have evidence of Yeshua's depravity as well as his power. She would come out of this covered in glory, and she would be able to name her own price, her own beat, her own stories from now on.

"Anything you say, boss," said Perry, rotating the remote cam dials to pick up the approaching squad of soldiers.

"Where's Yeshua?" Strategy asked, daring to peek out of her hiding place.

"His zombies are all around him," said Perry, concentrating on the second group of soldiers.

"And the other guy? Where's he?" Her curiosity getting the better of her, Strategy stood up cautiously. She was sure Perry could hear her heart thumping through the body mike. Peeking through some of the branches, she tried to spot Yeshua amid the chaos before her.

The approaching soldiers brought their weapons around to the firing position, and they came up behind their fellows. The leader of the second squad began to issue orders, deploying his troops to cover the occasional breaches in the first group's line. Another volley of shouts rang out, increasing the noise to impossible levels. More of the bodies reeled, careened, and fell, making it difficult for the rest of Yeshua's restored dead to move without stumbling over them.

Strategy dropped onto her face as a gobbet of muscle whizzed over her head. She was certain that Perry was right and that it wasn't safe to remain where she was, but she would not vacate her position, not yet, while Yeshua was still at large, and not while she had so golden an opportunity to be the first to interview him—or anyone else of significance—after this onslaught. That is, she added to herself, if the cops or the Army didn't show, scooping everybody up and clamping a security lid on the whole thing. "Where are the cops? Or the Feds? Shouldn't they be here?"

"Keep still!" Perry warned her. "The soldiers are fanning out. I think they're going to try to outflank Yeshua's zombies."

"That's great," said Strategy with heavy sarcasm. She could see her sleeve, and made a face at the mottled pattern of dirty blood on it.

"Steady there," Perry told her. "The zombies are heading for the rats now."

"Did they get the other guy?" Strategy asked, hoping they hadn't.

"I don't think so." Perry had centered his image on Yeshua, who moved among the dead, raising them up when they had fallen, and calling more out of the earth. "But the zombies are still keeping between him and Yeshua."

"I hope he manages," said Strategy. She felt something wet splat against her arm, and she wouldn't let herself look at it, for fear of becoming sick. This was the biggest story of her career—she wasn't going to screw it up now.

CHAPTER

52

DEE SCRAMBLED TO THE side of the mud and stepped onto the cracked roadway with a sense of relief. He had precious little time to spare, but for the moment he was in the clear. The grisly old woman and the others had forced him downhill toward a deep, newly formed crevasse. It was a gash in the slope about three furlongs in length. Yeshua's troops were maneuvering Dee so that he had to retreat toward the precipice. Dee looked around desperately. "I need a weapon to stave them off," he said to himself. The sound of the words led to action. He grabbed a stout, fairly straight tree limb, around seven feet long that had snapped off a fallen tree. He'd often placed high in cudgel fighting when, as a lad, he had participated in the Robin Hood Games in Gloucestershire. With the bough for a quarterstaff, he rammed into his opponents, aiming for their midsections and kneecaps; he propelled some of his pursuers into the gaping fissure. Despite his victories, he saw the odds were against him; eventually he would tire against these tireless dead.

He looked back behind him once, reasonably sure he

had but one option remaining: He charged the corpses ahead of him with the staff acting like a pike. He flattened a few and drove back those pressing most closely around him. Then with a shout intended more to overcome his own fear than to scare this soulless enemy, he turned on his heel and made a rush for the ravine. He held on to the long limb with all his concentration and extended it out in front of him. At the last moment he lodged the end of the staff in the soil and vaulted up into the air. His legs paddled madly as he sailed over the chasm, an ancient and still oft-used word for ploughing on his lips. He landed with a thud, knees and the heels of his hands sunk deep into the soft mud while the staff on the far side thudded its way down into the fissure. He quickly turned around and saw his attackers lined up on the opposite side of the crevasse, furious at his escape. Some three or four of them simply began the slow march down the side of the fissure; others began to look for alternate methods of crossing the gap to get him. "I know a trick or two that speaks well of my age," he congratulated himself. "A fig for you and your master. Aye, a Spanish fig!" he shouted, along with the accompanying finger gesture. He made a mock bow to his unappreciative audience and ran for cover.

In his descent down the treacherous hillside, Dee ducked behind the fallen canopy of treetops, burnt-out vehicles, shattered perimeter walls, anything that would keep him hidden from the sight of the false messiah and his minions. There was no doubt that Piper had kept his word and ferreted out Fawg set-ut. Circling back up behind the rear of the battle, he found an isolated gap in the ravine where he was able to lay down some long timbers and cross back to where the Roc was making his stand. The fighting made him move cautiously, doing his best to avoid the many bursts of bullets coming from the advancing rat-soldiers. He had to keep Yeshua in view, to prevent him from escaping from the confusion that roiled over the wide swath of hardening, clay-stiff mud. He observed with care, being particularly heedful of where the milling, resurrected multitudes were going. There were so many of them that Dee thought they were dangerous for numbers alone.

"Glory to God in the highest!" Yeshua shouted. "Come unto me, all of you! I will give you life everlasting!" He made a sweeping gesture as if to embrace everything on the hillside. "You, who live again in My Name, show your faith now, and your devotion. Stand against all who oppose me. Stand against these vermin from the Pit!" He was so close to his goal now that he couldn't imagine failure.

There was a long sound, half a sigh, half a moan, from the reanimated cadavers. Those who had not fallen were slowly grouping around Yeshua, forming a wall with their mud-covered bodies that was almost as impenetrable as stone, and aggressive.

Dee watched this, more appalled than fascinated, for the blasphemy of it struck him to the core. He wished he could get nearer to Yeshua, to observe him and determine what manner of madman he might be. On impulse he reached down and began to pat the drying mud from the road onto his face and hands, then dropped down and rolled until he was indistinguishable from the resurrected crowd around Yeshua. It was at the most a makeshift disguise, but he hoped it would be convincing long enough for him to penetrate the ranks of the restored dead. Entrusting his soul to God, he climbed onto the mudslide and pressed in among the walking corpses, his expression as blank as he could make it.

The living dead milled around him, crowding against him as they strove to guard Yeshua. Dee managed to work himself closer to Yeshua, taking care to stay out of his line of sight, for as confident as he was that he could deceive the restored dead, he was equally sure he would not be able to cozen Yeshua. This made him cautious, which was all to the good, for as Yeshua called out the names of those to be summoned back to life, the ground beneath his feet began to vibrate, and a moment later, a rift appeared in the hardening mud and an arm emerged, the hand wrapping around Dee's ankle.

"Jose de Soto, come forth! Praise Me!" Yeshua shouted.

The body clambered out of the earth, using Dee to lever himself upright. He immediately joined the knot of bodies around Yeshua. Dee shuddered at the cold touch of the dead man, and moved away from Jose de Soto as quickly as he could without making himself conspicuous. Beyond the living dead Dee could see a young woman he recognized from the vid, pale as whey, struggling to get nearer to the rat-soldiers, who continued their steady advance on the flailing, shambling dead.

Piper's soldiers wheeled about to get a different angle on the resurrected. They fired another volley of shots and watched as more of the bodies blew to bits.

"Who are you?" Strategy asked, a quiver in her voice, trying to get close to the soldier giving the orders. "Why are you attacking these dead?"

"We are not attacking them, we are attacking that imposter," said the officer, pointing directly at Yeshua.

"What kind of imposter?" Strategy pounced on this tantalizing bit of information. She saw herself not only saving her career, but bringing in the most exciting story

GNN ever sent out. She kept a wary eye out for unfriendly fire.

Yeshua held up his hands, and Dee could see the faint shine on his arms, and the suggestion of a pattern of scales. Yeshua shimmered in the sunlight, and Dee knew it wasn't a halo around him but his Rocness showing through his human form. "Follow me! I will give you all you need!" Yeshua shouted, his voice ringing with emotion, his body trembling. The unmistakable odor of musk emanated from him, filling the air. Dee immediately identified it as the same aroma that lingered in Dyckon's spacecraft.

Certain now that Yeshua was indeed Fawg, Dee slipped more deeply among the dead, hoping to avoid the bullets of the rat-soldiers while he determined what Yeshua was up to. An exposed arm caught Dee unawares and sent him reeling backward, falling gracelessly to the wet, trampled mud, where he slid a little. He looked up to see Yeshua not far from him, his face pitilessly contorted into a ruthless grimace of hatred; he smiled suddenly, but Dee saw it was a rictus of evil as Dee watched Fawg's serpentine tongue flicker over Yeshua's mouth. Finding his long-sought quarry this close, Dee sprang to his feet, bloody, bold, and resolute.

Suddenly three of the corpses collapsed, and Dee found himself standing directly in front of Yeshua, who staggered as the bodies fell against him, and the dark glasses fell from his face. Dee looked straight into the Roc's eyes.

"I knew it!" Dee cried in triumph, and in the next instant was sent flying as Yeshua's massive hand slammed into his shoulder and sent him sprawling.

LEETA O'CONNER ENTERED THE dining room of the Majestic with care. She had put on her deep-green velvet dinner suit for the occasion, and had donned her spectacular set of pearls—a seven-strand choker with a diamond clasp, drop earrings, and a wide bracelet to match the choker. She knew she looked smashing, but she wanted to be sure Boris knew it, too.

He appeared in the kitchen doorway, surprisingly good-looking in formal dinner wear. His hair was carefully combed; he had used a leather-based cologne, and his face was still shiny from his shave. "Thank you for accepting my invitation for a midnight supper, Leeta O'Conner."

"My pleasure, Boris," she said, coming toward the one table on which the candelabrum was lit. The dishes were genuine porcelain and the glasses were Hungarian crystal. "This is very impressive." She knew that was what he wanted to hear, and she liked being able to say it. She reminded herself that she had been handling men since she was fifteen—in all senses of the word. Men were pretty much the same the world over. It shouldn't be difficult to bring this Siberian to heel.

"You're kind to say so," said Boris. "But this isn't a shade to you."

Leeta knew this was blatant flattery, but she drank it up. As Boris came to hold the chair for her in a show of old-fashioned good manners, she said, "You are shameless."

"Only in that I cannot find sufficient praise for you," he said as he seated her. With an expert flourish the Majestic Hotel's owner whisked the ornately folded linen napkin off the table and into the lady's lap, then went back to his side. "You must be used to men telling you how lovely you are."

"What can I say?" she countered. "If I agree, I make myself a vain, self-centered egotist; if I disagree, I insult your graciousness." Actually, she felt like a parched plant that had finally been watered. Romulas had rarely given her compliments once they were married, and when he did, they were only a prelude to sex. She sat still while Boris poured wine into the smallest of three glasses above the two spoons and knife; by expertly rotating the bottle, he was able not to spill a drop of the wine on the immaculate tablecloth.

Boris filled his own glass and offered a toast. "To a most fortunate partnership."

"Are we going to be partners?" Leeta asked as she touched the rim of her glass to Boris's.

"I hope so," said Boris. "I think both of us would like the arrangement I am going to propose."

"Oh, dear," said Leeta, anticipating what was coming.

"I haven't been widowed long, and I'm not really ready for—"

"No, no," said Boris, laughing and waving his hand in protestation. "That is not what I intend, or not yet," he amended. "For now I have a business proposition—just business."

"Business?" She was mildly surprised, and a bit apprehensive. She had not come to this remote city for business, she had come to disappear. She wasn't sure she wanted to do anything that would make her come to anyone's attention.

"Yes." He leaned forward. "You and I could make a fortune"—he said *fortune* as if it were an enormous amount of money—"if you're willing to play along with what I must do."

She smiled. "I'm listening."

"Well. You see the trophies mounted around the rooms? Bear and cat and fox and wolf?" He pointed to a few of the heads adoring the dining room walls.

"Yes?" She had found the display a bit disquieting, but she had not wanted to say anything that might offend Boris.

"I said I hunt. I shot the bear in the front. I've shot almost all of the animals you see in the hotel." He smoothed the front of his brocade vest. "I want you to tell me, Leeta O'Conner—have you ever worn a genuine fur coat?"

Leeta stared at him. "You mean genuine, as from an animal?" She did her best not to gawk. Animal fur had been outlawed for at least fifty years.

"Yes." He lifted the lid of the tureen and ladled out a rich hunter's soup—venison, duck, and wild boar in a thick broth with mushrooms and baby cabbage. The aroma was tempting, and she could not conceal her hunger. "Have some of this. I think you'll like it."

Obediently Leeta picked up her soup spoon and sampled the rich, dark liquid, avoiding the meats for the moment. It was excellent, and she had to say so. "This is quite wonderful," she said.

He filled his bowl. "I am glad it is to your liking." He tasted it, his expression critical. "You know, it could use a few more shaved onions. Next time."

She ate in silence, waiting for him to speak again. When he finally did, she listened attentively.

"Siberians are allowed to hunt, but we are not allowed to export hides or furs. But we may wear our own furs when we travel." He nodded to her, then said in a rush, "If we were partners, you could wear fine furs anywhere in the world, and you might trade your genuine fur for an artificial one, and accept a little money to make up the difference in value. You would not be questioned, and we could have business in every part of the world."

"You mean go against the law?" she asked, feeling a mixture of shock and intrigue.

"Of course. And you would be well-compensated for the risk you take. I will supply you with the coats—not too many, nor too often—and we will set up special tours that will serve as a cover." He took a deep breath. "So. What do you think?" As he rose from the table, he held up his hand. "Do not tell me yet. I am going to get the stuffed partridges and the pickled beets. Think about it while I'm in the kitchen."

Leeta raised her glass, thinking this could be a way to get free of Mother O'Conner at last. If Boris paid her in cash rather than credits, there would be no banking records. Boris said he could handle the travel arrangements so her name would never be used. She could still be relatively anonymous. She smiled, and this time her expression was crafty, and so worldly that her features were quite transformed for a moment. Then she schooled her expression to a compliant one, and began to think of the best way to let Boris convince her.

CHAPTER

54

AS YESHUA BOLTED FOR the distant remnants of roadway, his shape began to change. He was shining in the iridescent slime, leaving a path behind him as bright as a snail's trail. His large, clawed footprints were growing with each step. His stride lengthened with his legs and soon he was covering ground at twice the speed of the restored corpses, many of whom strove to keep up with him, all without success. Moving quickly, Fawg's shoulders became more massive with every step, and his appearance continued to metamorphose into Roc form.

"After him!" Strategy shouted.

"How?" Dee asked. His head still rang from the blow he had been struck. "Employ one of the skimmers to go. I'm on foot."

"And let someone else get my story? No, thank you; I didn't go through the antechamber of Hell to give away everything I've made for myself," she said, her fears of danger now eclipsed by her fear of losing the story and all that went with it—fame, money, her own prime-time hour on GNN.

She surged past him, stumbling on the bits of bone and flesh that littered the landslide, inadvertently pushing against the small man. Dee staggered in the mire, barely staying upright as the newswoman ran after Yeshua, shouting to Perry and Natasha, "Get this on the air! Can you see him? I can't believe what he's doing!" She reached the line of rat-soldiers who were rushing after the fleeing Roc. "Let me through!" she bellowed, shoving one of the rats aside.

The line of zombies were still advancing, trying to grab anything that moved, and they continued to battle as they went. The sound of cracking bones was a counterpoint to the tramping of the rat-soldiers, with Strategy sounding a loud, solo note. Dee stood back, trying to sort out the snarl around him; he did his best to keep Fawg in.

"You!" Strategy shouted, looking at the chief officer of the rat-soldiers. "Why are you attacking these—?" She flung her hand in the direction of the walking dead. She slowed her pace a little to match that of the advancing rat-militia.

"Because they are unnatural, and they carry a virus that is dangerous to all of you, and us," said the officer, his nose twitching, and his tail curling up to show his distress.

Strategy was taken aback. "How?" she demanded, staring after the retreating, reptilian back of what was no longer Yeshua.

The officer signaled his troops to continue their charge at the reanimated corpses, and gave Strategy a curt nod. "We will discuss this later," he declared.

Frustrated, Strategy stepped back rather than be run over by the rat-soldiers. "Now, that's ironic," she said for her own ears, "rats trying to prevent the spread of disease." She looked about for someone she could interview, and hit upon Dee, who was now trying to reach the top of the mudslide, the better to survey the confusion. "You!" She ran toward him, mike at the ready. "I want to talk to you."

Dee retreated, mistrusting the attention the newswoman brought with her. "Waste not my time, woman. There is a dangerous alien abroad in Angel City."

"That's an unusual accent," said Strategy, determined to engage him in talk. "Where do you come from? And why are you here?"

"I come from London," said Dee, "and I am here to prevent a catastrophe."

Strategy's face lit up. "Tell me about it," she urged.

But Dee beat a hasty retreat over the trembling, hardening mud. He scrambled up the slope, occasionally using his hands to steady himself on the climb. Panting, he made it to the shoulder of the slide, where deep rifts scarred the grass at the brow of the hill, marking the place where the sodden earth had first pulled away from the rock on which it rested. There he stood, his hands shading his eyes, his attention on Fawg, as he rushed away from the pandemonium he had caused.

Wishing that Dyckon were here with him now, giving him insight into what such a rogue as Fawg might do. "If wishes were horses, beggars would ride," Dee muttered to himself, and did his utmost to still his thoughts, so that he would not embrace turmoil instead of reason. The fibres of his suit began to shed the mud he had rolled in, revealing a pattern like the charred grass and crumbing soil that was all around him. Very carefully he began to walk beyond the slide to the crest of the ridge, walking quickly along it, glancing down from time to time to observe what was happening below. Without Yeshua to rally round, it was clear that the rat-soldiers would defeat the restored dead, given enough time.

Mustering all Dyckon had taught him about the Roc, Dee concentrated on the actions Fawg would have to take if he had any hope of eluding his pursuers: It wasn't possible for Fawg to escape through the heart of the city, not in his proper form. And with this zombie army, he dared not resume human shape for fear that they would congregate around him, bringing Piper's men in their wake. Still, he was quite capable of imitating any shape, which was what made him especially dangerous. He must not lose sight of the towering gargoyle. As he crawled his way up the muddy hill, Dee was feverishly trying to devise a plan for apprehending Fawg before his contagion spread beyond the living cadavers.

There was a shudder under his feet, and Dee grabbed for the nearest outcropping of rock, clinging to the cold stones until he was certain there would be no slide. He saw an area of fresh mud, indicating that another, minor slippage had occurred. Satisfied that he was safe for a while, Dee kept going along the ridge, using the skills he had learned as a spy.

For a short while, Fawg disappeared under a canopy of trees that had not been near enough to the mudslide to be uprooted. Dee was worried, and tried to decide if he should go down the hill to find Fawg; but in little more than a minute, Dee saw Fawg emerge from the cover of the trees, barreling up the slope. A moment later Dee saw half a dozen rat-soldiers come rushing out of the trees, heading right toward Fawg, their weapons drawn and aimed.

"Nay!" Dee shouted, and rushed down the hill, determination in every risky step. "Nay! You mustn't!" He held up his hands as a sign of prohibition. "Cease at once!"

The rat-troopers paid no attention to him. "For Piper and victory!" the leader of the squad shouted. "Fire!"

A fast volley of bullets slapped into Fawg's body, whipping him around, roaring with pain and fury. He stumbled, then brought himself up, preparing to charge. Dragonlike, he reared up to his full height, the talons of his hands grasping at his attackers. The rat-troops were momentarily paralyzed by eons of superstition and innate dread. But unlike the dragons and basiliks of myth his kind may have inspired, Fawg had no fire to breathe on them to slow their advance.

Dee was almost at the side of the rat-soldiers. "Don't kill him! You mustn't! By Heaven, stay your hand! I must speak with it to know its secrets."

"We have our orders," said the leader, his whiskers quivering as Fawg lurched toward them, his tail lashing, his eyes wild with wrath. "Fire!"

The second burst of fire did more damage, and one of Fawg's legs collapsed. He writhed, bellowing and batting at the air with his front limbs, all the while glaring balefully at the rat-soldiers. Even this close to death, Fawg's glare was contemptuous. He had lived too long to be brought down by these ignorant mongrels. History would never accept it. He searched the skies and earth for something to hurl at them.

A third shouted order brought a last salvo from Piper's men, and the Roc's crest flew apart, leaving a spatter of red. Fawg kicked and spasmed and lay still.

Dee went to Fawg's shattered body laid out before him, a great apprehension rising within him. He turned around to the rat-soldiers, who were being given orders for the cremation of the alien corpse. "May Heaven forgive you, and all of us," said Dee.

"He was a danger to all of humanity—you and us," said one of the soldiers, "as long as he was alive. Now he is dead and the danger is gone." He shrugged before calling Piper's soldiers to attention.

"If he was the only one," said Dee, and had the wry satisfaction of getting the soldiers' undivided concentration. He took full advantage of the moment, knowing he would probably not command it again. "But, sirs, consider: What if there be more?"

"Is this likely?" The officer was impatient to sterilize the area.

"I have no desire to find out," said Dee, "but that may be out of my hands."

55

CORWIN TARLTON—OR AT ANY RATE, the Roc mimicking Corwin Tarlton—sat in his room at the Azzahzi Palms glued to the vid monitor watching the GNN newscast streaming in from Angel City. He had been watching for hours: Strategy Brooks was holding forth on the extraordinary events that had transpired during and after that day's mudslide in the Hollywood Hills. The vids that kept being broadcast every other minute clearly showed Fawg set-ut being gunned down by a horde of humani with heavy artillery. Like everything at the Azzahzi Palms, the vid monitor was old and in need of repair. The streaming video would sometimes cut out and he'd miss a chunk. Most of the murdering humani looked like rats, some even with tails—highly unlikely. But what was unmistakable was the footage of Fawg's body being ripped apart. Then the ratmen ignited his limbs and trunk. The images turned Corwin's stomach and left him immobilized. It was beyond horrible. It was unthinkable. At first his mind couldn't accept what it was being told. It was not possible that Fawg, clan leader of the set-ut, could be vanquished by a ragtag platoon of rat-humani—who looked like dinner. Fawg was a Roc, moreover he was the supreme commander of the set-ut; he was the god of these people. They wouldn't attack their own god. It was inconceivable especially on this day. This was the day Fawg and he had planned to release the virus and start the overthrow of the planet.

No, this could not happen to them today. Without his elder clansman, his master, to inspire and guide him, Corwin was at a loss to know what to do. Going ahead with their plan without Fawg was absurd. Corwin knew he didn't have the necessary talents to go it alone. What was worse was that when he and Fawg had separated, Fawg had insisted on taking the clan communication devices with him, which meant that Corwin was now stranded on Earth, alone, with no way to reach home. He was marooned on a hostile planet, and sure to be discovered eventually. His fate would most likely be that of Fawg, or worse. His mind churned on that nightmare for the first two hours as he sat in front of the monitor. He'd looked up at one point and caught one of the interviews with the humani fleeing his master. The humani was shorter than Strategy and vaguely familiar.

"Waste not my time, woman! There is a dangerous alien abroad in Angel City!" Dee had tried to shove the newsman aside.

"That's an unusual accent. Where do you come from? And why are you here?"

"I come from London, and I am here to prevent a catastrophe!"

There was something about his face that nagged at Corwin's memory, but then, all humani looked the same to him. After the third replay of the interview and the reiteration of the fact that the aggressor came from London, the realization struck him: The humani was Dyckon's pet, John Dee. Centuries before, he and Fawg had discovered Dee in suspended hibernation hidden aboard Dyckon's ship. They had planned to use the information they gained from him to increase their political leverage against the mission leader. Recently, Fawg had said that Dyckon had let the old humani go so as not to tarnish Dyckon's reputation. There was no question this was he. GNN had reported that after Fawg's incineration, Dee and the rat-men army had burned all the resurrected corpses. The funeral pyres had burned out hours ago, though an odor of charred, rotting pork hung on the air. As the fires finally extinguished, Dee and the vermin troops had disappeared.

"This is Strategy Brooks again. I'm here with Commander Darla Anderson of the California Security Forces who, for the last couple hours, have been taking charge of cleaning up the carnage and destruction caused by both the mudslides and the extraordinary battle that took place here earlier in the day. Commander Anderson," she said, turning to include the athletic officer in the frame with her, "what, in your opinion, was the creature that called itself Yeshua Ben David? Was it—he—a space alien?"

"Ms. Brooks, I am not a scientist, and I was not present this morning, so I cannot tell you what you thought you saw." The commander spoke crisply in spite of her obvious exhaustion.

"Thought I saw, Commander?" Strategy countered huffily. "We have shown the world what we all saw. Everyone knows what we saw. There is no question but that the creature changed from being a man to some kind of large gargoyle in front of us. That is not humanly possible. You can't argue that."

"With due respect, I can. The world has only your vids, and before I can express an opinion, those vids need to be investigated by the CSF."

Strategy Brooks suddenly turned full face into the vid camera, facing her audience. "Ladies and gentlemen, what you've been seeing all day has been genuine and verifiable. GNN and I have absolutely nothing to hide; you have my word as a journalist on that." With that she swung back to the commander, who was starting to rise from her seat. "Commander Anderson, before you leave, do you have anything you can tell our viewers about the identity and disappearance of the strange militia who attacked today?"

Commander Anderson mustered all her self-control and answered as calmly as she could. "Well, Ms. Brooks, we have every reason to believe that these were the Homeless people who swarm the Pit. Obviously, their deformities are the result of the area's radioactivity. Why they thronged here, we have no idea."

Strategy wasn't willing to let it stand at that. "We heard them invoking the name Piper. Do you think they were his troops?"

For the first time, the Commander smiled; her professional demeanor thawed and freckles crinkled around her eyes. "Ms. Brooks, we all know Piper, the Rat-King, is just an urban legend, just like alligators in the sewer. I'm sure Piper—if that is actually what they said—is in reference to something else. Excuse me." With that, Anderson shed her cordiality and moved purposefully away from the van and back toward her command post.

"Well, ladies and gentlemen," said Strategy, again staring into the camera. "We will take you now—"

At that moment Corwin was startled—nearly out of his skin—by a pounding on the door.

"Mr. Tarlton! Mr. Tarlton! I know you're in there!"

Fear of capture immediately turned to annoyance as he recognized the voice of Hamil Azzahzi. The humani seemed more agitated and more resolute than ever. What was it this time? With an effort, the Roc concentrated on reestablishing the Corwin Tarlton form. "Yes, Mr. Azzahzi. Have you found the source of your smell?" he called as he shuffled to the door, taking time to put on his sunglasses, which sat on a bookshelf by the door. "I'm coming. Just you wait." He made no effort to conceal the rancor in his voice; a withered humani hand slowly turned the lock and opened the door.

"Ah. Mr. Tarlton." Azzahzi looked up from a palm-held computer that he had been studying. "Yes, yes. We have indeed located the cause of the smell. Oh, my, what a mess. It will cost a small fortune to fix."

Tarlton sniffed disapprovingly to indicate that his time was being wasted. He indicated with his hand and eyes that he wanted to get back to the vid monitor.

"Oh. Sorry to disturb you. Strange happenings in Angel City. Allah must not be pleased."

Again Corwin sniffed.

"My apologies. I will not take much more of your time. We have large leaks in the pipes below the building. Snakes. Many snakes came. Got into the ventilation conduits and couldn't get out. The Inspector and Animal Control must do a full investigation. We will need you to vacate for two or three days. It's in the lease agreement." With that, the landlord thrust his palm computer in Tarlton's face. "You see? All legal. All there in black and white."

The Roc couldn't believe what he was hearing. With all that happened today, now this. He started to protest. "You can't just kick me out."

But Azzahzi would hear none of it. "Oh, yes, it is in the lease agreement—health crisis—read the fifth clause." Again he brought the small computer to Corwin's face, who just as quickly pushed it away.

"This is hardly a crisis!" Corwin said, preparing to close the door.

Undeterred, Azzahzi went on, "The inspection team starts tonight, while snakes are asleep. The sooner you're out, the better. I'm sorry, but I must insist you pack now. I'll make it up to you—I'll take two weeks' rent off your bill."

"But—" The words faded even before the Roc could say them. He realized there was no point in arguing, for it only drew attention to him.

The lack of rebuttal prompted Azzahzi to assume he had made his point. "Thank you for your cooperation, Mr. Tarlton. Thank you." He backed away as he was speaking and turned to scurry down the dank hallway.

Corwin Tarlton absently watched him disappear, his attention on the sinking feeling in his mind. Slowly he closed the door, shutting out the outside world; he found his way back to his recliner and the vid monitor.

On the screen Strategy Brooks was going on about a lost colleague: Corwin wasn't really listening. All her remarks seemed disconnected, having no meaning to him. He wallowed in his own confusion. He had no purpose, no path to follow, he told himself, and now he must find new shelter where he could keep his identity a secret. It was too overwhelming.

He opened the closet where he stored his luggage. He

threw one bag on the bed. He would fill that one with personal items later; first, he was more interested in the case that lay beneath it—a cold storage unit made of electronic fabric totally unknown to the people of this world. When properly charged, it could store things for days at frigid temperatures despite any outside climate. He checked the charge-gauge and saw that it would need a new influx of Skreeah if he was going to be out of the apartment for a couple of days. He peered inside the case. The carrier had a number of compartments with holding racks and zippered pouches; the racks were laden with plastic containers that stored the clear, jellylike substance that was the set-ut virus. Each container had a different Egyptian glyph that indicated what Earth city it was meant for. He had never thought he would have to lug the whole case around with him again. But he knew he couldn't leave it behind, for fear some humani might uncover its contents.

With that in mind, he unzipped the central pouch and walked over to the bureau that stood by the bed. He opened the middle drawer and reached in the back for the portfolio of documents that had been given to him by Fawg. They were more precious to him now that his master was gone. One of them caught his eye; it was the decoded formula for Fawg's timeslip device. Corwin picked up the sheet, folded it, and slipped it into his pocket as he prepared to leave.

ABOUT THE AUTHOR

ARMIN SHIMERMAN was born in New Jersey and relocated to California, attending Santa Monica High School and continuing his studies at UCLA. In 1974 he moved to New York to act. He has performed on Broadway and guest-starred on several television shows, but he is best known for his roles as Quark on *Star Trek: Deep Space Nine*® and Principal Snyder on *Buffy the Vampire Slayer*™. Armin is also the co-author of the *Deep Space Nine* novel *The 34th Rule*, and when not filming, he can often be found teaching Shakespeare.

CHELSEA QUINN YARBRO, a professional writer for more than thirty years, has sold over seventy books and more than sixty works of short fiction. She lives in her hometown—Berkeley, California—with two autocratic cats. When not busy writing, she rides her Norwegian Fjord Horse, Pikku, or attends the symphony or opera.